gmH ς

Ashley was working her way through her own epiphany…

And looking for Wyatt to share it, if the warmth in her blue eyes was any indication.

"I'm comforted by knowing my family and friends are there if needed," she was saying. "But maybe...they don't feel the same way?" Ashley glanced up at him, expecting an answer.

"Maybe they feel they aren't as important to you as they used to be." And boy, didn't that hit home!

"Oh, my gosh. You get it." Ashley laughed self-consciously, reining in that delicate laughter.

The trees seemed to move closer. The wind seemed to pick up strength.

But in the center of it all was Ashley. Bright red hair and sunny yellow dress a reassuring beacon that whatever had happened in the past...whatever was happening right now... nothing was as important as this woman in front of him and the soul-touching conversation they were having.

Dear Reader,

Do you like "twin switch" books? I do. How about hunky heroes? Yep, me, too. *The Littlest Cowgirls* deals with the fallout of a twin switch with a hunky hero.

Actress Ashley Monroe has often had her identical twin, Laurel, take her place, but never with results like this. Ashley asked Laurel to fill in for her on a date with action film star Wyatt Halford. And now Laurel's pregnant...and Ashley's got some explaining to do with Wyatt, who believes he went on a date with Ashley. Boy, is he in for a surprise when he comes to Second Chance as Ashley's wedding date and sees pregnant Laurel.

You can't have a romance with actors without a little Hollywood thrown into the mix. Ashley wants to produce and star in her own films, starting with *The Ballad of Mike Moody*, a project she'd like Wyatt to join her on.

I had a lot of fun writing this small-town series, which began with Laurel's story—*Snowed in with the Single Dad*. I hope you come to love the Mountain Monroes as much as I do. Each book is connected but also stands alone. Happy reading!

Melinda

WESTERN

The Littlest Cowgirls

———

MELINDA CURTIS

HARLEQUIN
WESTERN

HARLEQUIN®
WESTERN

Please Recycle — This Product is Recyclable

Recycling programs for this product may not exist in your area.

ISBN-13: 978-1-335-91776-8

The Littlest Cowgirls

Copyright © 2021 by Melinda Wooten

This edition published by arrangement with Harlequin Books S.A.

For questions and comments about the quality of this book, please contact us at CustomerService@Harlequin.com.

Harlequin Enterprises ULC
22 Adelaide St. West, 40th Floor
Toronto, Ontario M5H 4E3, Canada
www.Harlequin.com

Printed in U.S.A.

Melinda Curtis, prior to writing romance, was a junior manager for a Fortune 500 company, which meant when she flew on the private jet she was relegated to the jump seat—otherwise known as the potty (seriously, the commode had a seat belt). After grabbing her pen (and a parachute), she made the jump to full-time writer. Melinda's Harlequin Heartwarming book *Dandelion Wishes* is now a TV movie on the UPtv network! Look for it on DVD soon.

Brenda Novak says *Season of Change* "found a place on my keeper shelf."

Jayne Ann Krentz says of *Can't Hurry Love*, "Nobody does emotional, heartwarming small-town romance like Melinda Curtis."

Sheila Roberts says *Can't Hurry Love* is "a page turner filled with wit and charm."

Books by Melinda Curtis

The Mountain Monroes

Kissed by the Country Doc
Snowed in with the Single Dad
Rescued by the Perfect Cowboy
Lassoed by the Would-Be Rancher
Enchanted by the Rodeo Queen
Charmed by the Cook's Kids

Return of the Blackwell Brothers

The Rancher's Redemption

Visit the Author Profile page
at Harlequin.com for more titles.

PROLOGUE

SECRETS. GABBY KINCAID loved them. They made her feel like an adult.

Gabby was twelve, a talker, and practically a Monroe. Yes, one of *those* Monroes. Her dad was marrying one. As such, she knew the Monroe history and a few important Monroe secrets.

Gabby chewed on the rubber end of her pencil, reviewing the Monroes the way she carefully reviewed her homework for tests.

She scribbled a word in her notebook. *Money.*

The Monroes were wealthy. Or they used to be. Or maybe some of them still were. Laurel Monroe was pregnant and marrying Gabby's dad this weekend, but she didn't act stuck-up or bossy-up.

Gabby glanced over to Laurel, who was sitting with her twin sister, Ashley, and their mother on the couch in the Lodgepole Inn. They were talking about the latest trend in fancy shoes as if something big and top secret wasn't about to happen at any moment.

But it was. Gabby gnawed on the pencil eraser again.

"Gabby, don't do that," Laurel said in a kind way, which pretty much summed up her approach to life. That was no secret.

"I need a distraction." Gabby tapped her pencil on the check-in desk. Another word was added to the list in her notebook. *History.*

Harlan Monroe had been a total success story, kind of like King Midas. Oil, finance, moviemaking, yacht building, hotels. You name it. Harlan had made money doing it. Harlan had also been born in Second Chance, Idaho, where Gabby lived with her dad and ran the Lodgepole Inn. Though it was cozy, the inn hosted a lot of the Monroes when they came to town, and they complained it wasn't "The Ritz," which was when Gabby had learned they didn't mean the cracker. That still stung a little.

But when it came to the Monroes, Gabby was willing to forgive, because of the next word in her notebook: *Secrets.*

A long time ago, Harlan had bought the town of Second Chance. But he negotiated with folks living and working here, offering them the measly lease price of one dollar a year. Why would he do that?

Harlan was dead now, so she couldn't ask him. And he'd left Second Chance to his twelve adult grandchildren, also without a good reason. Didn't he realize people would have questions? Gabby had questions. And people didn't always answer them, which was why sometimes she had to just sit silently at the check-in desk, pretending to do homework while she listened.

And when she listened, she learned a lot of things, including other Monroe secrets. Because, yes, there were more.

Like the secret that Laurel's twin, Ashley, who was a famous actress and often referred to as America's Sweetheart, was going to make a western movie right here in Second Chance next year. Although…she'd recently told that to reporters. So, it was no longer a secret.

Bummer. Gabby picked at the end of her pencil, plucking apart the chewed eraser. That had been a good secret, too.

But an even better secret was that Ashley wanted Wyatt Halford, the hottest of hot action stars, in the western film with her. They were going to tell the legend of Merciless Mike Moody, who'd robbed stagecoaches in these parts, stabbed Jeb Clark, the blacksmith, and had been killed by a rock slide during one of his escapes. Ever since Gabby was a kid, people would talk about Merciless Mike and wonder what had happened to all his stolen gold. Well, a couple of months back, the Monroes had unraveled the truth behind the legend *and* found the bandit's gold! Which was way cool, and kind of a secret, too, since they hadn't officially announced it to the world.

Gabby stopped destroying her pencil and stared out the window at the blue summer sky.

Secrets. She loved them.

But there was one Monroe secret that was bigger than them all. Wyatt Halford, dubbed this year's sexiest man alive, was Laurel's baby daddy. And he was coming here. To Second Chance. Today.

Wyatt didn't know a thing about the babies that were on the way.

Dad should be pacing. He was marrying Laurel on Saturday, she was nearly thirty weeks pregnant and could deliver twins at any time, and Wyatt was coming to the wedding. But was he uneasy? No. He was in their apartment doing the books. And the Monroes on the lobby couch weren't even fidgeting.

Shouldn't their stomachs feel like they ate too much popcorn at the movies? Gabby's did.

Wyatt Halford. *Super Mega Crush!*

Was it possible Wyatt knew he was a baby daddy? Due to circumstances beyond Gabby's control—*stupid laptop*—it had kind of been posted on the internet—*totally not her fault*. That bit of information was down now, and Dad always said you shouldn't believe what was on the World Wide Web, so Gabby had been trying not to worry. But still… It also meant she had a secret of her own.

Secrets were so hard to keep.

The low sound of a large vehicle parking in front of the Lodgepole Inn made Gabby's heart beat really, really fast. She ran from behind the check-in desk to a front window to witness the arrival of Wyatt, the sexiest man alive, greeted by Ashley, America's Sweetheart.

It was all heady, complicated stuff to lay on the shoulders of a twelve-year-old.

Especially one who had access to the internet and wasn't good at keeping secrets.

CHAPTER ONE

ASHLEY MONROE STOOD on the porch of the Lodgepole Inn with her best smile planted firmly on her face as she watched Wyatt Halford's assistant park their SUV in front of her.

This meeting in Second Chance, Idaho, had been five months in the making.

Her sister's future happiness hinged on this meeting. She tried to squelch the fluttery feeling in her chest that thought caused.

Wyatt stepped out of the back seat of the SUV like the Hollywood royal he was—tall, proud and with a casual appearance that was anything but casual. More like practiced and perfected. Apart from that cowlick that looked like it couldn't be tamed. There was the tan skin. Those scuffed black cowboy boots. He carried a black cowboy hat. All time-consuming prep and props to create the impression that Wyatt was a genuine rough-and-tumble cowboy who'd become a genuine rough-and-tumble action film star.

She'd bet he'd never shot a real gun in his

life. Or learned how to make little sports cars drift in circles, stopping on a movie mark. Or...

Wyatt removed his sunglasses and glared at Ashley.

Cue dramatic music.

This man wasn't happy. And he wasn't trying to hide it.

Ashley's feet suddenly felt as if they were slipping on a steep slope. She curled her toes in her black suede booties and glanced behind her.

Three females crowded the inn's front window—her mother, Laurel and Gabby. Gabby was wide-eyed, cell phone in hand. Laurel looked worried, a crease in her brow. And Ashley's mother? Her disapproval was evident without so much as a downward turn of her mouth. As Ashley's agent, Mom felt there was more on the line for Ashley than for Laurel, and that Ashley's public image must be protected at any cost.

And that was just it. For too long, Ashley had been the daughter the Monroes protected, the one everyone considered too fragile to safely navigate a Hollywood career alone. No more. She'd stand on her own now and face the fallout from her mistakes head-on.

She turned toward Wyatt.

He won't break me.

Wyatt walked up the inn's steps, sunglasses held on top of his head by that artfully created cowlick. He still carried that cowboy hat.

I will not back down.

Not when Ashley knew her course to conquer Hollywood as a producer-director could only be charted with smarts, professionalism and a whole lot of luck. No way was she going to let the highest-grossing actor of last year see her sweat.

Begin as you mean to go on.

"Thanks for coming." Ashley stepped forward to greet Wyatt, rising on her toes to kiss each of his cheeks.

And...*yikes.* Wyatt did the whole celebrity bit well. He even smelled good, like the scent of a lush green forest.

Wyatt held on to Ashley's elbow with a light but firm touch. The look in his dark brown eyes... It hid nothing. Backed down from nothing. "How could I refuse the request to be your wedding date?"

Oh, that voice. So deep. So smooth. So dangerous. He was quite the package.

No wonder Laurel fell under his spell. Even if it would only last twenty-four hours.

Ashley was falling now. Standing too close,

staring into his eyes too long. She could feel his magnetism.

But she could pretend his charisma was a facade—a role he was playing—and resist. After all, Wyatt had been summoned here.

Playing the part of the summoner, Ashley brushed a thumb over the summonee's cheek. His lightly stubbled cheek. *Goodness.* "You look like you're waiting for me to feed you your next line," she said, without so much as a tremble in her voice. And then she stepped back, grabbed his hand and led him toward the door.

Anyone who saw them would think they were friends, maybe even dating. Through the window, Gabby held up her phone as if taking a picture. And Ashley, who was as camera-shy as Wyatt was rumored to be, had to work hard not to turn away.

"Hang on." Wyatt planted those boots. "We need to talk about…" He gestured toward Ashley's midsection.

He knows something.

Ashley's smile became strained. She could feel a break in character coming, barreling toward her like an avalanche. And then her acting training kicked in, upholding that fourth wall between herself and her audience. *Breathe. Relax. Focus on the emotion you're trying to project. Calm.* Ashley was calmer than a shallow pool on a hot summer day. No ripple of panic. No wave of guilt.

"I saw something on the internet," Wyatt said in that hard, angry voice. "A post on an encyclopedia website about your sister and me."

He knows everything.

"Ashley, I've never met your sister." His brow furrowed, making him almost human. "It had to be a typo, your sister's name instead of yours."

He thinks I'm pregnant? He knows nothing!

To her credit, Ashley kept on smiling. She shifted her head, as if trying to get a handle on the meaning of his words. "Is there a question in there somewhere?"

The door behind her opened. Laurel's cheeks may have filled out during the pregnancy, but her features were still nearly identical to Ashley's. Laurel patted her very round stomach and arched her very slim brows. "It'd be easier on everyone if we were more direct."

So much for breaking the news to him gently. Ashley sighed and faced Wyatt. "That was no typo. You've met my sister. And surprise." Those two words fell flat, just not as flat as the ones that followed. "You're going to be a father."

IT WAS HARD for anyone to throw Wyatt Halford off-kilter.

Mostly because, growing up, his father had excelled at shaking him to his core. Often people, especially those who knew who he was and recognized how powerful he was in the film industry, didn't make a run at him.

You're going to be a father.

Wyatt was off-kilter. Truth be told, he was so off-kilter he didn't know where kilter was anymore.

He allowed Ashley to lead him into the Lodgepole Inn, a two-story structure built from rustic round logs. The least she could have done was invite him to a swanky hotel before springing this news on him. That, in itself, was suspicious.

You're going to be a father.

News flash: This was a hoax.

Wyatt clung to that thought the way he'd clung to a fake ledge on a soundstage during a scene a few weeks ago. He was being punked. Nobody punked Wyatt Halford. He glanced around, looking for cameras. Bingo. A cell phone in the hands of a girl with strawberry blond hair and worship in her eyes.

Wyatt assembled his defenses in what he hoped was an intense scowl, the likes of which he used when the villain in a film had taken his love interest hostage.

The pregnant version of Ashley came to stand in front of him. She wore a fashionable gray dress that clung to her curves. It was hard not to look at the woman's stomach. It was sizable.

"I don't believe we've met," Wyatt said to all that roundness, channeling the stern, cocky tones of Ian Bradford, the top spy he'd played in three films.

"We've never been formally introduced." The pregnant woman hesitated. "I'm Laurel. And I... Sometimes I take Ashley's place in public."

You're going to be a father.

News flash: Cracks discovered in Wyatt Halford's hoax theory.

Wyatt resisted washing a hand over his face and tried to keep his gaze on Laurel's, tried to keep his spinning brain on the task at hand—damage control. He'd been in that mode since someone had posted the Wyatt Halford–Laurel Monroe baby news online. It had taken him days to get the post removed. And against his agent's advice, he'd decided he needed to accept Ashley's invitation to be her date at her sister Laurel's wedding. Why? Because he had to squash the rumor at its source.

It can't be true.

Ashley guided him to the lumpy couch and sat next to him, laying a hand on his arm. Her touch was a cool contradiction to her red-headed beauty. "That date you thought you took me on…"

"That was me," Laurel said bluntly. She placed her palms on either side of her belly. "And the twin girls here are the result."

Twins?

Wyatt's mouth went dry and his concrete belief that this was a baseless rumor continued to fracture.

A middle-aged, redheaded woman wearing a dress and heels more suited to Bel Air than a mountain hotel stepped in front of him. "Our team has given this situation a lot of thought, and in terms of a strategy, we've decided—"

Wyatt's assistant, Jeremy, banged his way through the door, carrying Wyatt's luggage.

The noise shook his attention loose. "I'm not marrying you." He pointed at Laurel and then jerked free of Ashley's hold. "Or you. I don't know what your game is, but—"

"You're not marrying anyone." A scowling man marched forward, putting his arm protectively around Laurel. "No one's asking or expecting or even wants you to do that."

"What a relief." And yet Wyatt worried because the situation could still spiral out of his control. "Your little dating game came at quite the cost, didn't it?" A glare at Ashley was called for.

"This is no game." The middle-aged woman narrowed her eyes at him. He recognized her now. The short red hair. The fierce expression. She was Genevieve Monroe, Ashley's momager. "We've brought you here to talk through the steps of how to explain this to the public and to the industry. We don't want anyone's future derailed by this news. Especially Ashley's."

"We want you to relinquish your parental rights to Laurel's babies." The scowling man must be Laurel's ever-so-lucky groom, Mitch Kincaid.

"Do we need to spring everything on him at once?" Ashley asked in that deceptively sweet voice of hers. "Look at him. He's in shock." She laid her hand on his forearm once more.

The last thing Wyatt wanted was for Ashley to defend him. This mess was all her fault. She should be defending herself! He brushed her hand away.

But maybe he was in shock. He couldn't seem to focus. Twins switching places... *dang*. And babies...*plural*. Wyatt had vowed *not* to repeat his father's mistakes and make a baby with a woman before deciding whether he wanted to get married or not.

How's that plan working out for you?

Was that his father's voice in his head? Wyatt gritted his teeth.

"We were all in shock when we learned the truth," Genevieve said sharply. "But Laurel's about to give birth and a way forward needs to be finalized."

At the check-in desk, the girl with strawberry blond hair handed Jeremy a room key without taking her wide eyes off Wyatt. She'd be asking for his autograph any minute. She was the one member of this ensemble who wasn't contributing to the scene. The one contradiction to the scam the Monroes were trying to sell.

"I'm out." Wyatt stood. "Nice try putting one over on me, Ashley, but not even your hack of a brother could write a screenplay this far-fetched." Jonah Monroe was well-known for his smarmy teenage rom-coms. Wyatt signaled for Jeremy to reverse directions. "Send all future communication to my lawyer." He couldn't get out the door fast enough.

"Wyatt!" Ashley followed him to the porch, closing the door behind her. "Hear me out."

Where had shy, timid Ashley Monroe disappeared to? Where was the subdued actress who almost always wore pink in public and never had a bad word to say about anyone? This woman was dressed in a white blouse and black leggings. And she stood her ground as if she'd been doing so all her life. While he... He was running away.

Wyatt squared his shoulders. He was Wyatt Halford and didn't have to explain himself to anyone.

Except he would if word got out. If the Monroes confirmed to the world that announcement he'd had removed... They lived in a cancel culture. Granted, his bankability was largely based on his playboy image. But this...

"I was wrong to send my sister on a date with you," Ashley said levelly. "I'm sorry about that. But you were wrong, too. You didn't call me back the next day. You didn't text. Or send flowers. What does that say about you?"

"I'm not on trial here." Not yet. "You are. You and your sister and—"

"We're at a crossroads, Wyatt." Ashley cut him off smoothly. "You don't want to be a father, right? This could be a public relations nightmare for both of us. Or you can just walk away. No strings attached."

Part of him wanted to do just that. But only chumps grasped at solutions they hadn't reviewed with their lawyer. And that man in there… Laurel's fiancé… If those babies were Wyatt's, who was to say Mitch would be a good father? Kids needed good fathers. He knew that better than anyone.

No. Wyatt wasn't signing anything. "Goodbye, Ashley." He shoved his sunglasses in place and his cowboy hat on his head.

Behind her, Jeremy hammered the door frame with their luggage on his way out.

"I'm sorry, Wyatt, but…you can't go." She sounded apologetic, but adamant.

"Really?" He stomped down the stairs. "Why not?"

"Because my cousin Shane removed your spark plugs." Ashley gestured toward the truck idling behind Wyatt's rented SUV with Shane at the wheel, right before he drove off. "I'm not going to make excuses for him. He's gone rogue."

Shane Monroe? Wyatt seethed. He hated that dude. He'd shown up on the set of Wyatt's film to hand-deliver a wedding invitation and a barely-veiled threat about what would happen to Wyatt's reputation if he didn't make an appearance in Second Chance.

Wyatt drew his cell phone from his jeans pocket faster than a sharpshooter in a gunfight. "I'm calling the police."

"If you won't listen, that's your right." Ashley shrugged and turned toward the door, sidestepping Jeremy. "Make sure the police spell your name correctly. It'll make it easier for the paparazzi to find us."

CHAPTER TWO

"YOU KNEW I WOULDN'T have enough cell phone signal to call the police." Wyatt spun toward Ashley, taking the porch stairs two at a time, long legs quickly eating up the distance between them.

"Well, I was hoping your phone carrier was prone to low signal and dropped calls." Ashley lingered near the door, refusing to acknowledge her pounding heart, staying in character. "If this were a horror movie, we'd send Jeremy down to the basement to access the only working landline."

Jeremy sagged against the log wall of the inn, looking horrified. He didn't know there was no basement.

Scowling, Wyatt continued coming toward Ashley, but he slowed.

"And then, of course, we'd send Wyatt Halford to find Jeremy's body." Ashley's chin was high. Her voice clear. Inside, she was trembling, every instinct urging her to flee. "There'd be a scuffle with the unholy terror that's plaguing this mountain town. But Wyatt would live to see another day."

Wyatt stopped in front of her, angry eyes only partially hidden behind those dark glasses. "I am not amused."

She shrugged. "I come from a large family. Twelve Monroe grandchildren. When we got together, which Grandpa Harlan frequently encouraged, there was a lot of drama. My grandfather taught me that you can face adversity one of three ways." She held up one finger. "Hide in the basement and wait for the ghost to come find you."

"I take offense to that remark," Jeremy mumbled, having been the example in her metaphor to hide in the basement.

She held up two fingers. "Charge into the basement ready for battle."

Wyatt crossed his arms over his chest. "Or?"

"Or collect the facts and make a rational decision." Ashley held up three fingers.

Wyatt smirked. "In this film of yours, you'd be the plucky, bookish character who helps the star save the day. A sidekick."

At this point in her career, there was no way Ashley was settling for a sidekick role that didn't benefit from a plot twist that made her the heroine on the last page. "It depends on whose story you want to tell, Wyatt. Personally, I prefer the unexpected one."

"I get it. You want me to read your indie script." Wyatt heaved a sigh. "You can't afford me, Ashley. Especially not now. Haven't you heard? I charge an annoyance fee."

Jeremy glanced from the pair to the SUV to the woods, and then sat on a suitcase, seemingly settling in for the verdict of whether they'd stay or go.

"Let me be clear, Wyatt." Ashley pointed toward the door. "The most important person in the world to me is inside this inn." Her sister, Laurel, to whom she owed so much. It was Laurel who'd made it possible for Ashley to retreat from the world when the pressure of stardom became too great. Those twin switches had allowed Ashley a safe space but had driven a wedge between the sisters. Still, wedges didn't have to be permanent. "I realize you don't want to be part of my project, Wyatt. But you have to be part of Laurel's, even if it's just to agree to step aside."

A car made a slow stop at the intersection and then turned toward the heart of Second Chance.

Wyatt kept his back to the vehicle, not even looking around. He had a reputation for vehemently protecting his privacy.

And Ashley couldn't blame him. Adoring fans could make even the simplest activity in life a stressful production.

The car was packed to the ceiling with luggage and pillows. The driver pulled into a parking space at the Bent Nickel Diner, two doors down.

Wyatt gave the car a sidelong glance. "Do you know how impossible this situation is to unravel? If word gets out, chances are one or both of us will be relegated to bit parts in B films and mediocre TV comedies."

"True." Ashley kept her voice just as low as his. "But we've had a few months to wrap our heads around the challenge, and we believe we've found a solution." A way to ensure Laurel's happiness. It just so happened that their course of action—Wyatt giving up a claim to the girls—also protected Ashley's career. And his.

"We? Your team?" he said sardonically.

"My family," she correctly gently.

He scoffed, nodding toward the nearest window, where her mother, Laurel, Mitch and Mitch's daughter, Gabby, gathered.

Ashley wished her so-called team wouldn't so obviously eavesdrop. "There's been some anticipation about your arrival."

"And there's been a leak on your end."

Then he said two words. The name of the online encyclopedia site that had reported Laurel's pregnancy with Wyatt.

Ashley had her suspicions about the post. Her cousin Shane was the most likely choice since he was meddlesome when it came to protecting family. He'd traveled recently to South America to find Wyatt filming on location, where he'd floated the idea of Wyatt being Ashley's wedding date. Wyatt hadn't welcomed Shane with open arms, and the inflammatory post had gone up almost immediately afterward. Yeah, that had to have been Shane's doing. But Monroes didn't throw each other under the bus. Instead, she glanced significantly at Jeremy, trying to cast suspicion on Wyatt's team.

"Nice try." Wyatt shifted his weight, easing between her and the Bent Nickel Diner. "But I have tight control of my staff. Take another shot at it."

Whether on purpose or not, he'd hidden Ashley behind his broad shoulders, away from the hungry travelers in the parking lot. She shrugged. "There's no point in casting stones."

"I enjoy casting a few stones." Wyatt's tone had regained its edge, and his body seemed to be expanding. Not the swell of an egotistical chest, but the bunching of muscles by an elite athlete.

"You can blow off steam at the river behind the inn," Ashley said. "There are plenty of rocks you can toss. And if you're hungry, there's the diner."

His features turned stony. Incredible talent, that.

"Lucky for you," Ashley continued, "Chef Camden Monroe is cooking at the Bent Nickel Diner part-time." She leaned to the side to speak to Jeremy. "They offer a to-go menu."

Her movement brought her closer to Wyatt. His anger hadn't diluted the smell of a green forest glade. Such a tranquil impression. So at odds with the tumultuous man before her.

Ashley smiled. "Or you can stock up on food items from the general store. Keep in mind that the inn only has a microwave for guest use."

Wyatt chewed the inside of his cheek. "Jeremy, you've got to find me a nearby house rental. ASAP."

"Best of luck with that." Ashley reached for the door handle. "Oh, and Gabby has a room ready for you. Apologies, but you'll have to double up." Like she was doing with her mother. Mitch's family was arriving soon, as were more Monroes.

Wyatt covered her hand on the doorknob. His touch was gentle, yet strong.

Ashley didn't move, soaking in the layers of his character as if she was reading a really good script. Under pressure, he seemed strong, steady and single-minded, although she'd heard he was also demanding, difficult and bad-tempered.

"Sharing a room with my assistant?" Wyatt tsked, lips close to her ear, warm breath tickling her skin. "That's not how I roll."

Gone was the instinct to push him away. In its place was the draw of a moth to an irresistible flame. There was a reason Wyatt Halford had earned the "sexiest man alive" title. In her experience, he was quite literally the sexiest man she'd ever encountered.

"Dave. Dave. Would you look?" a woman called from somewhere near the diner. "Isn't that Ian Bradford? I mean, what's his name? The guy who plays Ian in those films you like." The woman gasped. "And that girl from that show we watched as kids. The redhead. Ashley something?"

Wyatt didn't move, but he seemed to shrink in on himself, as if doing so would make him invisible.

Oh, he was vulnerable, all right. A man in need of soothing. Or shaking up.

She had him right where she wanted him. Ashley would have smirked…

If she hadn't given in to impulse, risen up on her toes and kissed him.

PREVIOUSLY, ON THE life and times of Wyatt Halford…

He'd kissed Ashley Monroe on New Year's Eve in Hollywood.

Or at least, he'd thought that woman was Ashley Monroe. That woman had been charming and soft, blushing when their eyes met, fitting the image of the former child television darling turned beloved rom-com star. He'd fallen for her the same way he'd fallen for the on-screen version of her. Growing up, her long-running television show had been his guilty pleasure.

The Ashley Monroe filling his arms in Second Chance, Idaho, wasn't charming or soft. She kissed like a woman who knew what she wanted, who'd laugh at his jokes without blushes, who'd return the heat of his kiss unabashedly and wouldn't stumble over her own two feet trying to stay out of his way.

Both versions of Ashley Monroe had bright red hair and a petite frame.

Wyatt opened his eyes to stare down at this Ashley.

Not that he stopped kissing her. He was a red-blooded man, for Pete's sake, not a fool.

"Get my phone out of the diaper bag, Dave," the woman in the diner parking lot said.

Wyatt tensed. People intruding on his privacy wasn't his favorite thing.

Ashley's hand curled around Wyatt's neck just as her eyes opened to meet his gaze. Her lips curled into a slight smile. All without breaking that heart-thumping kiss!

He felt as hot as if he were still in South America. His arms had somehow managed to wrap themselves around her. His brain forgot to care about their audience.

"Your phone's not in the diaper bag, babe," a harried man's voice said. "And Bobby needs to eat. We're going inside."

Ashley's smile expanded, reaching her eyes. All without breaking the intensity of her kiss.

Who smiled while kissing?

Who knew he liked women who smiled while they kissed him?

"No. Jeez, Dave. Come back here," the woman called out. "We can sell that photo."

"Sorry, babe. No can do."

Near the parked car, a door rattled open. A bell tinkled. A door clattered closed. Wyatt assumed that was the diner door. Someone made a sound of frustration and the door ran its lines again—rattle, tinkle, clatter.

And then everything slowed to a stop. The commentary. The smile. The kiss.

Reality came crashing back. He wasn't ready for fatherhood. He wasn't ready to be knocked off his Hollywood pedestal by scandal. And he really wasn't ready for this version of Ashley Monroe, because he was very much afraid that this woman could upset everything in his apple cart.

In the circle of his arms, Ashley took charge of the conversation the same way she'd taken charge of him with that kiss. "You're not in Hollywood, Wyatt. And much as I'm trying to make you comfortable, this is my sister's wedding week. The Lodgepole Inn is all booked up. Two twin beds are all they've got to offer."

Wyatt's arms fell away from her. "I'm not cowed by you or the Monroes."

Her gaze lost its appeal. "I wouldn't expect you to be. The only thing I ask is that you be my wedding date to help shield my sister and her babies from speculation. It seems far-fetched for you to be their father if you're with me at Laurel's wedding. For everyone's sake, we need the public, the press and our peers to doubt the rumor." Ashley opened the door for Wyatt much the way he'd planned to open the door for her before she'd kissed him, because his mama had taught him manners.

Though he didn't feel like using them right now.

WYATT HALFORD STOOD within touching distance.

Of Gabby.

At the Lodgepole Inn.

Wearing cowboy boots and a cowboy hat.

She should have been speechless. She should have held out her copy of that magazine with him on the cover, silently pleading for a signature. Instead, she was living up to her name as she came out from behind the check-in desk to show Wyatt and his assistant to their room. "The kitchenette over there is for guest use. Microwave, fridge, sink, single-cup coffee maker. The coffee, tea, cereal and oatmeal are free and available 24/7." Gabby pointed toward the alcove as she hopped up the first few stairs toward the second floor. "The Lodgepole Inn is old. I mean, really old. I've done a book report on it and my dad fought to have the spot declared a historical landmark."

"Not a minute too soon," Wyatt murmured over Dad's cautionary *"Gabby."*

You'd think Wyatt's remark and Dad's warning would have shut her up.

Nope. "Your room has a fantastic view of the Salmon River, a meadow favored by a family of moose, and the Sawtooth Mountains. It's okay to be a tourist and take pictures." Gabby skipped up a few more steps, hopping to places where the stairs didn't squeak, because moving around the inn silently despite the floorboards was a talent of hers, and Wyatt should appreciate talent, right?

"Down at the end of the hall, you said? We can find our room." That was Wyatt's assistant, Jeremy. He was dragging all their luggage up the stairs under the watchful gaze of Dad and the Monroes.

"It's okay." Gabby hopped up a few more steps to the landing, turned and beamed down at them. "I don't mind showing you where it is." What girl would complain about a few minutes more with Wyatt Halford?

Wyatt grabbed a suitcase and a backpack from Jeremy and took the stairs two at a time.

"Oh." Gabby hadn't expected them to get up the stairs so quickly with all those bags. She sprinted toward the end of the hall. But the tour must go on. She wanted Wyatt to love her home as much as she did. "Second

Chance has a lot of history. My dad signed me up for a couple online courses this summer." *To keep you out of trouble*, he'd said. Although both of them knew trouble had a way of finding her. "And I'm writing a paper on Merciless Mike Moody, a local stagecoach robber who terrorized the territory. You know, the guy Ashley's film is about. Anyway, everyone in town has a different take on the legend, but I'm researching the facts." Not completely true. She was mooching some of Jonah Monroe's notes, the ones he'd used to write the movie script for Ashley. "So, if you have any questions about him, I'm your girl."

I'm your girl? Was that too much? Boy, it felt like it. Inwardly, she cringed.

"Which room is Ashley's?" Wyatt marched right behind Gabby, as if the humongous suitcase was lighter than her laptop. "I hear she snores. I want to be as far away from her as possible."

"The Meadow Room. We just passed it." Gabby gestured toward the door on the opposite side of the hall from Wyatt's room. "And Ashley doesn't snore. She's too perfect to snore. Or to fall asleep while doing her homework." Never mind waking up to drool on her pages. "And she's too perfect to walk into walls." And practically break her nose. "Or drop her cell phone in the river." All flaws and calamities of Gabby's.

"Nobody is that perfect." Wyatt nearly stepped on her heel, causing Gabby to lose her balance and bang into the wall, where a stubby knot rose out from the log. "Ow."

Wyatt pulled up short, reaching to steady her. "Are you okay?"

Wow!

"I—"

"She's fine." Jeremy came to a halt behind Wyatt. He was tall and blond and slender and scowling, and nowhere near as cute as Wyatt. "No blood. No tears." He made a clucking noise as if Gabby were a horse and he wanted her to giddyap.

Wyatt sighed and gave Gabby the kind of long-suffering smile that said he understood what an annoyance his assistant was.

Gabby wanted to cheer, thinking about her celebrity crush and how she'd been right for months. Wyatt wasn't the jerk the Monroes had been saying he was. His assistant was!

"Here you go." She opened the door and stepped back.

Wyatt thanked her and went inside.

Jeremy snatched the key from Gabby's hand. "Are the linens clean?"

"Yes."

Jeremy poked his nose into the room. "I'll call you back up here if they're not. And the bathroom?" He dragged the suitcase behind him, swinging wide.

"It's clean." Mortified, Gabby bumped against the far wall in her haste to get out of his way.

"Thanks." Jeremy shoved a twenty-dollar bill into her hand and shut the door behind him before she could even tell Wyatt to enjoy his stay.

How rude.

Gabby crumpled the twenty in her fist and marched back down the hall, not caring that her feet hit every creaky board along the way.

CHAPTER THREE

"WHAT WAS THAT KISS?" Ashley's mother spoke in hushed tones that matched the austerity of her conservative wool sheath. She'd hustled everyone into Mitch and Laurel's apartment behind the check-in desk as soon as Wyatt disappeared upstairs. "That wasn't part of the plan. You're messing this up already. Look at Laurel. She agrees with me."

Ashley met Laurel's anxious gaze. Her sister worried about Ashley too much. And Ashley ached because of it. Laurel deserved her own spotlight and not to be in Ashley's shadow. Her sister had chosen to shine in Second Chance. So if kissing Wyatt helped bring the spotlight to town for her, so be it.

Like kissing Wyatt was a hardship.

Ashley pressed her lips together.

Like kissing Wyatt would win back her sister.

"He was going to leave," Ashley said. "We're lucky his cell service was spotty." And that he hadn't tried to start his rental. Shane couldn't find a spark plug, much less remove one.

"See? Ashley's got this, Mom," Laurel said, dropping carefully into a kitchen chair. Her bag of knitting and worn-edged sketch pad sat in the middle of the narrow table. The apartment was tiny—two bedrooms, a bathroom and the small kitchen. The lobby served as their living room. Laurel claimed she liked cozy, and when she did so, it was in a tone that brooked no argument.

"Ashley doesn't have control of anything," Mom insisted. She always spoke with authority and conviction, even if she knew she was wrong. "A man like Wyatt Halford isn't to be trifled with. We'll be lucky to get out of this mess without a lawsuit or a public relations fiasco."

Her mother's warnings struck a chord inside Ashley, but it was the same note she'd heard for years—control your image by not taking risks. Ashley was ready to hear a new tune. Heck, it was high time she banged the keyboards to make her own music. And she was trying.

Demoralized because she'd been pigeonholed as a one-dimensional actress, Ashley was starting her own production company to create her own roles. Ginger Monroe Productions was going to option scripts and books for TV and film, oversee those ideas through to completion and then sell them to streamers, television networks and movie studios for distribution.

"Everyone just needs to take a breath and calm down." And by everyone, Ashley meant her mother.

Ashley took her own advice, drawing a deep breath. She was reminded of Wyatt's subtle, contradictory scent. He should wear a musky cologne that marked him as dangerous. His kiss could certainly support that.

Gabby barged in. "That Jeremy is a jerk. He wasn't impressed by anything I said about the inn. He practically accused us of having dirty sheets and smelly toilets."

"Gabby." Mitch tried to enfold his daughter in his arms. "What have I told you about cranky guests."

"To let their comments roll off my back." The preteen wanted nothing to do with her father's hug. She stomped toward her bedroom and slammed the door, only to open it again almost immediately. "And Wyatt is super nice, except he thinks Ashley snores." She slammed the door once more.

"I don't snore." Ashley felt that needed to be said.

"Not often." Her mother couldn't let anything slide, but since they were sharing a room, Ashley couldn't argue.

"Welcome to the world of Hollywood assistants." Laurel reached for Mitch's hand, smiling softly. "The first line of defense for celebs. I'm sorry that Jeremy was mean to Gabby. I can talk to him."

"Leave that to me," Mom said in a hard tone that promised retribution. She was rather fond of Gabby.

"You warned Gabby about certain Hollywood types, but I don't think she listened." Mitch brought Laurel's palm to his cheek and smiled at her with so much love that Ashley had to look away.

Now that Laurel had Mitch, she didn't need Ashley. Or at least, Laurel wouldn't need her once the Wyatt issue was resolved. It was wrenching to realize she might never be close to her twin again.

"How are you holding up, honey?" Mitch asked Laurel.

"Laurel's fine. Let's return to the important issue of saving Ashley's career." Mom checked her pinging phone, missing Ashley's and Mitch's disapproving frowns. "Don't add fuel to this paternity bonfire, Ashley. You didn't have to kiss him."

"I did. There was an opportunity to shake Wyatt up, and I took it."

"He's not going to be in your movie." Mom headed for the door leading to the lobby.

"That wasn't why I did it." Wyatt Halford with both feet firmly on the ground would be a force to be reckoned with. Ashley's plan was to keep him unsteady and keep him in Second Chance until he signed away his legal right to Laurel's babies. She'd seen the surprise in his eyes when they'd kissed. Goal accomplished. At least for now. "But thanks for bringing us all down to earth, Mother."

"As the worst-case scenario thinker in the family, I live to serve." Mom made her exit with a dramatic flourish of her hand.

When the door clicked closed behind her, Mitch's expression turned somber. "Wyatt's not going to agree, is he?"

"He will," Ashley reassured him, because it was now her job to reduce the stress in Laurel's life.

She and Laurel exchanged glances. What was her twin thinking? Ashley's gut clenched. She didn't know.

When they'd been young and close, before Ashley's stardom separated them, they'd shared the infamous twin speak. But now, many years and many slights later, Ashley could only gauge Laurel's body language to infer what she was feeling. The raised brows. The pursed lips. A combination of disbelief and worry? About the unsigned paternity documents?

"Don't let Wyatt's refusal bother you, Mitch." Laurel reached for her sketch pad. "You wouldn't have signed the papers either. Not without reading them through and understanding them completely."

"True." Mitch's phone rang. He brightened. "It's the state's historic commission. I've got to take this. We're close to earning historic designations on another block of cabins." One swift kiss to Laurel's crown and he was out the door, too. He'd been trying to get several buildings in Second Chance on Idaho's historic registry to protect the town from being developed into a rich person's playground, like Aspen.

"I'm not sure Wyatt should give up his parental rights," Laurel said, almost reluctantly, as if she wasn't sure how Ashley would react to her opinion.

"That's a reversal," Ashley said with the utmost neutrality. In the few days she'd been here, she'd learned pregnant Laurel changed her mind more often than unpregnant Laurel. Her sister couldn't change one fact, though—

Wyatt Halford would make coparenting difficult. Ashley was sure of it. Why? Because Wyatt made movie production difficult. Why would coparenting be any different? "What happened to you worrying that he'd sue you for primary custody because of the way everything went down?" Because he'd thought he'd been on a date with Ashley and hadn't been given a chance to decide whether he wanted to be a dad or not.

"He's just… He didn't…" Laurel floundered, fingers clinging to the corners of her sketch pad. "When we told him, he didn't overreact."

"Doesn't mean he won't be vindictive when the shock wears off." It had to be said. Mom wasn't the only glass-half-empty thinker in the family.

Laurel fell silent, gaze focused downward.

"If you want to give Wyatt a chance to coparent…" Ashley softened her tone. "If you think it's what's fair to the babies… You know I'll support whatever you want." But until Laurel decided for certain, Ashley was going to continue to push Wyatt out of the picture.

"It would be easier if I knew what I wanted, wouldn't it?" Laurel's eyes were teary. "Or if I knew what was best for everyone…"

"Maybe you just need to sit down and think about what's best for *you*. Forget wedding plans. Forget wardrobe designs for my film. Think about what your heart is telling you. Think about it now. I'll wait." Ashley sat down at the small kitchen table next to Laurel, pulling out her phone to check her messages. There were lots, including a request for her to visit a local horse trainer in an hour. She was trying to put a preproduction team in place for the Mike Moody film. And she was in several message groups with coworkers from previous productions.

Laurel didn't say anything as Ashley scrolled, sorting and prioritizing. Her sister knew Ashley paid more than lip service to those she allowed in her social circle. When Ashley was sixteen, she broke up with her boyfriend only to wake up to the news the next day that he'd overdosed on pills. She'd collapsed. A few months later, the girl who was playing her best friend on the sitcom had tried to take her own life. She'd fallen apart.

Could Ashley have done anything to help them? She didn't know. But she came out of that dark place to become the mother hen of every crew on every project. Ashley responded to every shared high and low on those message loops, and she reached out to those who'd gone silent to let them know how awesome they were. But as much as Ashley was proud of her mother-hen role, it couldn't make up for the fact that she'd completely messed up her relationship with Laurel.

When she was done sorting, Ashley set down her phone and gave Laurel her complete attention. "Well?"

"He's a good kisser," Laurel said simply. She didn't so much as blush.

"So much for the Wyatt parenting debate." Ashley smiled indulgently. "I don't want to have this conversation with you."

"Who will you have the conversation with? Mom?" Laurel chuckled softly. "I'm not jealous. Mitch is a much better man. For me, anyway."

Ashley made a noncommittal noise. Was there any contest? Mitch was a former lawyer from Chicago, who'd bought this inn so that he could raise his daughter in a small town. The man had heart and clearly adored her sister. On the other hand, Wyatt had a reputation for being difficult, a player and an actor who focused on wealth and the material expression of it.

"That lip bomb was a smart move. You threw Wyatt a curveball." Laurel continued her not-so-subtle attempts at engaging Ashley in Wyatt-themed conversation.

There was only one reason Laurel would bring up this topic. "You're worried I'm going to get hurt."

"Yes." Laurel's eyes watered. "When you let guys get close, they tend to sweep you off your feet."

Ashley scoffed. This observation was only based on a sample size of one.

"I'm so sorry I've put you in this situation. You've worked so hard for your success, and now our twin switch could be what you're most known for."

That was one of Ashley's fears. But it took a back seat to Laurel's well-being. "No matter how this turns out, I'm not going to regret those two little nieces of mine." Ashley took her sister's hand in both of hers. "Don't you worry about me. I backed you into this corner by asking you to pretend to be me. There will be no more pretending for you. And no more hiding who I am and what I want from the world for me."

Ashley needed to repeat that last part every time she was made to feel her opinions and dreams weren't important. In Hollywood, people often considered their dreams more important than anyone else's.

"No more pretending." Laurel passed the palm of her free hand over her belly. "Conveniently, after this, my hips are forever going to be wider than yours."

"I envy you," Ashley blurted. She envied Laurel even as she'd been thinking home and family might not be in the cards for her. And since there was no taking back her words, she expanded on them. "You found the love of your life and you're going to be a mother. More importantly, you're going to do a better job at it than our mother did."

Although she meant well, Genevieve had molded them to succeed rather than to accept who they were and how to find their own measure of happiness. Their mother's drive had almost broken Ashley. Or it would have if not for Laurel's unconditional support and sacrifice.

"You think I'll be a good mom?" Laurel got all mushy-eyed, nose turning red.

"I do. With all my heart. And those girls of yours are going to be best friends forever." Another point Ashley envied.

"We're best friends." But Laurel's words rang hollow.

"We *used to be* best friends." Ashley forced herself to speak the truth, to stare into her sister's eyes and acknowledge the loss. "And I hope we'll be best friends again after I make up for everything." All the times Laurel had been pressured into a twin switch. All the times Laurel's needs had taken a back seat to hers. All the times their mother had forced Laurel to treat Ashley like an entitled celebrity instead of a sister.

"Ash." Laurel wiped away a tear. "It takes a strong person to start out their career at age five, much less thrive as an actor for twenty-plus years. Whatever slight you think you've caused me, I've forgiven you and moved on."

"I'm not asking for your forgiveness, although I'll take it." Now it was Ashley who wiped away tears. "It's more important that I make things right between us."

And to do that, she needed Wyatt to sign those paternity release papers.

"Whoa." Ashley brought her rented SUV to a stop in a swirl of dust, thoughts of Wyatt Halford fading at the sight before her.

A palomino clamped its teeth on the brim of a little cowboy's hat and lifted it off the boy's head. The horse ambled over to a woman and put the straw hat on her head, receiving a cubed treat as a reward.

Said cowboy was Andrew, five, and one of her cousin Sophie's kids. Said horse was

in a large corral at the end of a dirt drive-
way that led to the ranch proper. Said woman
had black hair and obvious skills as a horse
trainer.

Zeke Roosevelt, a slender, ginger-haired
cowboy who was part of the crew of stock
wranglers from the Bucking Bull Ranch
that Ashley had hired for her film, gave her
a friendly wave. He leaned against a corral
fence post. A few feet away from him, a tall
cowboy with a fringe of unruly black hair
was twirling a lasso around his boots with
an audience of young cowboys.

Ashley got out and joined Zeke at the corral
fence. "Looks like you brought every boy as-
sociated with the Bucking Bull Ranch." Five
boys. All under the age of ten or so. Two of
her cousin's kids, who were Zeke's stepsons,
and the three Clark boys.

Zeke chuckled. "You try leaving a kid behind when they know you're coming to the
Bar D, even if they aren't your own. It's like
coming to the circus." He caught the attention of the woman in the corral. "Cassie here
is a horse trainer. I thought you might be interested in what she can bring to your film."
He pointed toward the man jumping in and
out of the spinning lasso. "And her brother
Rhett is a champion roper. He coaches now.

I promised the boys lessons if they did their chores around the ranch."

"Ms. Ashley!" Little Adam Clark jumped up and down, holding a stiff coiled rope that was almost as tall as he was. "We're going to play a roping game. Want to watch?"

"You bet I do." Ashley gave the boy a big smile. Despite having a long to-do list, she always got a kick out of these boys and their energy. Even the stoic Wyatt Halford would smile at their banter and antics.

At the prospect of cowboy games, Andrew asked Cassie for his hat back and then scrambled between the corral rails to join the other boys.

"Rhett has an intriguing approach to keep kids interested in throwing lariats," Zeke explained. "Speed drills and multiple targets, like an obstacle course. He's coached a couple of junior champions. They'll start in a minute. In the meantime, Cassie, why don't you show Ashley the kind of horse stunts she can expect?"

"Sure. You always see horses going down in westerns." Cassie pointed finger guns at the palomino and said, "Bang."

The horse lay down in the dirt, as if shot.

"Good boy. Wake up, Romeo," Cassie said.

The palomino stood up and trotted over to Cassie for a treat.

Cassie stroked the horse's neck while he ate and then backed up. "Romeo, up." She threw up her arms.

The horse stood briefly on his hind legs.

"Good boy. Romeo, bow."

The palomino gingerly sank down on one leg and lowered his head.

"Come on, you show-off." Cassie gave him another treat when he stood and then gave him a series of hearty pats.

Ashley applauded. "Well done."

"Thanks." Cassie came over to the railing with Romeo trailing after her. "It helps that Romeo is a people pleaser. Did you have any stunts in mind?"

"I haven't gotten that far in the planning stage," Ashley admitted. "What in the world are you doing training horses out here in the middle of—" she almost said *nowhere* but corrected herself midsentence "—the Idaho mountains?"

"It's in my blood, I suppose. Our family used to run a traveling carnival, complete with a petting zoo and animal performances." Cassie gestured to a barn behind the field the little ropers were in. "We've still got a lot of the kiddie rides in storage. A small train, a miniature carousel. You know, that kind of thing."

"I tidied up a number of parts to use in roper training," Rhett cut in, pointing to a small wooden horse mounted on a hay bale and a metal train engine with a mannequin sitting at the controls. "People seem to like throwing at targets rather than the traditional practice steer." There was one of those, too. A metal frame with a horned bull's head on it.

"I like throwing at the train conductor." Adam jumped up and down, grinning. "We've only got a fake bull to practice roping on at home. I want to throw, Mr. Rhett. When can we?"

"Now." Rhett plucked Adam's cowboy hat off his head and then set it back in place. "But first, what's the most important thing to remember when roping?"

"Release!" All the boys chimed in.

Ashley smiled, infected by their enthusiasm. If Wyatt were here, it seemed unlikely that he'd enjoy it as much as she did. He was too uptight, stiffer in person than he was on screen.

"Yes, your release is the most important technique." Rhett nodded. "First time through we're going to throw while standing on a hay bale. You get three throws at the three targets—train, horse and bull. We'll go oldest to youngest."

Adam groaned and slowly fell to the ground, much the same way Romeo had done in his stunt. "Wake me when it's my turn."

Davey climbed up on the hay bale. A birth defect had left him with only one hand, but he didn't look as if it bothered him. He selected a coil of rope at his feet, leaving two others on the hay. With practiced ease, he began to twirl a loop over his head and his cowboy hat. And then he threw it toward the train conductor. It dropped smoothly over the mannequin's shoulders.

"Good job." Rhett gave the boy praise.

"I can do it faster," Charlie, Davey's younger brother, goaded.

Davey let out a groan as he lunged for the second lariat. "Speed. I stink when I throw fast." And as if to prove it, his next toss was rushed and went wide of the carousel horse's head.

"Rope me, Davey." Adam scrambled to his feet and ran out into the target area.

"That doesn't seem safe." Ashley took a step forward before Zeke stopped her.

"He'll be fine," Zeke said. "They do better with live targets."

"One-upmanship and fun." Rhett nodded.

"It's that competitive instinct and passion for the sport that stops a roper from over-thinking. And sometimes it makes them trust the throwing motion more than they otherwise would."

"My brother, the roping guru." Cassie scoffed, leaping onto Romeo's bare back. "Or should I say he's a roping man's spiritual guide."

But sure enough, Davey roped his brother. And later, when it was little Adam's turn, he returned the favor.

"I'M NOT GOING to be pressured into signing anything by Ashley." Wyatt eased onto the hotel room bed after having been outside with her. The mattress sagged nearly as much as his spirits. He was supposed to be rehabbing inflamed muscles around his lower verte-brae and clearing his head during this break, not facing moral dilemmas and sleeping on lumpy mattresses.

Do the right thing.

Was he a father? He denied the accusation. But denial wouldn't straighten out his feelings about Laurel Monroe's pregnancy. If this story went public with confirmed sources, his chances of landing the lead role in a sci-fi thriller franchise would be ruined.

Wyatt called his agent for an update on film negotiations.

"The news is grim," Brandon told him. "Jess Watanabe's people told me he was put off by the Monroe baby rumor." Jess was going to direct a sci-fi thriller. He liked calm, serene sets and avoided controversy at all costs. The only drama he wanted was the kind that he filmed. "Their decision regarding you as the lead is on hold. I know I didn't want you to go out there, but pictures of you dating slender, not pregnant Ashley Monroe is the best way to banish these rumors. I know you hate to share your personal life to the public, but in this case, please send me photos for my team to post on your official fan page."

Wyatt suppressed a groan. "That's playing right into the Monroe hands."

"I know, but we need some play, buddy."

Wyatt promised to keep his agent in the loop before hanging up.

"We'll need more hangers." Jeremy surveyed the room's small closet. He'd already placed Wyatt's cowboy hat on the top shelf. "And an ironing board. Does your phone need charging? Do you want to shower and change into clean clothes?"

Wyatt stared at the ceiling. His personal assistant wasn't interested in Wyatt's career.

He was interested in his wardrobe and his calendar and keeping people at a distance, the way he'd done with little Gabby earlier. Jeremy's role was clear. Wyatt's path out of this mess was not.

He wished he could just close his eyes and make the entire situation disappear.

"After I unpack, I'll head downstairs so you can rest." Jeremy did a double take, his attention caught by something outside the second-story window.

Rest. Sometimes Wyatt felt like the pampered creature his father accused him of being.

Point of fact, he was tired. It had taken nearly two days of travel to get here from South America, where he'd been filming. He couldn't remember the last time he'd had a full eight hours' sleep.

But rest? The Monroes had a plan. And he'd bet it wasn't a plan where he was a priority. Wyatt could feel a double cross in his bones better than his coal-mining father could feel the earth tremble before a cave-in.

Jeremy continued to stare out the window the way most people stared at their cell phones during a tweet storm.

"Jeremy?"

"Do you remember when the little girl was babbling about our view?"

"About the Sawtooths and the wildflowers?" Oh, yeah. He remembered. She'd reminded him of his older sister Natalie when she was a kid, who could talk a mile a minute if you let her. Much as it pained him to do, Wyatt needed to get back to West Virginia to see his family before he began shooting his next film.

Do the right thing.

He and his family were no longer close. A few years ago, he'd bought his two older sisters and his father each a small ranchette, and his mother a fancy headstone at the cemetery. The gifts didn't make up for his estrangement, but they eased his sense of duty. His mother had always told him that family came first. But his father...

"You'll regret spending money on me when folks realize you got no talent other than your good looks," his father had said when Wyatt handed over the keys. He'd never been supportive of Wyatt's chosen occupation.

If it hadn't been for his mom and older sisters hauling him around as a kid for modeling and small roles in commercials, Wyatt might never have pursued acting at all. He'd be working as a miner now, riding horses and ATVs on the weekends. But they had, and his father's staunch disapproval fueled his need to be the best action star Hollywood had ever known.

"You should come see this," Jeremy said. "I didn't pay attention to the scenery when I was driving."

And Wyatt had been dozing the last half of the trip. He rolled out of bed and sauntered the few steps to the window.

The Salmon River meandered past the inn, its rocky bottom clear from above. On the opposite bank, the carpet of wildflowers began, blue and yellow blossoms swaying in the breeze. Beyond that, a pair of moose meandered across the meadow as if out for a leisurely stroll. And across the valley, the grandiose Sawtooth Mountains rose up to the sky.

It was postcard pretty. But according to the media, so was Wyatt. The difference was that nature had created all that harmonious beauty spontaneously, while Wyatt's presentation was polished by a team of stylists—hair, fashion, fitness, social media. Sometimes he felt there was nothing genuine left about him, inside or out. Nothing but his broken-in cowboy boots and his cowlick.

He returned to the bed, muscles protesting, feeling twice his thirty years. He shifted, lying sideways across the mattress, his head, neck and shoulders hanging off one side of the bed, his feet hanging off the other. "What's the likelihood we can set up my inversion table in the corner?" He needed to release pressure on his vertebrae.

"Slim to none with two beds in here." Jeremy unzipped a suitcase and began shaking out Wyatt's shirts. "Do we have to stay? It's so provincial."

It was a small town, much like the one Wyatt had grown up in. Other than this being the setting for the Ashley-Laurel debacle, he had no gripe with it.

Wyatt stared at the log wall as he tried to relax his muscles to maximize the stretch. But all he saw was Ashley's smile while she kissed him. All he heard was her play on the situation as a movie script. All he felt was her softness as she filled his arms. She surprised him when he thought no one could anymore.

Wyatt Halford from West Virginia would have grinned.

Wyatt Halford from Hollywood scowled.

"THANKS FOR MEETING me here." Shane addressed the group he'd assembled at Egbert's fly-fishing shop at the north end of town.

Ashley checked the time, wondering what

Wyatt was doing. Or more specifically, what he was thinking…about her, her movie-making venture and that kiss. She frowned. The only wondering she needed to be doing about Wyatt involved speculation as to when he'd sign those paternity papers.

On the back porch, Egbert shouted instructions to a pair of tourists who'd stopped to try their luck fishing in the Salmon River. "Flick your wrist. Yes, snap it. Careful of the trees. Pick up that slack with your free hand. There. Good. Better. Isn't that relaxing?"

It didn't sound relaxing to Ashley, but it was a welcome distraction from thoughts of handsome actors. She sat on a bench between her brother, Jonah, and Gabby. "You've got ten minutes, Shane." And then Ashley had a call with the man she wanted to hire as her director of photography.

"I won't waste words." Shane was in casual corporate mode today, wearing a black polo shirt and tan khakis. He might no longer be running Monroe luxury hotels, but he was running things in Second Chance, trying to revitalize the town's economy. And he'd challenged the eleven other Monroes who'd inherited with him to do something—anything—to help him.

At the end of the year, the twelve Monroe heirs were voting on what to do with the town—keep or sell. Currently, the vote was split down the middle. Ashley was voting to sell. She could use the influx of cash to fund her movie production. At the same time, she was rooting for Mitch to obtain historical protections for certain structures so that whoever bought up the land couldn't bulldoze all Second Chance's charm and history.

"We've hooked the big fish." Shane meant Wyatt. "And now we're going to reel him in." Shane was wasting time with metaphors. He tended toward the melodramatic when he had an audience.

Ashley rolled her eyes.

"We got Wyatt in town. Now our goal is for him to perform in the Old West Festival," Shane continued. He'd changed the date of his little street fair so many times, but now it was the day after Laurel's wedding. "And to do that—"

"I thought the goal was to get him to be in our movie," Jonah said only half-seriously, because Jonah was rarely serious about anything. He nudged Ashley.

"I thought the goal was to get him to sign Laurel's paternity papers," Ashley said with a straight face, joining in. She nudged Gabby.

"I don't know what you guys are talking about." Gabby grinned because she was a player when it came to yanking Shane's chain. She was such a great addition to the family. "My only goal was to meet Wyatt Halford. I don't even know why I'm here."

Shane washed a hand over his face. "I'm going to assume this is redheaded humor." Because those seated before him all had red hair, while Shane's was walnut brown. "Focus, all of you. If we can link Wyatt's name with Second Chance, tourism goes up. If we link his name to the Old West Festival, Ashley gains leverage in Hollywood. And if Wyatt becomes fond of the script Jonah's written, Wyatt might decide to play Mike Moody on the big screen, double bonus for Ashley, Jonah and Second Chance."

"But that still doesn't mean he'll give up his legal claim to Laurel's babies," Ashley pointed out.

"That's where Operation Snaparazzi comes in." Shane smiled at Gabby. The duo had created a network of residents to pose as Wyatt Halford fans, snapping his picture with Ashley around Second Chance and posting them to social media as a way to boost attendance at the Old West Festival this weekend. Not to mention, the world would be abuzz with curiosity if Wyatt and Ashley were together in a charming, romantic mountain setting. "He'll be so relieved at the positive press your fake dating creates, that he'll sign those paternity papers. Trust me."

"Now you've done it," Egbert called from the back porch. "Your lure's caught on that log. No…no. Don't step in the…" There was a splash. "Don't fight the current," he shouted. "It'll take you to a sandy shoal down by the inn." And then Egbert muttered, "And this is why I insist clients wear life preservers."

And wasn't the situation out back an apt metaphor for the state of things in Second Chance? It didn't matter if the Monroes were Second Chance's safety net. Sleepy towns, like rookie fly fishermen, were just not bankable. And bankrolls funded films.

"I want to trust you, Shane," Ashley said, channeling her mother's inflexible tone. "But I don't trust Wyatt to play into your hands." He was just too stubborn. "Why can't you write a press release about the gold you found in Mike Moody's hideout?" She checked the time again. "That will create more interest in Second Chance and your festival. And Wyatt might find it intriguing enough to read the script and sign on. I don't want him to feel like he's being manipulated and then put us into a grudge match where the only move he has is his right to those girls. Luckily, he doesn't seem interested in them at the moment." And he was on record in the press as saying he wasn't ready to settle down.

Shane crossed his arms over his chest, brow furrowing. Shane was a dear, but he preferred unquestioned leadership to collaboration.

"Or we could just hand Wyatt the script and cut to the chase," Jonah said crisply. "I tried to leave him a copy when we tracked him down in South America, but Shane wouldn't let me."

"Wyatt would have turned you down in South America." Shane's furrow deepened to a frown. "And then we wouldn't get any buzz from people wondering what he's doing out here."

"Okay. I agree with your handling of buzz in principle," Ashley allowed. "However, Operation Snaparazzi goes too far. Not only is it invasive of Wyatt's privacy, it's deceitful. I'm, uh…trying to change my tactics in that regard."

"No Snaparazzi?" Gabby drooped, pulling at a string in the hem of her teal sundress. "That's the best part. Other than Wyatt Halford being here, that is." She was the operation lookout, the spy who'd alert Shane when Wyatt and Ashley were together.

"Someone's got to post pictures of Wyatt to social media," Shane pointed out. "And it can't come from a Monroe. I'm not including Gabby. She can post, even though she'll be an official Monroe family member after the wedding."

"Sweet." The preteen glowed. "No more *practically* a Monroe."

"I want to go on record as saying this is a bad idea," Ashley said. "Imagine if Wyatt found out that on top of Laurel pretending to be me six months ago, that now I'm positioning him for photo opportunities."

But since there was a snowball's chance that it might work, Ashley was willing to let Shane give it a try.

CHAPTER FOUR

"WHAT ARE YOU DOING?"

Gabby nearly fell off the stool at the front desk.

Jeremy had come silently down the Lodgepole Inn's stairs and was trying to peek over her shoulder at her laptop screen.

She banged it shut. "I'm doing my homework." That was a lie. She was sending a private message to Shane about there being no sign of Wyatt. But she gamely tried to sell her cover. "My dad enrolled me in college prep courses this summer. Weren't you upstairs? I didn't hear you come down."

Gabby glanced over to her soon-to-be-grandma Gen, who sat on the couch and held a magazine up in front of her face as if she had no interest in their conversation.

Jeremy didn't turn to see who she was looking at. "When you checked us in, I noticed how you walked silently up the stairs and down the hall. I retraced your steps." Wyatt's assistant was dressed in pressed khakis, loafers and a red polo shirt with the collar turned up. He had blond hair with dark roots that was flipped up in front like an ocean wave about to crash on top of his head. He was just as foreign to her as the Monroes had been when they'd first arrived last January. And *ew*. He smiled at her as if they were good buddies.

Had he forgotten what a jerk he'd been to her when he'd arrived?

Should she? He'd tipped her and he probably knew what Wyatt was doing. It was her top secret job to find out what that was.

Still undecided, Gabby leaned over to glance up the stairs. "Is Wyatt coming down soon?" If he was, there'd be no need to suck up to Jeremy.

"He's resting, trying to get adjusted to this time zone." Jeremy's smile was faker than his blond hair color. "I bet you know everything that goes on here."

"She does." Grandma Gen set down her copy of the *Hollywood Reporter* and turned to face Jeremy from her position in the corner of the couch in front of the fireplace. She smiled at Jeremy, but it wasn't a smile meant to warm anybody's heart. "Can I help you, Jeremy?"

Jeremy straightened up the way Gabby did when Dad suspected she was surfing the internet when she was supposed to be studying. "I was just wondering where to get a good cup of coffee."

"The Bent Nickel Diner," Gen said coolly.

"Let me rephrase." Jeremy cleared his throat. "Where can I get a soy latte?"

"The Bent Nickel Diner," Gen repeated.

Jeremy hesitated. "And what about—"

"The Bent Nickel Diner," Grandma Gen said a third time without even waiting to hear what the question was.

Gabby suppressed a giggle.

Gen stood in one smooth motion, as if she'd been born in high heels. "As Mr. Halford's assistant, you need to know two things. If you go out this door and turn right, you can find the only services that matter in town— the grocery store, gas pumps and the diner."

Jeremy nodded. "And the second thing?"

Gen passed a hand through the air in Gabby's direction. "This young lady is going to be my granddaughter."

Gabby waited for Jeremy to ask what that meant, since she had no clue.

He must have known what Gen meant, because he nodded and went out the door, turned right and went down the porch stairs, out of sight.

"What was that for?" Gabby asked Gen. "If

you were trying to protect me, don't bother. I've been dealing with Monroes for months without your help."

Grandma Gen walked over to Gabby and laid her soft palm on Gabby's cheek. Her breath smelled like harsh-tasting mouthwash, not the minty kind. "Protecting my family is what I do."

"Don't you think he was just trying to be friendly?"

"No." Gen tsked. "He was trying to milk you for information. I know his kind."

"His kind?"

She nodded. "Yes. What information do you have that he's not supposed to know?"

Like all her Monroe secrets? "Um…" Gabby hedged. "You mean like the Snaparazzi?"

"Yes. And what else?" Grandma Gen made a "gimme more" gesture with her hand.

"I know about Mike Moody's gold."

"And…"

"I know who you invited to the wedding." People who hadn't been on Dad and Laurel's guest list. Gen had slipped in some envelopes to stuff with invitations, which had been Gabby's job. And Grandma Gen had sent out more invitations last week when Wyatt Halford confirmed he was coming.

Gen straightened. "I'm impressed. But you

can't tell Jeremy any of those things. They'll be our secrets. Yours and mine. Try to keep them that way, okay?"

Gabby nodded, pleased with this new partnership, yet she worried.

Could she keep these secrets any better than the one about Wyatt becoming a dad?

ASHLEY SAT WITH Jonah at a rear booth in the Bent Nickel Diner, eating lunch.

On a call earlier, she'd come to a tentative agreement with a director of photography. It was time to celebrate. She was enjoying a strawberry-and-walnut salad, while Jonah picked at a plate of steamed vegetables. They were reviewing a tricky emotional scene Jonah had written, a pivotal moment between Mike Moody's sister Letty and her love interest, the town blacksmith, Jeb Clark.

"We've got to expand this moment that Letty faces." Ashley found a plump section of strawberry hiding in her lettuce. "Jeb offers the traditional life—love, home, children. But although Letty loves him, she feels an equal, if not stronger, pull from the riches that robbery offers her."

"A classic struggle between the safe path and the unpredictable road to potential wealth." Jonah nodded.

In that respect, Ashley felt as if she was wrestling with the same struggle—stay the course as an actress earning a paycheck, or take a chance as a producer gambling her own money and future on a dream.

Jeremy entered the diner and glanced slowly around the room, taking stock.

Ashley evaluated the Bent Nickel as if through Jeremy's eyes, from the perspective of a personal assistant to a megastar. Jeremy was probably thinking the Bent Nickel was a classic roadside dive—green-pleather-and-chrome bar stools at the lunch counter, booths flanking either side, checkerboard linoleum flooring. He'd be wondering if the food would be a pleasant surprise—if Cam was cooking, it was—or if the menu was going to make pleasing his boss more difficult—no doubt, it was.

Predictably, Jeremy turned up his nose. But before he could turn to go, Roy burst through the door behind him. The elderly town maintenance man wore threadbare blue coveralls and a black baseball cap. According to Shane, he'd been preparing several abandoned cabins for rental, which she was grateful for since housing would be vital to her film production.

"She's back," Roy said breathlessly.

Several patrons turned at his words.

"Great opening line," Jonah murmured. And then he said louder to Roy, "Who's back?"

"That Mama Grizzly." Roy pushed Jeremy out of the way to reach their table. "She comes down the mountain every summer."

Behind the counter, Ivy, the proprietor of the Bent Nickel, gasped. "She pushed my huge trash bin into the river last year while she tried to get it open."

"That she-devil," Jonah murmured, catching Ashley's eye, trying to make her laugh.

Ashley refused to take the bait.

Roy nodded. "She broke into a car parked by the highway two years ago just to reach an open bag of potato chips."

"Barbecued?" Jonah gave Roy an innocent look.

"Salt and vinegar." Roy didn't miss a beat.

The smile on Jonah's face grew to misbehaving levels.

"Remember the year she ransacked my kitchen." This from an older man at the lunch counter. "I left my windows open when I drove to the store for milk. When I returned, she'd torn out my window and the door on the fridge."

Jonah leaned toward Ashley. "Maybe we should write a bear encounter in the script."

Ashley shook her head. The script was already long.

"And then there was that IRS woman who came to visit Egbert." Roy removed his cap and held it over his heart, as if honoring her passing. "He warned her about wearing fruit-scented lotion during grizzly season."

There was a moment of silence, making Ashley wonder what had happened to the poor woman.

"Can I help you?" Ivy asked Jeremy, who still stood near the door. His eyes were wide and his stance uncertain. "Bathrooms are in the back."

"I'm looking for a soy latte." Wyatt's assistant's voice shook. "And a black coffee."

"I'm sorry. Our latte machine is broken." Ivy pointed over her shoulder to her fiancé, Ashley's cousin Cam. He had the unit open and was poking around inside.

"Look!" Roy charged toward the front plate-glass windows. "There she is!"

Jeremy spun. He gasped. He gasped louder than anyone.

And then he was gone.

WYATT WAS JUST finishing his yoga floor work to strengthen and stretch his back when Jeremy burst back into the room.

"There's wildlife here." Jeremy backed

against the closed door, as if the wildlife was on the other side.

"It is the mountains." Wyatt got to his feet with only minimal joint pops and cracks. "We saw moose."

"There are *bears*." Jeremy tugged at his polo collar. "Grizzlies."

"Not in this room." Wyatt glanced outside. The only wildlife he saw were butterflies.

"I'm talking about out there," Jeremy whispered, as if there was a bear in the hallway and he was afraid it might hear him.

"Calm down." Wyatt suppressed a smile. "What's wrong? Wildlife doesn't faze you. You just spent four months with me in the jungle."

"We only saw monkeys and parrots." Jeremy held up a finger. "And we went back to the hotel every night, where I could get you your morning coffee and my soy latte. My one indulgence."

Wyatt scratched the back of his neck. "I'm not sure I follow."

"There were no *bears* in South America." Jeremy's gaze swept the floor. "I'm deathly afraid of bears."

"Deathly." Not just plain afraid. His assistant was *deathly* afraid of bears.

Jeremy's frightened gaze landed on Wyatt.

"That bear is as big as a Volkswagen. And it walked through town as if it owned the place. No fear whatsoever."

Wyatt searched for the right thing to say. He patted Jeremy awkwardly on the shoulder. "That must have been…scary." Scarier than being sent down in a dark basement to find a working landline?

Oh, yeah. Ashley's horror-movie example came to mind.

Oh, no. Do not laugh.

Wyatt tried to hold on to a too-brief flashback of Ashley's kiss. Tried and failed.

"You think this is funny." Jeremy knocked the back of his head against the door. "There are bears *in town* and…" He swallowed in an obvious attempt to regain his composure. "Do you know all the irons are checked out downstairs? And the one latte machine in Second Chance is broken? I can't work in these conditions."

"These conditions?" His good humor faded. They had beds, electricity and running water. "You mean no irons, no lattes, and…*bears*?"

"Yes." Jeremy bolted for his bags, which had yet to be unpacked. "I need a bear-free vacation. I've worked for you for a year and I've never taken one. And I need one. Now."

"By all means." Wyatt stood back, clearing the path to the exit. "I'll let you know when I'll be returning to LA. Can you make it back on your own?" He had to ask because just then Jeremy didn't look as if he'd make it out the front door.

Jeremy sniffed. "They may have stolen our spark plugs, but I'm sure they'll help me find a ride to the Boise airport." In no time, he was banging his way out the door, down the hall and on his way to vacation.

Leaving Wyatt with a room all to himself, which, all things considered, was a relief.

Jeremy didn't know Wyatt's back regimen was anything more than part of his regular strength and conditioning program. Wyatt's back pain was currently chronic, but with a few days' rest and the right care, he hoped he'd be fine. And it wasn't as if he couldn't lift things, like a suitcase or a mattress, as long as he practiced good form.

At least, that was what he told himself as he moved Jeremy's mattress and box spring against the wall, and broke down the wooden antique bed frame to make room for his inversion machine.

Now he just had to find a way to get the heavy equipment out of the SUV and upstairs.

No pep talk was going to convince him he could do that alone.

INSOMNIA WAS A movie producer's best friend.

Or at least, Ashley's. She couldn't seem to shut her brain off and go to sleep.

In the kitchen alcove downstairs, Ashley turned on the electric kettle and then searched through the tea options for something calming with only the hall light for guidance.

A figure appeared in the shadowy doorway.

Ashley's heart scaled up her throat.

"Wyatt." She swallowed it back down. "You scared me half to death."

"Your scream got that message across." He wore black basketball shorts and a Los Angeles Clippers jersey. His dark hair was mussed and his gaze more alert than it should be at midnight, although he seemed as surprised to see her as she was to see him. After all, he'd jumped.

"I didn't scream." Did she? She tore into a package of chamomile.

The door to Laurel and Mitch's apartment flew open. Mitch stepped out, surveying the pair, short dark hair mussed. "Who screamed?"

"Do I look like a screamer?" Wyatt demanded.

"You do," Mitch said, without taking time to think about it. "If you're having trouble sleeping, might I suggest reading and signing those paternity papers? I could get them for you."

Wyatt's jaw worked, but he only said stiffly, "No, thanks."

"You'll have to review them sometime." Mitch closed the door, leaving them alone.

Alone with the sexiest man alive.

The very air between them felt thick. Why couldn't his being stubborn hinder his magnetism?

Focus. And not on the sexy.

She'd start with his clothing. Thankfully, he was wearing some. A Clippers jersey, in fact. And snap. Ashley was wearing a Lakers tank.

She held her shirt out, glancing down at it. "This must be where we agree to disagree."

"About?" Wyatt rubbed a hand over his hair, teasing that cowlick.

"Basketball. Screaming. Your involvement with my nieces." She should hold meetings in the middle of the night more often. Exhaustion made her much sharper.

"I didn't get Laurel pregnant," Wyatt said wearily.

"Why do I feel as if this is a murder mystery and I'm the unlikely detective interviewing my prime suspect?" Ashley tossed the tea bag into a mug and poured hot water over it.

"Have you been spiking your tea?" Wyatt pointed to the trash and a small, empty bottle of vodka. Coincidentally, it was a brand of vodka her mother favored.

Ashley regrouped. "Do you have an alibi for the night my nieces were conceived?"

He scowled at her.

She decided to scowl right back. "This isn't a case of 'he said, she said.' Laurel is willing to take whatever test you want to prove her case. But honestly, Wyatt... Are you trying to say my sister might have slept with someone else but wants to pin it on you?" Ashley attempted to laugh. "Laurel loves Mitch. She could have bypassed the public repercussions of a one-night stand without ever telling you and put Mitch's name on the twins' birth certificates. It would have been easier all around. But Laurel doesn't like to lie."

"Except when she's pretending to be you."

It wasn't rage that welled up inside Ashley at his retort. It was guilt. And shame. And tongue-sealing self-reproach. Because of Ashley, Laurel's character was being questioned. Laurel's character was the epicenter of Wyatt's doubt. Ashley could argue until she was blue in the face. It would do no good. She was going to have to come at Wyatt another way.

And since she didn't know what that argument was, she could only reply with a flat "Good night."

She trudged up the stairs, leaving Wyatt in the kitchenette. When she was in her room, she inched her way along the wall to her side of the bed she shared with her mother to set down her tea.

"You're losing much-needed beauty sleep over this passion project of yours," Mom said, without removing her hydrating sleep mask.

"Producers don't need beauty sleep."

"You say that now. Wait three more years until you're thirty. You'll sing a different tune."

"Will I?" She'd rather be happy in her own skin and with her own choices.

And she had to make sure Laurel had a chance to do the same.

CHAPTER FIVE

MORNINGS WERE ASHLEY'S busiest time of the day.

When most people were still asleep, she could get a ton done.

Two mornings after Wyatt Halford came to Second Chance, Ashley unlocked the Bent Nickel Diner at 5:00 a.m., carrying a stack of folders and her laptop. She had her comfy sweats on, her hair in a braid, a baseball cap on her head and a metal water bottle dangling from her finger.

Cousin Camden turned on the kitchen lights just as Ashley turned on the dining room lights. He'd given her a key, because she couldn't work in the cramped room at the inn she and her mother shared. It was a toss-up as to who showed up in the diner first—Ashley or Cam. Today, it was a draw.

"Morning. Hot water for tea coming right up." Cam plugged in the electric kettle as Ashley took her seat in a booth near the back. And then Cam went about his morning kitchen prep, leaving her alone.

She checked her social-media groups first. The production team on her longest-running television show was excited about a spin-off Ashley was in the process of pitching to a streaming network. Her cast mates from her last rom-com film checked in from the sets of their latest jobs. Her favorite hair and makeup team posted pictures from a historical film they were working on. All those ringlets. Ashley had hair envy. Not to mention, she hoped to hire them for her film if she could knock their price down. Seeing everyone safe and well gave her just the boost she needed to seize the day.

A jogger moved past the window, catching her eye. It was Wyatt. Sweat dripped from his hair and darkened his shirt. He spotted her inside and came to a full stop.

Oh. My. Word.

Her heart raced when their eyes met.

She swallowed, trying to find some detachment. Maybe if she regarded him more the way a producer would and less like a woman.

That's it. Her pulse settled as she looked at him with a more critical eye.

He was magnetic, not just because he was

gorgeous and muscular, but because his dark gaze was intelligent and intense. It was why the camera loved him. Ashley took a moment to drink in the art that was Wyatt, because art had to be appreciated, even if said master-piece was hardheaded and was rumored to hold a grudge. Even if for one brief moment, she allowed herself to mourn the fact that he wasn't committed to her...*film*, that was.

Cam set a mug of hot water in front of her, along with a tea bag.

"Thanks." She'd needed a reminder that it was time to work. There'd be enough time to address Wyatt complications later in the day.

While her tea steeped, Ashley opened the file Laurel had emailed her with wardrobe sketches for the film. Ashley was playing the role of Mike's sister Letty. She wanted the dresses Letty wore in the beginning of the story to reflect the sharpness of her character, the cunning she hid beneath her pretty curls and innocent smile.

She could see Letty walking through the wagon train's staging area before it left on its westward journey, admiring the posses-sions of her fellow travelers and charming the wagon master into teaching her how to fire his Sharps rifle.

Wyatt sat down across from Ashley and waved to Cam. "Water, please." He was a sweaty mess. "I think I slept two days straight. I needed it after the push to finish filming and the time it took to get here. I'm assuming someone would have told me if Laurel had given birth."

"No babies yet. Can you toss him a towel, Cam?" Ashley barely looked up from her screen, but she was 100 percent aware of Wyatt. The way his chest heaved. The way he rearranged his limbs in the booth. The way her brain wanted to focus on him, rather than her work.

Jerk, her brain said.

Not so fast, her body said.

"You're up early, Ashley. Did you already get your workout in?" Wyatt eased back into the seat.

"I don't work out. I walk."

Keep those eyes glued to the screen, girl.

Impossible.

She lifted her gaze. She needn't have looked. The artwork hadn't changed. Its impact on her hadn't changed.

"It's always work first for Ash. I'm Cam, by the way." Her cousin set a large glass of ice water and a hand towel in front of Wyatt. "If they had a treadmill at the inn, she wouldn't have to hike around Second Chance every afternoon."

"I actually like breathtaking views," Ashley said, still staring at Wyatt. Not all eye-popping vistas were outdoors.

Girl.

Ashley frowned. She couldn't afford to be swept away by Wyatt's devastating looks and happier mood. Where was cranky Wyatt?

"You hike around the valley with bears about?" Wyatt raised his glass to Ashley in a mock toast. "I take it you don't have a deathly fear of the beasts. I lost my assistant to arkoudaphobia." He lowered his glass and his voice. "That's a deathly fear of bears, even the friendly panda. I looked it up."

"Ash knows no fear." Cam winked at her, possibly remembering the time she'd run screaming when he'd held a lizard in her face during a childhood camping trip with their grandpa Harlan.

"I don't carry any food when I walk," Ashley told Wyatt, trying to ignore her cousin. "And I tend to stay in the meadow." Which so far had been bear-free.

"Hey, superstar." Cam tapped the table near Wyatt. "Just FYI. We're not open yet."

"But you're serving Ash." Wyatt drank more water.

Ashley sighed. "I come here early to work in peace." Instead, she was going to have to assemble her defenses and disassemble Wyatt's. "I don't order breakfast until the diner is officially open for business. And in return Cam leaves me alone." Hint, hint.

"Sorry. I forgot." Cam headed toward the kitchen. "I'm supposed to be the silent prima donna chef, not the chatty diner cook."

Wyatt wiped the sweat from his face and hair, waiting until Cam was in the kitchen to speak. "About this situation we find ourselves in…"

Ashley closed her laptop, almost grateful for another legitimate excuse to look at all that gorgeousness. "Let's cut to the chase. Do you accept the idea that the girls are yours? Do you want to be a father?"

"Maybe?" Wyatt winced. For the first time that morning, he seemed deflated. "But that's not the issue, is it?"

"Isn't it? Let's say they are yours. If you want to be an involved dad, there is visitation and child support to be arranged. The entertainment reporters will have questions and search for surface-level dirt, but we can get out ahead of them before your name goes in the public record on the babies' birth certificates. Because you know you can't keep this a secret. Someone is going to see your name while processing the babies' paperwork and see dollar signs and leak that to the press." Had she laid that on too thick? "But if you don't want to be a father, you can take care of that with a simple signature. There will be nothing to link you to the girls but DNA. There will be no scandal. No speed bump put in front of our careers." It was what Ashley, her mother and Mitch wanted.

"You think I should sign." How quickly Wyatt became closed off. "For the good of both of us."

"I didn't say that. I stand behind what's good for my sister." But her conscience wouldn't let her forget Laurel's indecision regarding Wyatt's parental role. He deserved the choice to be involved or not. "Those babies my sister is carrying... Their well-being and happiness should be more important than our acting careers."

Wyatt's expression gave nothing away. He glanced up at a yellowed, framed photograph of a prospector and his mule. "My agent thinks

I should sign." His statement alone indicated he was considering fatherhood.

Dang it.

Ashley tugged at the neck of her T-shirt. "You know… I don't always do what my agent says."

Wyatt returned his gaze to hers and raised his eyebrows. He obviously knew her mother's reputation.

"It's a fairly recent development." Ashley didn't add that she planned on firing her mother after Laurel's wedding. She needed an agent who shared her vision for the future. And, of course, she needed to work up the nerve to let Mom go. "Seeing as how it sounds like you're not going to give up your rights—"

"Not just yet, no."

"—you need to be my date for the baby shower this evening." Where guests would have the opportunity to snap his photo.

"I'm not the baby-shower type." Wyatt regained some of his deprecating attitude. "Nor did I bring a gift."

"You can mooch off mine."

Wyatt scowled. It was becoming clear that he wasn't going to be agreeable, even if it was good for him.

He's not right for the role of Mike Moody.

It was a niggle of a thought, just a feeling, really. And because of what was at stake for her—funding, distribution, word of mouth—Ashley squashed it. She wasn't going to openly pursue Wyatt, but she wouldn't turn him down outright if he wanted the role.

"And how, exactly, does the dating ruse help the situation?" He wiped at his damp hair with the towel, distressing his trademark cowlick.

"The ruse offers an explanation as to why you're around Laurel and the babies when they arrive." Which could be any day now. Twins were notorious for coming early and Laurel was about thirty weeks along.

"An explanation will only be necessary if people find out I'm here." He grimaced. "Which they will, if, let's say, pictures were to circulate."

Was he suspicious about Operation Snaparazzi? Since he'd been recovering from filming and jet lag, the town's amateur photographers had been standing down, awaiting Gabby's signal.

"I can't very well institute a no-photo policy at my sister's baby shower." Ashley schooled her expression to mimic a slightly harried school secretary, one reluctantly charged with upholding the rules. "This isn't a closed movie set. And you *are* the world-famous Wyatt Halford. People are bound to take pictures with you." And post them, complete with the hashtags #SecondChance, #OldWestFestival, #WyattHalford and #AshleyMonroeMovie. "Look at it this way. Our *dating* gives you a chance to think about what you want to do next. Being a parent comes with a lot of responsibility. You don't want to let your kids down."

"Parenthood." Wyatt looked flummoxed, as if he truly didn't know what to do. "My own parents... My mom was great, but sick a lot. And my father was...not the greatest. But he was responsible. Brought home a paycheck every two weeks and was around some of the time."

Saying a father was around some of the time wasn't high praise. Ashley felt sorry for him.

"I know something of factory-defective parents." Ashley had two. "And I understand a little of your dilemma. Acting isn't a nine-to-five, home-every-night job."

He nodded.

It was odd how between catching sight of

Wyatt jogging and talking through his options in this crisis, he'd become less of an icon and more of a person. But she was being too fair, too wishy-washy, like Laurel. She needed to be more like her mother and maneuver him the way that was best for her sister.

Ashley's phone sat on the table. A message popped up.

He leaned forward. "Checking in with your friends. That's nice."

Nice? The word was Ashley's hot button.

Ashley Monroe is so nice. Not: *Ashley Monroe is so talented.*

Grrr. "It's not *nice*, Wyatt. It's what you do when you care. And in this business, all aspects of this business, people can get beaten down by just about everything. Sometimes, you need just one person to listen and validate you." Best leave it at that before she dumped more emotion in his lap. Ashley opened her computer. "Sorry. I need to get through some work stuff before seven."

Wyatt shifted in his seat, twisting his back as if his muscles needed stretching. "Reviewing that precious script of yours? What's the working title?"

"*The Ballad of Mike Moody.* And I'm not reading it this morning. I'm reviewing wardrobe designs Laurel created. She's very talented." She tapped the pile of folders on the table next to her. "Lots to do." That was his invitation to leave.

Instead, Wyatt took the top file folder and began flipping through it.

He's not Mike Moody.

Wyatt was too bold for the tailor turned stagecoach robber. Too in-your-face. It was Letty who ran the gang, not Mike. Wyatt's ego wouldn't let him play a believable second fiddle. It would come through on the screen, clearer than that cowlick.

His dark gaze pivoted to her, tinged with disbelief that stung sharper than the "nice" label. "This is a list of film support companies. Lighting. Sound. Craft services. And you were talking with Zeke about horses for the movie. Are you acting *and* producing this film?"

"You don't have to sound surprised," she said evenly, trying not to snap. Was it so farfetched that she'd produce a movie? "You may have heard I'm starting my own production company."

"I hadn't. So, it's to be a comedic western?" Wyatt tossed her folder back on the pile. "Or a romantic saga?"

"Not a comedy. Not a romance." It galled her that he'd have that impression. Not that the entire world wouldn't have the same expectation. Rom-coms and lighthearted romance made up Ashley's adult acting credits. Drama? No one would expect it in her wheelhouse. And that was why she had to come out of her shell and sell the idea. "It's a western." Ashley busied herself with her tea bag. "The good westerns—the classics—fire on all cylinders around the key themes of justice and the struggle of surviving in the frontier. It's the reason people love the genre." She loved filmography and would have studied it in college if her career or her mother had allowed her time to attend.

"The former child star wants to take on a would-be classic." Wyatt arched in his seat the way Laurel did when her back bothered her. "This probably wasn't the best time to ignore the advice of your momager. I'm assuming she disapproves."

"Yes." And so did he. It was all there in his sharp little barbs. Didn't he know that her father ran Monroe Studios? Didn't he know she'd directed TV episodes of her series when she was sixteen? And had executive produced episodes when she was nineteen? But more important, didn't he think she was capable of navigating her own career?

I am more than a Hollywood cliché.

The affirmation did nothing to calm the frustration thrumming through her veins. But it was a reminder to don her battle armor and her strongest, most impenetrable weapon— her acting talent.

Drawing a breath, Ashley drummed her fingers on her laptop and regarded Wyatt with a veneer of calm that felt as thin as crumbling salt around the rim of a margarita glass. "Mike Moody and his sister came from Philadelphia. He was a tailor and hoping to settle in San Francisco, but he was unsuited for the hardships encountered on a wagon train. He and his sister were accused of stealing. They were kicked out of the wagon train and settled in Second Chance."

"You'll be playing the part of the sister." Wyatt grinned. "So, you're looking for a leading man who can play the gentle tailor who morphs into a cold-blooded killer."

She didn't tell him his guess was close, but wrong. "Whoever plays Mike and Letty Moody must be able to handle the hallmarks of the genre—horse chases—"

"Check." He finger-checked an air box.

"—and gunfights."

"Check. Check." He continued to make light of her project.

I will not grit my teeth. I will not grit my teeth. "And be able to portray both the expectations of the character's facade and drop subtle clues in their performance as to their true nature." Mike's onset of blindness and resulting meltdown. Letty's unbridled greed, and her belief that life owed her more than she'd been given.

"Check, check, check. Too bad you can't afford me." Wyatt sipped his water. "If you're looking for atmosphere, I saw the town's historic blacksmith shop down the road. You might add a horseshoeing scene."

He had no idea how important that smithy was to the story. Blacksmith Jeb Clark would fall hard for Letty, but ultimately his love would lead to her bloody demise.

Ashley filled her lungs with air and stayed in character as the Ashley Monroe no one could rattle.

Her phone vibrated. A text came in from Emily Clark at the Bucking Bull Ranch.

Wyatt leaned forward, irritating in his interest in her private correspondence.

Still up for riding and shooting this morning?

He lifted that dark gaze to hers, and for the first time, it was filled with mischief. "I am."

"You weren't invited." But her heart beat faster at the thought of him coming along. Not because she was interested in him romantically, but because if he joined her, he might soften up about taking the role of Mike Moody.

And like clockwork, just the thought of Wyatt playing the role activated that niggle of doubt. Her grandfather had made several fortunes by following his instincts. Might just as well get this gut feeling out on the table now. "Don't take this the wrong way, but I think you'd be miscast in the role of Mike Moody."

Just saying it out loud brought her tremendous relief. She grinned. Not as Ashley Monroe, America's Sweetheart, but as Ash Monroe, confident, soon-to-be accomplished producer. And later, a respected director.

"Nice try, but reverse psychology doesn't work on me." Wyatt drained his water glass and stood, not as smoothly as she might have thought. His muscles must be stiffening after his run. "You'll take me riding and shooting this morning to foster this impression that we're dating." He sauntered out of the diner as if he was the Mike Moody of legend.

Darn.

"GOOD MORNING." GABBY greeted Wyatt from behind the check-in desk. "Did you have a good breakfast? Isn't Cam a great cook? Do you need anything? Coffee? Tea? Water? The internet password?"

Wyatt hurried past his young, fawning fan. "I'm good."

A lie. He was still smarting over Ashley's comment in the diner. How dare she tell him he wasn't right for the part of some two-bit bandit from the Idaho mountains? He was going to show her just how good he was on horseback later today. That would change her mind. Not that he planned to change his mind about taking the role.

"Gabby." Laurel stepped out of the apartment behind the desk. She wore a stylish, flowery blue dress. For a pregnant woman, she had style. "Give the man some space."

Wyatt hadn't seen Laurel in two days. Was it possible she'd grown larger? Or maybe that was just him, panicking when confronted by what might be his doing.

Do the right thing.

His mother would want him to accept Laurel at her word and stand up to the consequences of his actions. His father would laugh at his predicament and demand the same thing.

Wyatt couldn't ignore the situation. He turned to face it and Laurel head-on. "Gabby's fine. Fans have presented me with much worse questions."

"Like what?" Gabby asked.

Laurel gently shushed her.

There was a "pregnant" pause where the three of them stared at each other.

And then Laurel laughed. A hearty *hardy-har-har*.

Wyatt remembered that laugh. He remembered thinking on their date that it wasn't the laugh of his teenage TV crush. On-screen, Ashley had a melodious laugh, one that matched the sweet characters she played.

His body went cold.

It's true. I'm a father.

Laurel must have seen a change in his expression, an acceptance of fact, because she sobered. "Do you hate me?"

He shook his head, trying to regain some semblance of composure without admitting he was responsible for Laurel's situation. "My mother always told me it wasn't right to hate anyone." She'd told him that in regards to his father. "Are the babies healthy?"

"Yes." Laurel nodded. "When I first found out I was pregnant, I was terrified you'd seek out revenge against me and Ashley." She took a step closer, lowering her voice, although Gabby would hear anyway. She was mere feet away. "I was afraid you'd take my babies from me." She cradled her belly. "Actually, my mother put that idea in my head. But once it was there…" Laurel blew out a breath. "I couldn't get it out."

"I heard that." Genevieve stepped out of the kitchenette, wearing a blue satin bathrobe. Her short, bright red hair was in clips, and her face was covered with a green facial mask. She carried a cup of tea. "I make no apologies. I'm paid good money to be the worst-case scenario thinker in the room." She stomped upstairs.

"The walls here aren't much good at keeping secrets," Laurel said plainly. "When there are walls."

Wyatt gave Gabby a significant glance. "Should we take this conversation elsewhere?"

"Why?" Laurel reached over to smooth Gabby's strawberry blond hair. "This young lady's already heard everything I told you. And she'll only find a way to hear whatever we talk about if we relocate."

"Being plugged in is a gift," Gabby said unapologetically. "But in my defense, those are my baby sisters. I need to watch out for them." Her expression was so earnest, Wyatt had no doubt she would.

There was another pregnant pause, during which time Wyatt realized he shouldn't have a conversation about Laurel's babies if he wasn't willing to at least admit there was a possibility they were his babies.

Her apartment door was open. He poked his head in for a better look. It was clean but sparsely furnished, mostly because it was as cramped as a New York walk-up.

"All five of you are going to live here?" he asked. Laurel, Gabby, the babies and the overprotective Mitch?

"We're still trying to figure that out." Laurel smiled weakly. "An innkeeper needs to be on the premises. But I doubt guests will appreciate babies crying at all hours of the night."

"You realize that if those babies are mine, this setup is completely inadequate." So much for staying quiet on the subject.

Gabby scowled.

Laurel's eyes looked a bit watery. "I know. But I'm not going to lie to you about our situation and the challenges ahead. Just like I wouldn't expect you to lie to me."

Touché.

"You can't judge mine and Ashley's actions without seeing it from our shoes." Laurel squared her shoulders and blinked back her tears, giving Wyatt the impression that in the Monroe family, she was Ashley's protector, not Genevieve. "Ashley has always cared deeply for others. It's what makes her a good actress, but also what makes her so vulnerable in relationships. It's why I would stand in for her. As with most actors, her greatest strength is also her greatest weakness."

Before he could fully ponder Laurel's words, her phone rang.

She glanced at the screen, the icon of which was a big, beating heart. "It's Mitch. He's down in Boise pitching the historical commission again." She entered the apartment and closed the door as she answered, leaving Wyatt with Gabby.

"Can I do something for you?" he asked since she was staring.

"That's my line." Color rose in the girl's cheeks as she reached in a desk drawer. "But since you're asking, will you autograph my copy of this magazine? You're on the cover. It's the one where they crowned you the sexiest man alive. Or should I say SMA? That sounds cool, doesn't it? Like a secret?"

It sounded like a professional abbreviation—PGA, Producers Guild of America; DGA, Directors Guild of America. Let Ashley chase after credentials. Wyatt would chase after cash. He reached for a pen on her desk. "I'll sign. But after that, no more hero worship. I'm just a guest here, okay?"

"You could never be *just* anything." Which made Wyatt feel better about Ashley's rejection of him for the Mike Moody role, until Gabby yanked the magazine out of his reach. "Unless you try to take my baby sisters. And then you'd be just plain bad."

CHAPTER SIX

To Wyatt, the Bucking Bull Ranch, where Ashley took him to ride, looked like a movie set but felt like home.

An old but well-kept white two-story farmhouse with a broad front porch. A big barn. Massive pine trees. Pastures in the distance filled with cattle. White clouds drifting lazily across the blue sky.

Wyatt could feel the atmosphere of the ranch soak through his cowboy boots, adding a strut to his walk. He settled his cowboy hat more firmly on his head. It felt good to get away from the inn and the dad conundrum. And his back was rested, loose even. It had been two years since he'd last ridden, but when he got in the saddle, Ashley was going to see he'd be a natural as Mike Moody.

Closing her SUV's door, Ashley took him in with a quick glance and a roll of her eyes. "Jeez, can you tone down the movie-star chutzpah, please?"

"Nope. Wyatt Halford is a movie star *and*

a cowboy." He upped the wattage on his strut if only because it annoyed her. On the drive over, she'd listened to a lengthy weather report on unspeakably high volume, which had annoyed him.

"Movie stars make appearances with wrinkled shirts now?" Ashley teased.

"Perhaps you can loan me your iron."

"And have you *forget* to return it? My mother would kill me." Her blue eyes sparkled.

Wyatt curbed the urge to smile. It wouldn't do to let on that he enjoyed their banter.

A brunette greeted them from the barn door. Three young boys milled around her. They all wore hats and boots. They all gawked at Wyatt, but not like his fandom, who hoped for something from him—an autograph or a hug captured in a photo. No. This bunch stared at Wyatt as if he were a seldom-seen curiosity, like the world's biggest ball of yarn. Something to be gawked at and then forgotten.

"That's him," said the tallest boy. He must have been about ten or eleven. He tilted back his cowboy hat with his...wrist? He was missing a hand but didn't seem self-conscious about it.

Some of the cock drained from Wyatt's walk.

"He's just a city slicker, like Jonah," said

the second-tallest boy, sizing up Wyatt and finding him wanting. He looked to be about eight or nine, the same age as Wyatt's nephews. "Look how new his boots are."

"They're not that new," Wyatt murmured, catching Ashley's eye.

"If you can't say something nice…" The youngest boy seemed about kindergarten age. He swung the arm of the brunette cowgirl, hardly interested in Ashley or Wyatt.

Ashley made the introductions. "Wyatt, this is Emily Clark, and you've met her nephews—Davey, Charlie and Adam. Emily is the stock wrangler for my production. Zeke works for her."

"And she's the one who's been giving you riding lessons, I presume." Wyatt shook Emily's hand.

Little Adam grinned up at Wyatt, still swinging his aunt's arm. "My granny Gertie likes you."

"Oh, my goodness. Wyatt Halford." As if on cue, an old woman stepped out on the farmhouse porch across the ranch yard. She wore a blue chambray shirt, frayed blue jeans and scuffed red cowboy boots. "It really is you. Can I get a picture?" She didn't wait for permission. She gripped the stair rail and made her way toward them in a careful but hurried walk.

"If only I were twenty years younger," Charlie said in a falsetto, clearly trying to replicate Gertie's words.

"Granny Gertie likes your movies." Davey, the oldest, grinned and slugged Charlie, the middle boy. "Be nice."

"I'm. Your. Biggest fan," Gertie said, winded.

Gabby would no doubt argue with Gertie as to who held the number one spot.

"I even liked you when you played the baddie in your last film." Gertie came to a stop in front of him. She wore false eyelashes but the end of one was waving in the breeze. "Folks need to stretch themselves, whether they be a cowboy or they play one on TV."

Did no one believe he was an authentic cowboy? Wyatt turned on the charm for Gertie. "Thank you for your appreciation of my work."

"Hang on. You've got a flyer." Ashley swooped in, gently pressing the false eyelash back in place for the elderly woman. "There you go. Picture-perfect."

"Almost ready for my close-up." Gertie yanked up her bra straps. "Em, take my picture with these two stars."

"Snaparazzi." Little Adam snapped his fingers like castanets. Over and over.

His brothers chortled.

While Wyatt wondered what "snaparazzi" meant, he and Ashley were herded into book-ending Gertie while Emily took their picture. Oddly enough, Ashley's smile seemed strained. He wondered why, since these were her people. Could it be she was thrown off because Gertie was his biggest fan and not hers?

"You know—" Gertie turned with those careful steps of hers to face Wyatt "—my Percy was one of the original—"

"Descendants of the founding fathers of Second Chance." Ashley cut her off. "Percy was related to Old Jebediah Clark, the blacksmith whose smithy you saw in town." She barely acknowledged Wyatt's nod before continuing. "What are we working on today, Emily?"

"It's a gallop to pick up gold." Emily settled her hat more firmly on her head and grinned at the boys before marching off. "The arena is already set up for the stunt. Granted, it's a bit short, but we don't have to worry about gopher or prairie-dog holes."

"We all tried it and ate dirt," Adam piped up proudly.

"You didn't have to tell *him* that." Davey turned away from Wyatt, blushing.

"I practically fell on my head. In slo-mo," Charlie admitted, removing his hat to show

Wyatt where it'd been creased. "Auntie Em said next time I have to wear a helmet."

Wyatt smiled and made all the appropriate responses young boys liked to hear. "So this isn't a trail ride or a simple riding lesson?"

"It's work," Ashley said, bristling. "Stunt work. You should enjoy this, Wyatt, since you do all your own stunts."

And he had an aching back to prove it. But this stunt couldn't be that risky if the kids were giving it a go. It should be fun.

"Make sure you stop by before you leave, Wyatt," Gertie said over her shoulder as she headed back to the house. "I've got cookies in the oven, just in case I lose a bet."

The boys chortled and roughhoused their way to the arena.

Ashley followed Emily. No cowboy hat for Ash. She still wore the baseball cap from this morning. Her long red braid swung across her shoulders with each step. She wore a bright green T-shirt proclaiming herself a fan of human kindness. But her boots and blue jeans looked well-worn.

Wyatt wasn't fooled by the worn boots and blue jeans. They were a fashion statement in Hollywood, faded in the factory, not by use. He fully expected Ash to bounce in the saddle like the Hollywood princess she was.

The youngest Clark latched on to his hand and skipped to keep up with Wyatt's long stride.

Wyatt's heart unexpectedly skipped a beat. Kids didn't grab on to his hand, not even his nephews. But this small boy had seen something in him, felt confident enough to place his hand in Wyatt's, almost as if he were a trusted friend or uncle or...*father*.

For years, Wyatt had shied away from serious relationships, wanting his career to be the most important thing in his life. He needed to reach the pinnacle in Hollywood before he slowed down and did justice to a marriage and kids. And nothing had made him doubt that decision until this runt of a cowboy had taken his hand and made him feel as if he was missing something.

Do the right thing.

"Do you have a horse at home, Mr. Wyatt?" Adam asked, staring up at him as if he'd known him since birth.

"I don't own a horse anymore." Not since he'd left home for Hollywood. He owned a Ferrari now, which had close to one thousand horsepower at the top end.

"Boys, don't you have chores to do?" Emily opened the arena gate.

"Yep." Davey climbed up on the metal

railing. "But Granny Gertie bet me a batch of chocolate chip cookies that Ian Bradford could complete the stunt when I said he couldn't."

"You bet against me, Davey?" Wyatt caught Ashley's eye and grinned.

"Yep," Davey said.

And wonder of wonders, Ashley grinned right back, as if they hadn't been at odds with each other since his arrival in town.

And in that grinning mental space, he remembered the exception to their sparring ways—the heart-thumping kiss they'd shared on the Lodgepole Inn's porch. Talk about good memories. And he wanted to make another. But there was an audience and a challenge ahead. "What is this course you're talking about?"

"It's a scene from the movie." Ashley entered the arena, still grinning. "Mike Moody and his gang are robbing a stage. One of the passengers collects everyone's valuables in a small burlap bag and drops it. Someone gallops up, leans over and snatches it from the ground. Do you want to give it a try? I won't judge you if you don't want to. After all, it's not your film." Spoken like he had an open invitation for it to be.

He made a show of planting his booted feet.

Hitch his train to Ashley Monroe's wagon? Not in this lifetime.

"Should I have had him sign a waiver?" Emily asked, a glint of mischief in her eyes. "I don't want to be sued if he gets hurt. And after all, Charlie almost fell on his head."

Adam swung Wyatt's arm. "I'm with Granny Gertie. Mr. Wyatt can do it."

"Sure can." And with Adam's confidence, Wyatt almost felt like he could do anything. What would it be like to have two little girls who called him Daddy and believed in him?

"Such confidence." Ashley stared at Wyatt over the back of a compact brown mare. That grin hadn't faded in the last few minutes. Not so much as a smidge. She was itching to see him try the stunt.

And he was itching to show her what he could do. Just not in this arena.

"You can give it a go on Bumblebee." Emily checked the girth strap on a huge black horse. "He's run the course before." She cleared her throat. "And he'll slow down if you start to fall. Right, Charlie?"

"Right." Charlie found this hilarious.

"It seems like the wiser choice is the shorter horse." Wyatt was many things, but when it came to stunts, he tried not to be a fool.

Emily shrugged and went to adjust the

stirrups on the small brown horse. Ashley stepped back to give her space.

Meanwhile, Wyatt did a few squats to warm up and swung his arms. That gave the boys the giggles. They laughed harder when he stretched out his quads and hips.

"Just like a professional athlete." Ashley wasn't laughing. In fact, she was no longer smiling. She was looking at him with an expression of concern. "Are you sure you want to do this? You look a little stiff. I don't want you to get hurt."

Wyatt paused. "Because you need a wedding date to dance with?"

"No." Ashley scowled.

"Because I'll be cranky with you if I'm hurt?"

"No." There came the trademark eye roll.

"I've got it." Wyatt snapped his fingers. "Because I won't play Mike Moody if I eat dirt."

"No!"

There was suddenly something different about Ashley. He couldn't put his finger on it. Except to realize she hadn't lectured him on a movie genre once.

"I may tease you, Wyatt, but I never want anyone to get hurt." Ashley crossed her arms, but her eyes… Those blue eyes told the truth.

She was serious about the no-injury thing. "Just because you've done stunts before doesn't mean you'll be successful at this."

Contrary to what most people thought, Wyatt hadn't excelled in the industry on the strength of his body's resiliency to take a licking and keep on ticking. He'd taken acting lessons privately and he'd honed his ability to intuit a character based on a few clues of dialogue and script footnotes.

He had a vested interest in learning more about the real Ashley Monroe, and she kept dropping hints, like bread crumbs in an enchanted forest. Snatches of conversation drifted through his head.

Sometimes, you need just one person to listen and validate you. She'd been so earnest about answering her silly social-media messages, as if they hadn't been silly to her.

Look at him. He's in shock. On the day he'd arrived, she'd told the other Monroes to back off and then she'd laid her hand on his arm.

Ashley has always cared deeply for others. Laurel had said it was her biggest weakness.

And then his memory jogged further back. Not to a conversation, but to a news report: Tragedy for Ashley Monroe. When Ashley had been a teenager, a guy she'd dated, someone from one of those boy bands that girls raved over, had overdosed.

Despite the confrontational situation they were in, Ashley seemed genuinely concerned when she said she didn't want Wyatt to be hurt. He couldn't remember the last time a woman he'd kissed had been so concerned about *him*.

"I can do this," he reassured Ashley, determined she not worry.

Emily gave him an approving nod. "Although I can appreciate your can-do attitude, Wyatt, let me explain what you're doing before you accept." She marched out to a cone in the middle-left of the arena. "You're going to start over by the gate and gallop straight across the arena. When you reach this cone, grab on to the saddle horn with your left hand, keep that right foot in the stirrup and bend that right knee, stretching out your right arm in time to grab the gold." Which sat near a cone in the middle-right of the arena. "That gives you twenty feet to get down, and then you've just got to pull yourself back in the saddle and turn or stop before you smash into the fence on the other end."

Where the boys sat watching.

His mouth went dry as he imagined all

kinds of collisions. "Boys, move to the side." He waited until they shifted over.

"There's still time to back out," Ashley said quietly.

"Wyatt Halford doesn't back down." That was his father talking.

His father was old-school. "You skinned your knee playing soccer? Rub some dirt on it and get back out on the field." Dad's disparaging voice often shored up Wyatt's resolve when other folks might have quit.

That was why, despite his misgivings, Wyatt mounted the average-looking brown mare and walked her to the far end of the arena.

"Watch out for Missy," Emily cautioned. "She's a slow walker but a speed demon when you give her free rein."

As far as Wyatt was concerned, speed was good. There'd be less time to think if things went fast. Because if he allowed his mental wheels to turn, he'd think about Ashley's big heart and how much he wanted to prove that he could take on any role she tossed his way. Or he might think that soon-to-be fathers didn't take foolish risks just to prove they were strong.

But he didn't think. He turned Missy around and took a deep breath before snapping her reins and pressing her flanks with his heels.

The mare leaped forward, practically giving him whiplash. And she had wheels, speeding toward the first cone like a startled squirrel being chased by a hungry cat.

Wyatt started leaning to the right too soon, before he'd even reached the first cone. His back protested his acrobatics, spasming. He tumbled to the dirt and rolled until he stopped and was afforded a good look at that big open sky.

Footsteps and hooves thundered, near and far. Pain gripped Wyatt's back with strong, bony fingers that didn't want to let go.

"Is he dead?" Adam tugged the toe of Wyatt's boot.

Charlie dropped to his knees next to Wyatt's face, sending dirt into his ear. "Naw. He's making wheezy noises."

"Great. Now I don't have to make cookies." Davey sprinted away in triumph.

"Missy's fine if he wants to try it again." That was Emily, who'd caught his flighty steed on the far side of the arena.

"Wyatt?" Ashley moved over him, blocking the sun, which created a halo around her face. "Are you all right? Say something."

"Just let me lie here a sec." And stare into her pretty blue eyes. "Got the wind knocked out of me." And his spine rattled. "Just so you know, this is my manly smile. Not a grimace of pain."

"Whatever you say." Ashley's gaze cataloged his body parts, but not with the kind of heat he'd prefer to see in her eyes.

"Need a hand up?" That was Emily again. She'd led Missy over to him, perhaps assuming it would be easier for Wyatt to get back in the saddle if he didn't have to walk far. "Or should we call for a doctor?"

Ashley glanced up at her, moving her head far enough over that the sun blinded Wyatt once more. "I thought there was no doctor in town."

"There's not," Emily said. "We'd have to load him into the back of a truck and—"

"Ow!" Pain shot through his shoulder. "What was that?" He writhed on the ground, much to the boys' delight.

"Missy," Emily scolded. Tack jangled. "Sorry, Wyatt. She gets impatient for her rider sometimes and gives them a love bite."

"Love bite?" Wyatt stifled a curse. "Am I bleeding?"

Ashley tenderly touched his arm. "No blood, arterial or otherwise. My grandfather would say it's time to walk it off."

Closing his eyes, Wyatt took stock of his

back and shoulder. "Give me a second. Seriously. I can do this on my own."

"You take one arm, Em," Ashley said, matter-of-factly. "And I'll take the other."

Without giving him time to protest, the women heaved him to his feet.

He bit back a groan, contorting his torso to work out the kinks. "Whatever happened to human kindness?" The saying on Ashley's shirt.

"We're busy ladies with schedules to keep," Ashley said briskly. "You want me to try on Missy, Em?"

"The demon seed? Don't do it, Ash." Wyatt walked painfully to the edge of the arena where the boys had returned to their seats on the top rung.

"Do you need help up to the rail, Mr. Wyatt?" Adam asked.

"No. I got it." He would climb to that top rung if it killed him. His back spasmed and his shoulder throbbed, but he made it in time to see Ashley swing into Missy's saddle.

She walked the brown mare a few steps and then released her into a trot, moving with Missy as if she'd been born a cowgirl.

Every impression he'd ever had about Ashley Monroe, America's Sweetheart, was wrong. She was tough, multitalented. She sent Missy galloping around the perimeter of the arena. Again, Ashley looked like a natural. And he hated that no one in Hollywood had captured this strong, capable side of her. That no one really knew her.

Finally, she slowed to a stop on the far side of the arena and lined herself up with the cones and the bag of pretend gold on the ground.

She's going to nail this stunt.

And when she did, Wyatt would feel his whole life shift.

"Think about your center of gravity," Emily said encouragingly. "Don't go down too far or you'll eat it like Wyatt did."

"Wyatt didn't get any tips," he grumbled.

But there was no time to complain. Ashley leaned forward and let Missy run.

Wyatt held his breath. There was no way Ashley could do this. She'd have to be part spider and part fly, sticking to the saddle and darting down and back with the prize.

Ashley passed the first cone, contorted herself low and reached, just missing the bag of gold. "Whoa." She managed to bring the mare to a stop, although she hadn't regained her seat. "Shoot."

The three boys vocalized their disappointment. Wyatt took a deep breath and made a concerted effort to loosen the knots he'd made of his muscles while worrying about Ashley.

What was going on here? He never worried about other people doing their stunts. He applauded their skill and professionalism for making the attempt, the same way his father had taught him to admire professionals of all types for giving it their all on the job. But now, when watching Ashley, he felt...worried.

"Are you okay?" he asked her.

Ashley gave him a curt nod. There was a fire in her eyes he hadn't seen before, an intensity people often said he had when the cameras were rolling. This was the Ashley Monroe who'd kissed him, and he felt privileged to finally see her.

"You took too much time adjusting your grip on the saddle horn." Emily had Missy's reins. She demonstrated the numerous ways Ashley had held on to the horn.

"My grip on the saddle horn is the only thing keeping me in the saddle." Ashley stared at her bare hand. It was red. "Can I borrow your gloves?"

"Let's try them on the fence rail first." Emily handed Ashley the pair of gloves hanging out her back pocket. "Gloves are tricky. Too loose and you'll fall out of them. Too tight and you can't close your grip."

Ashley tugged the tan leather gloves on. She came over to where Wyatt was sitting, grabbed hold of the top round pipe rail and hung from it, lifting her knees off the ground. She went back to Missy and tested her grip on the saddle horn. "Let's try this."

"She's gonna do it this time," little Adam said.

Ashley mounted up and trotted back over to the starting point. She ran her hand around the saddle horn a few times before kicking Missy into gear. In no time, she passed the cone, dropped to the side and grabbed the bag of gold, only to drop it while trying to return to the saddle. She brought Missy to a stop and consulted with Emily some more.

"Mike Moody's gold is heavy." Davey chuckled, elbowing Charlie.

Wyatt gently pushed Adam's cowboy hat down on his head. "How long has Ashley been taking riding lessons?"

"This is the second time she's come." Adam peeked at him from under the brim, not as impressed as Wyatt was at her not being new to horsemanship. "Do you think Gertie's cookies are done yet?"

"No cookies until you muck out your horse stalls." Emily pointed a finger toward her nephews without turning around.

"Auntie Em has eyes in the back of her

head." Davey climbed down the outside of the fence.

"Where are you going?" Charlie asked.

"To get my chores done." Davey disappeared around the corner of the barn.

"Come on, runt." Charlie made to follow his older brother. "You want cookies, don't you? Can't have none without chores done."

"Cookies and ice cream," Adam said wistfully. He blinked up at Wyatt. "Do you know 'bout Mike Moody?"

"I do." Wyatt supposed he shouldn't be surprised that so many others in Second Chance knew about him, too, since Ashley had told him the bandit had settled here.

"Have you been to his hiding spot?" Adam straddled the rail, ready to climb down.

"I haven't."

"Or seen his gold?" Adam nodded toward the bag Emily dropped by the cone. He reached into his jeans pocket, as if he had something to show Wyatt.

"Nope."

"Adam!" Charlie called from the barn. "Come on."

"Ride with us to his hideout," Adam offered with an enthusiastic grin. "When we take all the Monroes this week."

"I'll clear my schedule."

"And I'll show you my gold if Mom says I can." Adam giggled as he climbed down the fence rails.

Before Wyatt had time to respond, thundering hooves told him Ashley was making another run at her own bag of gold. This time, she was successful. A joint-jarring drop. A swooping grab. And then she was back in the saddle.

It was exhilarating and annoying at the same time. A great stunt well executed. He was happy for her. But Wyatt wanted to be able to do it himself. Subtly, he stretched his back. Probably not a good idea to try again today.

"Yeehah!" Emily cried, tossing up her hands.

"Woo-hoo!" Ashley brought Missy to a stop in front of Wyatt, smiling like they were best buds. And that smile. Hello, Human Kindness. She was gorgeous. "Do you think audiences will like it?"

"Yeah." Wyatt swallowed his pride. "Yeah, I do." He gave her his most winning smile, the one that used to charm his high school math teacher to give him points for trying. "How long have you been practicing this?"

"Just this week. It was Emily's idea. She did some trick riding when she was on the rodeo circuit." She patted Missy's neck. "You're not just paying me lip service, are you? You've probably done much more dangerous stunts, but..." She was digging for compliments as if he was an old hand at stunt work.

Which he supposed he was after a decade in the business. But when had he become the elder statesman of stunt actors? He was only thirty.

Elder statesman.

Father.

Do the right thing.

He washed a hand over his face. Something was shifting inside of him, a perspective on himself and life, and it had been shifting since he'd joined Ashley on that porch when he'd arrived in town. It was just a premonition, really. An inkling that one of these days, he'd look in the mirror and find a gray hair. And his indestructible self-image, the one he used as a shield against his father's bitterness, would crack. Then his position on top of Hollywood would tilt and crumble. Meaning his father's prophecy of him riding on only his looks would come true.

What was Ashley Monroe doing to him?

"Seriously, Wyatt." A frown flitted across Ashley's face. "What do you think?"

She was a horsewoman? A stuntwoman? An actress turned producer?

What did he think?

He thought he'd been set up. Kind of like the date he'd had with her sister.

CHAPTER SEVEN

GABBY'S LAPTOP PINGED on the check-in desk, announcing an incoming message. "Oh, my goodness. Adorable."

Emily had sent her a picture of Gertie with Ashley and Wyatt. They all wore cowboy boots. She uploaded it to her anonymous Wyatt Halford fan page with all the proper hashtags. Operation Snaparazzi was officially off the ground.

"Sweet!" she said.

"Are you sneaking looks at kitten videos again?" Dad asked from the kitchen. "You're supposed to be doing your homework."

"I'm not watching cat videos."

The front door opened, but instead of a tall cowboy with world-famous good looks, Shane came in. He held a stack of papers and books in the crook of his arm and headed straight for Gabby. "How's my favorite future world leader?"

"Good." Gabby beamed, tapping the top of her laptop, trying to send a message to Shane that Operation Snaparazzi was in full swing without alerting Dad. He always thought she should mind her own business.

"Don't get Gabby out of the flow." Dad came to stand in the kitchen doorway behind her. "She's doing her homework."

"I don't want to interrupt. Future movers and shakers need to be serious about their studies." Shane sorted through his stack of things. "As one experienced mover and shaker to another, though, I found something Gabby might like."

Gabby rested her elbows on the desk, paying closer attention to the old books and yellowed papers he was carrying.

"I got you a planner." Shane set a small, thick calendar in front of Gabby. The cover was teal and embossed with flowers. "Half the year is gone, but a girl like you can easily fill up the remaining pages with your schedule and dreams for the future."

"Thank you." Gabby opened the planner, cracking the binding. On the first page, Shane had written a note.

To Gabby Kincaid, who knows the value of information. Never stop being curious about the world and the people in it. Shane Monroe.

Dad leaned over her shoulder. He probably read the note, too, because he sighed. "In case you need help interpreting that dedication, Gabby, it means you should keep studying, not become a nosy meddler like Shane."

"I think I should be offended." But Shane grinned when he said it and handed over the rest of the stack he carried to Dad. "I requested a search of Idaho history from a resource I have. I thought you might find it useful in your campaign to protect some of Second Chance's old cabins."

Dad hesitated before taking the pile. "Do you ever sleep?"

Shane chuckled. "You should know the answer to that question. I spent four months living in the room above your quarters, wearing a track in the carpet."

Instead of answering, Dad flipped through the pages on top, turning slowly and heading back into the kitchen.

"There are all kinds of stickers in the back." Shane tapped the planner. "But I took the liberty of marking some dates from earlier this year." And then he followed her dad, closing the apartment door behind him.

Gabby turned to January and found the first sticker—Important Day. Beneath it, Shane had written *Monroes come to town*. There was another sticker in February—a snowflake. That was the day of the huge blizzard, when they'd been snowed in. It was when Dad started to fall in love with Laurel. There were more stickers, more notes. But in June, he'd placed two stickers—Very Important Day. One was a few days ago. *Met Wyatt Halford.* And one was placed on this Saturday. *My first official day as a Monroe.*

Another message sounded on her closed laptop. Was it another photo of Ashley and Wyatt? Gabby opened her email.

She groaned.

"And my language arts professor just sent another assignment." Gabby huffed. "That man knows how to suck all the fun out of summer." This assignment had two parts. Interview two people about their careers, and then write a paper on how their experiences could be applied to her own decisions about her future. Gabby's mood lightened.

She knew the perfect two people to help her out—Ashley and Wyatt.

THE STUNT WORKED!

Ashley felt like celebrating.

Instead, in her mind's eye, she pictured how she'd position the cameras to capture the action. The wide-angle lens to summarize the robbery's devastation and bloodshed, the mid-range shot to convey the excitement of a daring galloping getaway, and the close-up to illustrate Letty's cold determination. She'd end with a wide shot of Mike and Letty making their escape.

"Remind me, Wyatt," Ashley said to him as they walked from the arena to the shooting range Emily had set up. "Have you done any trick riding?"

"No." Wyatt's nose was bent out of shape.

Or was it his back? He walked like a man who'd just been through a grueling football practice. She refused to believe it was because of that one tumble. His movements had been rigid before that.

Could he meet the physical demands of Mike Moody? Horse chases. A few fistfights. His fans expected authenticity.

"I applaud you taking shooting lessons," Wyatt said to Ashley when they reached the gully in the forest behind the Bucking Bull's barn, a place where stray bullets would only go into the mountain. "It helped me look more realistic when handling firearms."

Ah, lip service. A sure sign that his pride was smarting from being unable to complete the gold grab. And, jeez, the bag had been heavy. Emily had put some of Mike Moody's real gold nuggets inside.

"For luck," she'd told Ashley.

"It would make our grandfathers happy," Ashley had replied.

Their grandfathers, Percy Clark and Harlan Monroe, along with Harlan's twin brother, Hobart, had found the gold decades ago. But a string of bad luck and the death of Hobart had them putting the gold back. They'd left behind clues and a gold coin in Gertie's possession to prove the trail was real. And just a few months ago, the Monroes and Clarks had joined forces to find it again.

Ashley raised her rifle, a Sharps that was a replica appropriate to the time period of Mike Moody. She took aim and fired.

"Bull's-eye," Emily said, grinning.

"I should have known," Wyatt murmured, a trace of reluctant admiration in his tone.

Ashley took a moment to imagine her character hidden in the trees next to the dirt stage road. Circumstances and mistakes would have made Letty desperate for money but perhaps still hesitant to kill. How would she show these conflicted feelings from beneath a burlap sack with hand-cut eyeholes? Perhaps with a physical display of nerves. The wiping of sweaty palms on the man's suit she wore. The subtle readjustment of tense shoulders. The belabored breathing, raspy to indicate her dry mouth.

Ashley took aim again. Fired again.

"Bull's-eye," Emily crowed.

"You know how to ride. You know how to shoot." Wyatt crossed his arms over his chest, clearly unsettled. "What else do you know how to do?"

She liked Wyatt stripped of his cocky poise. She could more easily imagine him as Mike Moody, the man who let his sister dictate an increasingly dark path. "Are you still recovering from stunts you did on your last film?"

Ashley wasn't just concerned as one actor to another, as one person to another. She had to quell her instinct to nurture and think like a movie producer. Was he taking pain meds? And if so, was he managing them responsibly? In short, was he going to be a reliable cast member a year from now?

She hated that she had to judge him. But that was the hard-core truth of directors and producers. They had to hire and fire people. They had to care and sometimes give people the hard truth when it was warranted.

It was just… She wanted Wyatt to be well, physically and emotionally. She'd spent much of the morning with him. To her, he was no longer film icon Wyatt Halford. He was a man with aches and pains and prickly opinions.

"Wyatt?" Ashley glanced at him because he hadn't answered her.

"No. Comment."

But he'd have to disclose any health concerns if he were to participate in her production. Her contracts and insurance teams would demand it.

"Do you want to take a turn?" Ashley took aim for a third shot. She steadied her breathing and thought of Grandpa Harlan. He'd built not one empire but many. And he'd taken twelve grandchildren on adventures without any other adults. If he could do all that, she could juggle the roles of actress, director and producer. The toughest task would be convincing the people in the film industry that she could do it all.

"Bull's-eye!" Em was Ashley's strongest proponent.

"Yes, I want to take a turn." Wyatt rolled his shoulders and cracked his neck. "But first, answer a question. Who are you and what have you done with the real Ashley Monroe? Is she the pregnant one sitting back at the inn?"

"That's more than one question," Emily pointed out.

Ashley fired again, hitting the second circle. She chalked it up to her being unable to control her laughter. Wyatt was beginning to see her beyond the Hollywood facade. If she could change his opinion of her, it gave her hope for the rest of her peers.

And then her laughter died away. She couldn't say the same for her insight into him. Again, there was that niggle of doubt—was he up to the role of Mike Moody? Could he believably portray an emotionally vulnerable tailor who was going blind?

"She's not going to answer any of my questions." Wyatt scuffed his boot in the dirt. "I'm on to you, Ms. Monroe. Give me a turn with that rifle."

Ashley took pity on him. She even praised his shooting skill because he never missed a bull's-eye.

But she didn't answer a question. Not a one.

"YOU GUYS WANT some lemonade?" Gabby greeted Ashley and Wyatt upon their return from the Bucking Bull with a tray of iced drinks. "You look thirsty." And incredibly dirty, especially Wyatt, as if he'd been rolling on the ground. "I poured you each a glass when I saw you drive up."

Wyatt eyed the tray of icy drinks she carried to the coffee table. "Does every guest receive the gold-star treatment?"

"Only guests who are also friends," Gabby said, taking her computer from the coffee table and putting it in her lap. She gestured toward the fireplace and its mammoth hearth. "Dad told me it was the original cooking kitchen. Big enough to roast a pig on a spit. Sit. Drink. Take a moment to help a summer school student."

"I sense an agenda." Ashley paused a few feet away to check her phone. "But that's an easy guess, because Gabby always has something going on."

She did indeed.

Wyatt raised his eyebrows instead of asking Gabby to explain.

That look made Gabby feel weak because, yes, folks, the best-looking film star, ever, was staring at her. "I have to interview two people for my language arts homework. It would be so cool to interview you two."

Ashley and Wyatt exchanged glances.

Ashley shrugged. "Is my mother around?" She tucked her phone in her back pocket, took a glass of lemonade and sat on one end of the hearth.

"She's upstairs napping. Why?"

"Because actors usually bounce interview proposals off their managers." Wyatt took a glass and sat on the other end of the hearth from Ashley.

So much for sneaking in a picture of the two of them sitting together. Gabby wanted to thunk her head. She should have sat on the hearth and let them take the couch. But that didn't address her confusion. "I don't understand why you need to ask Grandma Gen."

"Interviews need to be on brand, basically published where our fans can access it, and the interviewee needs to agree to terms." Wyatt sipped his lemonade and looked toward Ashley, as if waiting for her cue.

Cue to what? Adults were so complicated.

Pay attention, Gabby!

Yikes, that was her dad's voice in her head. "This is my homework. It's not going anywhere. And what did you mean by…terms?"

"Terms are subjects that are off-limits." Ashley took off her cap and wiped her forehead with the icy glass.

"Like Laurel and her babies," Wyatt said, tipping his cowboy hat back.

"Oops. It's not that kind of interview." Gabby was relieved, because for a while there it seemed like they were going to drink her lemonade and not do the interview. "I should have explained. These are questions that are supposed to help me think about what I want to be when I grow up. The first question is, when did you know you wanted to be an actor?"

"Oh, I didn't really aspire to be an actor," Ashley said quickly. "I enjoyed reenacting movie scenes because it made Laurel laugh. Since my dad was a studio head, he'd slot me in as an extra. I think I was Kid Number Four on a Playground once. Oh, and Kid Crying at a Birthday Party. Stuff like that. And then suddenly, I was in a sitcom and had a career."

Wyatt angled his body toward Ashley. "Your parents didn't give you a choice?"

"You've met my mother, right?" Ashley shifted toward him.

Oh, man. Gabby wished they were sitting closer together, because when they looked at each other, it was like watching a movie where two people looked at each other and you just knew they were going to get married at the end.

Gabby forced herself to pay attention, because Ashley was still talking and she was supposed to type up her interview notes.

"My mother never asked me if I was happy," she said. "How about you? How did you become a superstar?"

"I didn't dream of being an actor early on either." Wyatt spared Gabby a smile that was

just a smile one friend gave to another, but
he was so beautiful it kind of made Gabby's
heart melt a little. "People told my mom I was
cute enough to be on camera and she believed
them. She and my sisters naively took me to
auditions where kids were being prepped to
be actors. And me? I just did whatever they
asked and often got the role. It doesn't seem
fair, does it?"

He and Ashley stared at each other as if
thinking what Gabby was thinking—they
were more alike than they seemed. But that
wasn't what Gabby was supposed to be thinking. She was supposed to be "analyzing" their
comments. "So, you sort of fell into acting
because you were good at it?"

Wyatt raised his glass of lemonade but held
the glass in front of his mouth as if he'd just
thought of something he had to say. "Or because we just looked good on camera." He
took a drink.

"What was your first steady job?" Gabby
frowned. "These questions aren't written for
actors."

"Maybe you could ask what was our biggest break?" Ashley supplied helpfully. "I
played a darling little sister on a television
show. I laughed on cue. I cried on cue. And
they wrote plots where I got into all kinds of

trouble. And when that show finished, I had my own show playing an average girl with an unusual set of friends. And, of course, we got into all kinds of trouble. But we worked everything out before the credits rolled."

"And so begins the legend of America's Sweetheart," Wyatt murmured, staring into his lemonade.

Gabby was glad she could type without looking at the keys—thanks to Dad and another online course—because she could watch them and enter her notes at the same time. "Wyatt, what about you?"

"After several commercials and clothing ads, my big break came playing the younger brother in one of those streetcar-racing, crime-solving films."

"Is that really a genre?" Ashley asked sternly.

Wyatt shook his finger at her, inching closer. "Almost all streetcar-racing movies have an element of crime in them."

"They are classified as action films." Ashley shook her head, but somehow, she managed to move closer to Wyatt.

They were no longer miles away on that hearth. And they were smiling at each other.

"Anyway…" Wyatt shrugged, which was supercute and made Gabby want to reach for her phone to take a picture. "My character died in a fiery crash in the climax, so I didn't get picked up for a role in the next half-dozen films in the franchise, but I was such a fan favorite that the producers cast me in a teen-age tearjerker film."

Ashley scoffed. "You very wisely did not call that movie a romance. It was a modern take on Romeo and Juliet, a tragedy, since you both died at the end."

"I'm sensing a theme," Gabby said, and then blurted, "Oh, my gosh! You have to play Mike Moody. He dies at the end."

"Kismet." Ashley laughed. "Or in Wyatt's case, a tendency toward tragedies."

"Oh, we're going to have words, Mon-roe." Wyatt shifted over toward Ashley on the hearth.

"Bring it, Halford." Ashley helped him close the distance.

"Before you rumble, can I ask one more question? Or take a picture and then ask a question?" Gabby didn't wait for permission for the picture. "I get extra credit if I submit a photo." Too bad she couldn't also post it to her fan site. But Wyatt would know imme-diately it came from her. "Why do you stay in your career?"

"For the money," Wyatt said, at the same time that Ashley said, "For the challenge."

There was a moment of silence, where the pair frowned at each other.

And then footsteps rang out on the porch as Wyatt said, "I was kidding."

But Gabby didn't believe it, and neither did Ashley. She rolled her eyes.

"I was kidding," Wyatt said again. "I love that every character I play offers me the opportunity to spread my wings."

"You're referring to your stunts now." Ashley finished her lemonade and stood.

Mackenzie burst through the door. "Mail, Gabby." She put it on the check-in counter. "More RSVPs for the wedding." And then she ran back out. Mack ran the general store, gas station and post office. She was always running around.

"More RSVPs?" Ashley went to the desk and tore into an envelope. "I hope these are regrets, since we've already planned out the number of chairs and entrées. Hold up. Jess Watanabe? Who invited him?"

Gabby set her laptop in its usual spot on the desk. "That would be Grandma Gen." Who was right. Gabby was no good at keeping secrets.

"Jess Watanabe is a director." Wyatt joined them, picking up another RSVP. "I'm up for a role with him. He's coming?"

"Apparently." Ashley shook her head. "Here's one from Tom Conners. He's a casting director for some of the biggest names in Hollywood. I've read for him a few times but never... Well, never mind." She fixed Gabby with a hard stare. "When did these invitations go out?"

"I can't remember?" Because if she told them last week, Grandma Gen wouldn't be happy.

The handful of RSVPs were more of the same. More Hollywood movers and shakers. And they were all coming.

"I need to call my agent." Wyatt headed toward the stairs. "Hey, Gabby, send me a copy of that picture you took just now." He rattled off his number.

Gabby nearly fainted. *I have Wyatt Halford's telephone number.*

"I need to wake my mother." Ashley looked ticked off. But she didn't move. She just stared at the RSVPs. "What is she up to?"

Gabby gathered them up. "I'll put these somewhere safe and tell Cam to expect a dozen more guests."

"Somewhere safe?" Ashley said slowly.

"What? You want me to show these to my dad and Laurel?"

"WAKE UP, MOTHER."

Ashley stood over the bed. She knew Mom had heard her come in. The Lodgepole Inn's floors creaked and the doors didn't fit right in the jambs.

"Let me exit from my yoga trance as peacefully as I went in." Mom did some deep breathing exercises.

Ashley breathed deeply, too. She picked up Mom's empty tea mug and sniffed. Mom was spiking her tea, all right. Now Ashley breathed deeply to keep from shaking her mother awake.

"I feel so refreshed." Her mother sat up and turned to hang her legs over the edge of the bed, smoothing her navy dress. She hadn't given up a single fashion statement to mountain living. "How has your day been? You look overheated and like someone dusted you with dirt."

"I've been busy," Ashley said through gritted teeth, wanting to be calm. "But you've been busy, too. You sent out some last-minute invitations to *Laurel's* wedding."

"Yes, I did." At least she wasn't denying it. "The mother of the bride is entitled to invite guests."

"And did you also jot a little note on the invitation?" Anger thrummed in Ashley's veins. "Something like *Wyatt Halford will be Ashley's wedding date*?"

"You know, I worry about what will happen to you when I retire from my role as your manager, but I shouldn't." She ran her fingers through her short hair, giving it a good fluffing. "You know exactly how to play the game. That's exactly what I did."

"But it's not what I'd do. This is no game. It's Laurel's wedding. It should be a small ceremony with family and close friends. It shouldn't be a networking event."

"Oh, come on." Mom stood, and by some miracle, there were no wrinkles in her dress. "I listen to your struggles every day. You can't get the best in the business to take your calls, much less sign on to work with you. Well, I'm bringing them here for a face-to-face meeting."

"At Laurel's wedding? No. You need to call these people up and tell them they're uninvited."

"I could never do such a thing. It would ruin your reputation almost as much as the news that Wyatt and Laurel are having babies together." She slipped into her black pumps and then slipped into the bathroom and shut the door.

"They're not having them together," Ashley

mumbled. "Can you just do what I'm asking you? For once, can we not argue? I'm the client here. What I say goes."

"Not if it's against your best interest. Then I step in. I always have." Said the woman who'd locked herself in the bathroom and wasn't stepping anywhere.

"Mom, I hate to do this. In fact, it might be better to do this after the wedding."

The bathroom door swung open. Mom had floss wrapped around her two index fingers. "Don't tell me you're having Wyatt Halford's babies, too."

"No." Ashley scowled.

"What else could be so bad that you wanted to wait until after the wedding to tell me?" She wrapped the floss tighter around one finger. "Don't tell me you've decided to stay in Second Chance. I tell you, there is something about this place... It must be in the water."

"I'm not moving to Idaho, Mom." Ashley took her mother by the shoulders and gave her a little shake to make her pay attention. "I'm thinking about firing you." She frowned. That could have come out stronger.

Mom scoffed. "You can't fire me."

"I can." She should. If she was the confident Ashley she presented to Wyatt, she would.

Mom wrenched herself free of Ashley's grip and tossed the floss into the trash. "I've laid this out beautifully, as if you're the next big Hollywood power couple."

"A lie." It was Ashley's turn to scoff.

"You can pretend for photos you post online that you're a couple, but you can't ride that wave to network among your peers?" Mom grabbed her empty tea mug and clutched it to her chest as she walked to the door. "You're going to ruin that, too."

"Too?" Ashley struggled to keep from shouting. "What else are you claiming I ruined?"

"Everything." Mom whirled at the door. She may have been drinking. She may have smelled like distilled spirits. But she had the balance of a cat in heels. "We could have signed an eight-figure deal to do three rom-coms this year. A few years back, you turned down a lucrative television role that is now netting an actress five million dollars an episode. And before that, you had to drop out of a film and threatened to quit a television series because of some boy."

"Caleb. Say his name, Mother. It was Caleb." Ashley felt sick inside. "You've been holding a grudge for eleven years because a boy I loved died and I was grieving? You thought at sixteen that I should just pick myself up and return to the soundstage the next day?"

"Yes." Her tone was icy. "It's what professionals do. And you didn't love him. You broke up with him the day before."

"Because I discovered he was addicted to opioids. Because I told you, and you said I should give him an ultimatum." To go into rehab if he wanted to be with her. "What horrible advice that was."

"I was afraid he'd get you hooked on pills." Her mother's eyes took on a faraway look and the icy tone warmed to a chilling fog. "And you were afraid, too. That's why you told me he was using. That's why you broke up with him."

"I shouldn't have left him at a hotel. I should have driven him to rehab." Tears rolled down Ashley's cheeks. Big, ugly tears. That was what they felt like because her guilt was big and ugly.

"Now who's carrying a grudge?" Mom's voice had softened, as much as her voice could. She came forward and wiped away Ashley's tears with her thumbs. "Darling, you have immense talent. But someday, you're going to fall in love and have babies of your own. You need to grab the brass ring now before something else distracts you."

"Mom, I haven't dated seriously in eleven years." She wiped her nose. "What makes you think Mr. Right is going to present himself? I have commitment issues bigger than Wyatt's. Something inside of me is broken and I...I don't know how to fix it."

"There's nothing wrong with you." Her mother's expression relaxed until she looked exactly the way Ashley had always wanted her mother to look at her—with love and understanding in her eyes. "Once you caught the acting bug, you elbowed us all away, even Laurel. And when those teenage hormones kicked in—" she gave her head a little shake "—you noticed boys, but deep inside you couldn't shake free of the desire to work. Bringing fictional characters to full bloom was more important than anything else."

Ashley agreed, but she felt cold. All the way down to her toes.

"You see it now, don't you? It's a sign of all the great creatives. They love deeply, but most of them don't love well or for long stretches of time." Mom touched Ashley's cheek gently. "For people like you, people blessed with great gifts, life is one big empty canvas that is filled with opportunities, achievements and, yes, a backdrop of those left behind."

This wasn't the speech Ashley had been expecting.

"As long as a handsome action film star doesn't come along who isn't going to let you keep your guard up—" her mother paused to let that sink in "—you'll be fine. We'll get you a little dog to fill the empty places. And we'll discuss how to gracefully exit all those little friendship circles of yours."

"Those people are my friends. They need me."

"At a distance, yes." Mom sighed. "I suppose we could hire someone to respond and pretend to be you."

"That's not happening." And Ashley needed to talk to Mackenzie over at the general store, because her mother didn't need to be drinking and jumping conversational tracks at the speed of an express train. "I'm not going to get distracted by my friends."

Mom gave a little shrug. "But someone will slip out of your circle whether it's because of your work or a man who wins your heart." She smoothed Ashley's hair away from her face. "And when that happens, you can't beat yourself up inside. Do you understand what I'm saying?"

Ashley nodded. She understood. She understood more than her mother realized. She understood that Mom's heart beat differently than hers. Mom's drummed in crisp, staccato beats, and Ashley's pounded a great booming rhythm. They lived differently and they loved differently.

"Good." Mom patted Ashley's cheek, as if she was still five and worshipped the ground her mother walked on. "Now, take a bath and get cleaned up. You've got a date with Wyatt in an hour. Give me the high sign if you need rescuing."

Mom turned and almost made it out the door before Ashley said, "I should still fire you."

Because they didn't see eye to eye on anything.

"That won't change anything for you." Her mother paused, not turning. "In fact, it might make things worse."

CHAPTER EIGHT

"YOU CLEAN UP WELL," Ashley told Wyatt when he came downstairs to escort her to Laurel's baby shower.

Wyatt reached the ground floor of the Lodgepole Inn and stopped.

Not because Ashley hadn't cleaned up pretty darn well herself. She wore a yellow sundress with a white sweater that had tiny flowers stitched around the edges. Her deep red hair cascaded over her shoulders like fine silk. And the small smile she gave him almost made him forget why he was going to a baby shower.

But no. It wasn't Ashley's beauty that stopped him at the bottom of the staircase. It was the quiet.

No one was around.

"Come on." Ashley reached out a hand. "Everyone else has already left." Her words sounded warm, but her smile didn't quite reach her eyes.

"The place is empty." Wyatt came forward,

not sure whether he should follow his impulse and take her arm or play it like friends and head for the door. "Our words echo."

The inn was empty, but so, it seemed, was Ashley. It was as if a light inside of her had extinguished.

"You found an iron." She straightened his tie. All without meeting his gaze. "You know what this feels like?"

"A date?" Because that was what it was supposed to be—on the exterior, at least.

"No." Ashley hurried toward the door and opened it herself. "A dream sequence in one of those apocalyptic films. You know, where everything looks normal but then the hero notices something is off, like you just did. That jars him awake and into the world of the apocalypse."

"Why do you do that?" He closed the door behind them and followed her down the steps at a slower pace.

"What?" Ashley waited for him at the bottom, hair lifting in the breeze.

"Put situations into the context of a film genre." When she quirked her brow, he took her hand and placed it in the crook of his arm. "Which way?"

"To the medical clinic." She tugged him forward, not checking for traffic before crossing the road. There was rarely any passing traffic in Second Chance, and tonight was no exception, so she was safe. But he wondered what went on in her head to distract her so. "We thought it would be cute to hold the shower at the clinic. And there's the added bonus that it's just been updated."

"Not to mention, no doctor is living there at the moment." He'd heard Emily say that as he lay in the dirt this afternoon.

"You paid attention." She graced him with one of her slow-building smiles.

"Hey, this is not just a pretty face." He leaned down so he could whisper in her ear. "I have good ears, too."

That brought a more natural smile to her lips.

The clinic was in sight. A log cabin built on the hillside across from the diner, it had a nice big porch. Baby-shower guests were milling about on the porch and inside, illuminated by soft lighting and the setting sun.

"Wait." He tugged Ashley to a stop. "What is it about you and movie genres?"

She stalled, only for a moment, but in that way that told anyone acting opposite her that something had gone off script. A forgotten line. An unexpected change in dialogue. A crew member moving into her line of sight.

Wyatt glanced around, but they were alone.

"I was raised in movie speak." And Ashley was the master of the brush-off, looking away when he wanted to see into her eyes to read what was going on in that sharp mind of hers. "Raised…" She huffed. "Lately I've been feeling as if I was raised like Rapunzel in a locked tower without a key to the door." Her gaze swung around Second Chance. "Do you know my father canceled my studio contract in January, because if he didn't, he wouldn't inherit twenty-five percent of my grandfather's wealth? And my mother sees my lips move but doesn't seem to hear a thing. What does that mean?"

"I take it you argued with your mother?" Wyatt said tentatively.

"Yes. And I almost fired her. Twice." Ashley glanced up toward the clinic, where people were chatting and laughing. "She's up there now, pretending to have a good time."

The same way Ashley was going to, he would bet. "Or maybe she's relieved she's almost been fired. I hear Ashley Monroe is a handful to work with."

She squinted up at him. "Are you making fun of me?"

"I'm making light of the situation." He rubbed her upper arms, because a cool breeze was kicking up as the sun was going down. "Ashley, you're one of the most generous people in this business, made even more amazing because most people know your mother received the Grinch model of hearts."

"Two sizes too small." But she didn't fill the air with her lyrical laughter. "Do you have many close friends?"

He drew back slightly, a learned response to any question that bordered on the personal.

"This isn't an interview," Ashley said softly. "I really want to know. I realized today that I nurture a lot of relationships, but none of them are close, not even the one with my sister."

He ached at the regret in her tone and reached to smooth the silken hair over her shoulder because he wasn't sure he could smooth whatever was bothering her inside. "I used to have a circle of friends from high school. In between movies, I'd take them somewhere fun, like the Bahamas or the Cayman Islands, where we could cut loose. I'd pay for everything, of course. But then their lives tied them down—work, spouses, kids. And they seemed so torn that they had to refuse my invitations." He shrugged. "So, I just stopped inviting them. Now in between films, I sleep. I rest. I visit my family."

"And stay in a hotel when you go home, I bet."

The gates he'd locked around his private life threatened to shut, but not before one last admission. "They have their lives, too." And hurt feelings no amount of money could erase.

Ashley wasn't focusing on him. And there was a faraway look in her eyes that told him she wasn't following the thread of conversation.

"What's wrong?"

"Something my mother said." Ashley's gaze brushed over the town before painting over him. "I'm probably boring you."

"A phrase taught to you by your parents to cover a momentary mind drift. Either I was boring or a bright shiny thought refused to be ignored."

That earned him a smile. "It was a thought, although perhaps not so bright and shiny. You probably experience this, too. When I'm working on a project or even evaluating a role, and I'm digging down deep to fathom the nuances of the character..." Her gaze drifted once more.

But he thought he knew where she was going with this. "When you're concentrating on bringing someone to life by more than words on a page."

"Exactly." She nodded, smile growing. "In those moments, I need time alone, time apart, sometimes big stretches of time where I live mostly in my head."

Wyatt nodded. He wasn't going to admit out loud that those instances were rare for him lately. This conversation was pointing out flaws in the quality of his work. Or at least, what his critics and peers termed as his short-comings. He had a type of character that audiences paid to see—flawed and tough, with a strong moral code. It was lucrative. Why deviate from the path?

And right there—in the middle of their conversation, in the middle of Second Chance, with whispering pines and a glorious mountain sunset framing a beautiful woman within reach—Wyatt acknowledged an unwelcome thought.

Playing to type isn't just lucratively safe. It's stupid.

And, of course, he dismissed that thought almost immediately, because who was going to turn down tens of millions of dollars to play the same character type in a different plot and fictional world? Not him.

But while he fought through a crisis of confidence, albeit briefly, Ashley was working her way through her own epiphany, and looking to share it with him, if the warmth in her blue eyes was any indication.

"I'm comforted by knowing my family and friends are there if needed," she was saying. "But maybe…they don't feel the same way?" Ashley glanced up at him, expecting an answer.

"Maybe they feel they aren't as important to you as they used to be." And, boy, didn't that hit home?

"Oh, my gosh. You get it." Ashley laughed self-consciously, reining in that delicate laughter.

The wind seemed to pick up strength. The trees seemed to move closer. But in the center of it all was Ashley. Bright red hair and sunny yellow dress a reassuring beacon that whatever had happened in the past… whatever was happening right now…nothing was as important as this woman in front of him and the soul-touching conversation they were having. Because Wyatt didn't have deep conversations with anyone. Nor did he look deep inside himself very often. He was too busy rehearsing, reading scripts, working out, planning his life twelve to eighteen months out. Sometimes more. And yet this woman—

the introverted actress who'd made a muddle of his life—she was splashing around for a personal life vest and towing him along with her, expecting this experience to bond them somehow. And the mind-blowing part was that Wyatt wasn't taking a step back and having none of it.

"Having my father cancel my contracts was like having a rug pulled out from under me," she was saying. "And while I was picking myself up, I realized there were some relationships I couldn't keep tethered at arm's length."

"Like Laurel." She'd told him her sister was the most important person in the world to her. And she was doing something about mending that rift, unlike Wyatt with his family.

"Yes." She ran a hand down his arm, as if needing to touch the person who was on the same wavelength as she was. "It's easy to hide myself in my work. I feel the temptation of it even now with this new direction I'm taking. But I have to tread carefully. I don't want to make the wrong choices again. I mean, Laurel…" Her expression turned pained.

"Loves you. Anyone can see that. Your relationship with her isn't a switch, flipped on or off."

"But if it's a dial, I've turned it too far to

one side." Her fingers knotted together at her waist.

"Maybe. But if it's a dial, you can turn it back until you find the right balance. Isn't that why you're here now?"

Ashley nodded and then drew a deep breath. "Listen to me. I'm the one being maudlin when we're about to go to a party." She graced him with a smile that millions of fans would recognize. "I'm sorry. I didn't congratulate you earlier on being in the running for a Jess Watanabe film. I was a little distracted by my anger over my mother turning my sister's wedding into a Hollywood East meet and greet."

"Thanks."

"But..." Ashley worried her bottom lip. "Here I go again into downer territory. I hear he's a stickler about not wanting any trouble around his set."

Wyatt nodded. "He replaced Amanda Fox two days before filming was to begin on his latest movie, because her divorce proceedings blew up in court. A couple of people were even arrested." Everyone in Hollywood knew this. "Can I assume your mother extended Jess an invitation because she wants me to go down in flames on Saturday?"

"Actually, she claims she thinks we'd make

a great power couple. And given the number of acceptance RSVPs we received, other people in Hollywood like the idea." Ashley heaved a sigh, but it was a corny, over-dramatic one. "If people only knew the truth about the two of us. For example, I resent you for trash-talking my film knowledge, and you resent me for being a better horseman. We could never be a power couple. We're too different."

Wyatt chuckled. Hadn't she listened during Gabby's interview today? Or taken note of their conversation just now. They were fundamentally more alike than they were different.

"Hey, Ashley!" Gabby leaned over the railing and waved. "We're waiting on you to start the games."

"Duty calls." Ashley hurried up the path.

Wyatt lingered, checking out the crowd. Ashley was an intriguing woman. Not perfect, as Gabby had so staunchly told him. But she was determined to reach for her dreams and not afraid to try new things to get there.

"You're lagging, Wyatt," Gabby said, still leaning on the railing. She wore a pink dress and white Keds and was ignoring the view of the valley, which was as good as the one from Wyatt's room. "Come on. I'll give you the nickel tour. As you can tell, the clinic is a glorified log cabin." She led him inside. "Small kitchen, small living space and two small exam areas. That ladder goes up to a loft for sleeping."

Pink balloons, pink streamers and colorful flower bouquets hung from the walls and porch rails. There were gifts stacked on what looked like a small dining table, making Wyatt wonder which one was from Ashley. And there were people mingling, swapping stories, sneaking glances at Wyatt and taking turns fawning over Laurel, who sat in a chair in a corner, simultaneously looking happy and uncomfortable with all the attention.

Ashley and a brunette with glasses organized the women into a circle and began explaining a game. Emily joined the circle, as did the woman who ran the general store and several others of different ages.

"Laurel's doctor is here. She's the blonde with the nerd glasses handing Laurel a glass of water. Our last doctor used to be a sports surgeon. But he moved to California." Gabby took Wyatt's picture with her phone. "And that's the nickel tour."

Wyatt placed a hand on her shoulder. "I thought you were going to stop treating me like a celebrity."

She shrugged and said, "I'm the official

baby-shower photographer. It's my job to take everyone's picture so the twins can look back on this someday." Gabby hiked her thumb at the refreshments table. "You should get some punch and cookies. The games might take a while."

He headed toward the table, checking out the assortment of frosted cookies—storks carrying pink swaddled babies, pink baby rattles, pink baby buggies—and cupcakes—pink or white. The punch was pink. The plates and napkins were pink. All in all, it was a smothering amount of pink.

Or it might have been, if it hadn't made him think of his mother and how much she loved to dress his sisters in the color. "Because it's so cheerful," she'd said when Natalie wanted to go Goth at the mature age of eleven. His mother had been the upbeat counterweight to his father's downbeat persona.

"In case you didn't know, it's a girl." Mitch appeared next to Wyatt and handed him a bottle of beer. "Times two."

"You've been through this before." Wyatt gestured toward Gabby.

She noticed them standing together and took their picture.

Wyatt felt like he stood on a precipice staring down into that big black hole Ashley had been splashing around in earlier. Someday, Laurel might have to explain why there were two fathers at her children's baby shower. Or not. It was his choice.

Do the right thing. He couldn't get his mother's words out of his head.

"My ex-wife's baby shower looked very similar," Mitch was saying. "But thankfully they make more than just pink clothes nowadays. And even if girls do want pink, I've recently discovered that my daughter is very capable when it comes to ordering her clothes online. Beats taking her to the department store. I just have to look at what she's put in her basket and approve or delete."

Should Wyatt decide to be involved, he'd need to settle on an amount for child support to help feed and clothe his children. And then Mitch would approve or delete the things they'd need. A disconcerting thought.

Wyatt looked away. Two baby quilts hung on the wall. One with dramatic black, teal and sand patterned material, and one with bright purple, teal and a soft white patterned material.

Mitch followed the direction of his gaze. "Laurel made those with Odette. Laurel has a slight aversion to pink."

"That used to be Ashley's signature color," Wyatt said absently.

"A point you might avoid in conversation with Laurel or Ashley." Mitch pointed out a slight older woman who stood next to Genevieve, staring at the agent's high heels with a perplexed look on her face. "That's Odette. She and Laurel run the Mercantile together. They sell local handmade goods."

"And paintings," a woman said, before taking a cookie and returning to Ashley's circle.

"Can't forget your paintings, Flip." Mitch took a drink of beer. "The brunette with the glasses is Sophie Monroe Roosevelt. She runs a store in what used to be the Fur Trading Post. Now it's a shop full of oddities and collectibles Harlan Monroe had stored up here in various buildings around town. It's the shop with the front end of an Edsel in the entrance."

"Across from the inn?"

Mitch nodded and gestured toward a thin old man who wore a baggy pink Hawaiian shirt and blue slacks. "That's our maintenance man, Roy. The town is incorporated with an unusual ownership situation. Anyway, Roy found a cabin full of antique sports equipment last week. Golf clubs. Lacrosse sticks. Old football uniforms. The week before it was steamer trunks and antique lockboxes, the kind they kept gold in on stagecoaches. Personally, I think it's trash, but Sophie finds buyers."

"Why are you telling me all this?" Wyatt looked closely at Mitch, searching for traces of his previous bitterness. "And more importantly, why are you being nice to me?"

"You should know the kind of community Laurel wants to raise the girls in. We help and support each other." He raised his beer bottle and then lowered it again without taking a sip. "I probably owe you an apology for the way I reacted the first day you were here. I take my future vows to love, honor and protect Laurel very seriously."

"Huh." Wyatt smiled as an idea took shape. "Community."

"You find that funny?" Some of the animosity that Mitch had just apologized for crept into his tone.

"As a temporary member of your community, I find this the opportune moment to ask for your help moving something into my room."

"You two look like you need a referee." Ashley slipped in between them. "Sophie's going to run the last game."

"That's my cue to mingle." Mitch left them alone.

Ashley shifted, maneuvering them around into a space where they could see the room and those out on the porch, but they were out of the way of traffic to the refreshments. She drew her cell phone out of her dress pocket.

Wyatt lowered her hand. "Whatever messages you have, they won't be as important as being present for Laurel's shower."

Ashley hesitated and then tucked the phone back into her pocket. "You're right."

"Wyatt Halford." Roy, the old man in the pink Hawaiian shirt, joined them. "As I live and breathe. I heard you were in town. Let me feel your biceps." Roy gave Wyatt's muscles a squeeze. "I wasn't sure if they made your muscles bigger in the editing room. You never know about technology nowadays."

Wyatt put his free arm around Ashley's waist and kept smiling. Gabby snapped their picture.

"Impressive. You're the real deal, Wyatt Halford," Roy said before moving on.

"Wyatt…" Ashley leaned closer, angling her face toward his and keeping her voice low. "Don't tell me you regularly get groped like a piece of fruit in the grocery store."

He shrugged. "You know how it is. When

you're famous, strangers think they're your closest friend."

"I do know." Ashley's eyes gazed at him compassionately. And then she flashed him a grin, putting a bit of distance between them. "But this… This is definitely rom-com material."

"Oh, don't start with the movie references." Wyatt groaned.

"Come on." Ashley nudged him with her elbow. "A couple at a party filled with unusual characters? Next thing you know, we'll be—"

"Do you wear sweater-vests, young man?" Odette appeared in front of Wyatt with a ball of black yarn in one hand. She pulled out a length and wrapped it around Wyatt's waist, as if she was hugging him. "I'm going to make you a sweater-vest. You look like you could pull it off. And once I make one for you, they'll sell like hotcakes in the Mercantile."

Gabby snapped another picture. And then Odette moved on.

Wyatt prided himself that his smile never wavered. "This isn't a rom-com, Ash. Or a misfit film." He guessed that genre was where Ashley was going next.

"Are you sure?" Ashley smiled but it wasn't

a smile for him. She gazed out over the gathering.

"How much would it cost to license your image?" Mackenzie, the brunette who ran the general store and had delivered the inn's mail today, ambled by next, looking Wyatt up and down. "I can see your face above a caption on a T-shirt, like, *Ian Bradford approves of Second Chance. You should, too.* Well, that was bad, but you get the idea."

He did. "If you take a picture of me, you own the intellectual property." Wyatt stared down at Ashley, feeling a chill that had nothing to do with her. "But I wouldn't use the name of a fictional character created by someone else. Ever."

"Great advice." Mack snapped a picture. "Thanks." She moved on to the punch bowl.

"Are we there yet?" Wyatt asked softly. "Because I have no idea what genre of film we're in."

"Close. Laurel's opening gifts." Ashley nodded toward the corner where her sister sat. "And then we'll clean up while you escort people safely up and down the path."

"What people?"

"Just my mother." Ashley opened a nearby cupboard, empty other than a half-full flask of vodka and a woman's small purse. "I saw her spike her punch. We're lucky she didn't spike everyone's." She closed the cupboard.

From the patio, Genevieve laughed a little too loud and tilted back on her thin heels.

"She'd have hysterics if she heard this, but I think she's having a midlife crisis." Ashley's brow clouded with concern. "She thinks none of us notice she's spiking her tea."

"I saw her making tea this morning." And he'd thought it odd that Genevieve had been walking around in public in her nightgown with a facial mask on. "That explains a lot." His arm curled around Ashley's waist. It felt so natural to draw her close, to have her gaze into his eyes. So natural to...

"A double stroller! And it comes with car seats and a bassinet." Laurel punched the air. "Thank you, Ashley and Wyatt. Thank you so much."

"I spent a lot of time picking that out," Wyatt teased Ashley, earning a grin.

"You're very thoughtful, not to mention generous," Ashley teased.

Wyatt craned his neck to get a good look at the stroller. Or rather the big box it came in. "I hope that's no assembly required." It was a humongous box. And a fancy stroller. More like a Transformers toy in all its iterations than what Wyatt expected of something to move kids from one place to another.

"Of course it requires assembly," Ashley said, as if it was no big deal. In Wyatt's experience, nothing was ever as easy to put together as it seemed. "It came from Sweden, and with all the accessories, it requires its own storage closet. I had to order it months ago just to make sure it arrived on time."

Months ago? Ashley had known about this months ago?

Wyatt stiffened.

Of course she had. He just hadn't thought through that fact. "Why didn't anyone tell me about Laurel and the babies sooner?"

"Laurel and Mom wanted to talk to you back in February, but you'd already left the country." Ashley patted his arm as if in apology. "You have good people around you. They wouldn't let Mom have access to your personal information. And Mom wasn't going to tell just anyone. But Laurel wanted you to know the truth before the babies came, so it was up to Shane to track you down."

"Shane." It always came back to that guy.

She glanced up at him and then reached up to smooth a worry line on his forehead. "Why? Did you think we planned to wait until the last minute?"

"No matter how I answer that question, you won't like it."

"True." She inched away from him.

Or she tried to, as if she was lost in thought about work and needed space. Wyatt brought her close once more. His attraction to her was far from convenient. At the moment, he didn't care. Holding Ashley in his arms was the simplest, clearest thing about his time in Second Chance.

Finally, all the gifts had been opened. Laurel thanked everyone for coming. Outside, the sun had set, bathing the valley in a warm glow. On the porch, Genevieve drained her punch glass and headed inside.

"Here we go." Ashley drew Wyatt forward. "Mom, the party's over. Can you make sure Wyatt finds his way back to the inn?"

"Smart," Wyatt murmured.

Her mother glanced toward the cupboard where the flask was located. "I need to get my purse. A woman should never be without her purse in case she gets fired and kicked out of her hotel room on the same day."

"Mom," Ashley warned.

She stalked away.

A few minutes later, Wyatt held Genevieve's arm as they walked down the steep dirt path to the road. His cell phone's flashlight app lit the way. Others headed the other direction or straight down to cross the road to vehicles parked in front of the diner. Their laughter filled the crisp night air.

"I don't know why you couldn't find your way back." Genevieve smelled like a distillery. "That hotel of ours rises from the earth like a brontosaurus."

"It's easy to get turned around in a new place." He slowed to help her step over a rock jutting out of the ground. "You always seem so sure-footed, though."

"Are you talking metaphorically, Mr. Halford?" Genevieve's tones were as formal as her regal movements. "If so, I have always had the gift of vision when it comes to career guidance. If not, my mother used to make me wear heels and walk with a book balanced on my head."

There was no sense beating around the bush with her. "What are your intentions toward me, Genevieve?"

She let out an uncharacteristic shout of laughter. "I have no idea what you mean."

"I think you do." He anchored her through a particularly steep patch in the path. "Ashley wants me here to protect Laurel. My agent wants me to stay here to protect my career. But you... I'm not certain if you want to ruin me or box me into a corner with Ashley and take credit for the greatest acting duo of all time."

"You're overselling your talent, Mr. Halford."

Now that they were away from the others, he could make out the effect of alcohol. The slurring of her words. The dampness of her palms.

"I've seen one or two of your films," she added.

He would bet she'd seen them all. "You know what I mean. I've seen the additions you made to the guest list." When he'd told Brandon, his agent had begged to attend. "Why?"

"Because you get it." She stopped in the trail and took mincing steps so that she could look up at him, so close behind her. But it was too dark to make out her expression, and he wasn't going to blind her by shining a light in her face. "You understand the Hollywood game. And Ashley is pushing me away. She needs someone to watch out for her, no matter what you decide about my granddaughters. You'll always have this shared experience to bind you. And that tie—"

"I'm not interested in finding a wife." The statement burst out of him on instinct, like yanking back a finger that had been shocked. Yes, he felt he knew Ashley on several levels, but that was different than the love one should have to commit to a serious relationship.

"I'm not trying to convince you to find a wife." Genevieve turned carefully away as if realizing there was nothing to gain by staring at him in the shadows. "But you could create a mutually beneficial understanding between yourself and Ashley. Watch over her as if she were a sister."

What he felt for Ashley...

He didn't want to put a name to it, but it was nothing like what he felt for his sisters.

He wanted no part of Genevieve's scheme and said so.

A deep grumble filled the air.

Genevieve teetered and clutched at Wyatt's arm. "What was that?"

Wyatt glanced around, aided by the flashlight feature on his phone. It hadn't been a truck rumble. It was more like...

Branches snapped. Something snuffled in the darkness.

Bear.

The hair on the back of his neck rose.

More snuffling and branch snapping. His phone's flashlight only illuminated a few feet into the woods. He hustled down the path, practically lifting Ashley's mother into his arms, making his horse-bitten shoulder bruise ache. Whatever was out there was interested in them. The pace of the noises increased, accented by a grunt.

Wyatt did a quick mental inventory. He had no food. Were bears attracted to alcohol? Because Ashley's mother did have that air about her. There was another possibility. "Genevieve, did you put any cookies in your bag?" Could any fit with that flask of hers in there?

"It isn't polite to ask a woman about her sweet tooth. But, yes, I took two."

Wyatt stopped mere feet from the two-lane highway. He grabbed her purse and opened it.

"What are you doing? Those are for later." She tried to reclaim her small bag. "If you wanted cookies, you should have taken your own."

Bingo. Two cookies sandwiched her little vodka flask. Wyatt flung them into the woods. Something big moved slowly out of the shadows. He aimed his flashlight toward the sound.

"Look at the cute little bear cub." The size of a Labrador retriever. Genevieve bobbed her head, trying to get a closer look. "Are we supposed to feed the bears?"

"Nope." Wyatt hustled her across the road and to the safety of the inn.

All without telling her that behind that bear cub had been a much larger bear.

Arkoudaphobia. The fear of bears. It was real. And now Wyatt had it, too.

"WHAT'S THAT SOUND?" Laurel was sitting in her chair, supervising the baby-shower cleanup.

Ashley stopped bagging the trash to listen. The others—Mitch, Gabby and Dr. Carlisle—stopped their cleanup efforts, as well.

"It sounds like someone's banging a pot." Mitch went out on the porch to look. "What are you doing?"

Wyatt climbed up the porch steps, a saucepan in one hand and a metal serving spoon in the other. "There are bears in the woods. When I was a kid, we used to scare them away with noise. I wouldn't leave any trash or food out."

Fear raced through Ashley's veins. Although she'd seen bears when she'd been camping with Grandpa Harlan, she'd never seen one as big as the grizzly hanging around Second Chance.

"Nobody panic." Mitch went to Laurel's

side. "That mama bear prefers easy pickings, like trash cans that don't lock."

"I knew there had to be a drawback to this place." Dr. Carlisle was Laurel's doctor, based in Ketchum. Shane had contracted her to update the clinic in the hopes that she'd realize Second Chance would be a wonderful place to practice. She had planned to stay the night in the clinic, but at the moment, she looked pale. She adjusted her thick glasses and tucked her blond hair behind her ears. All nervous gestures.

Shane wouldn't be happy to hear Dr. Carlisle was rattled by wildlife. Second Chance was in the middle of a forest.

Wyatt handed off his noisemaking kitchen items to Gabby and asked her to stand on the porch and continue to sound the alarm. He came to stand near Ashley. "This is not one of your horror movies."

Ashley nodded. "It's just life in the mountains."

"Yes," he said, sounding reassured. And Wyatt was reassured, encompassing her in a heated, almost passionate, gaze.

Ashley inched away. Given their intimate conversation before the shower, levity was called for. "It's more treacherous to navigate a career in Hollywood than escort my mother to her hotel."

"Yes, even without bears."

They both laughed and the moment passed.

Laurel stared their way with concern in her eyes.

"I'm fine," Ashley said in a loud voice. "In case anyone was wondering." In case anyone thought she'd forgotten that she and Wyatt were acting as if they were dating to create photo opportunities for Monroe accomplices.

Mitch began organizing. The food was packed up and put away in the refrigerator. The trash would be carried down and put in the inn's large metal bin. The presents would be left in the clinic. And they'd all march down together.

"I'll stay here." Dr. Carlisle looked much calmer than she had when Wyatt had first announced the bear's presence. "I'll be fine. Everything is clean and put away. I'll lock all the doors and windows."

"Are you sure?" Ashley glanced out into the darkness. "If I was staying here, I'd jump at every noise all night long."

"I'm sure." Dr. Carlisle had a confident smile, which probably helped her when she guided women through childbirth.

They left her in the clinic and made their way back to the inn without incident.

The group milled about the lobby, wide-eyed and smiling, as if they'd just accomplished a grand feat, not walked home without encountering wildlife.

"Nicely done, Halford." Mitch shook Wyatt's hand.

"I may not have the mad horseback riding skills of Ashley," Wyatt said half-jokingly. "But I know a thing or two about living in a small town in the woods."

Other things Wyatt knew a thing or two about: scaring away bears and charming the ladies. Ashley filed that under things she shouldn't think about when she thought about Wyatt Halford.

Laurel sent Ashley a silent look that was worry filled.

And maybe it was justified, because somehow Wyatt had taken hold of Ashley's hand without her realizing it. And maybe she was letting her guard down too much where he was concerned, because their hands fit together.

"Gabby, is your homework done?" Laurel asked, still watching Ashley.

"No." Gabby stared at her phone, spinning

her hips back and forth, making her skirt eddy around her legs.

Ashley tried to gently extricate her hand without causing a fuss. Wyatt held on. And Laurel saw that, too. The worry lines in her forehead deepened.

Laurel thought Wyatt was trying to muscle past Ashley's guard, the way Mom had warned. But he was only doing it to keep up the deception that they were dating. Anyone could come down the stairs or through the front door and see them. Mitch's mother, for example. She didn't realize that Ashley was like Letty Moody and Wyatt was like Jeb Clark. There was an attraction, but it was a train wreck of an attraction. Never destined to be.

Ashley leaned away from Wyatt, hoping to slip her hand from his, hoping to reestablish some space.

No dice. If his grip had been this firm on the saddle horn this morning, he wouldn't have fallen off the horse.

Laurel's frown was in full force now. "Gabby, did you do the dishes?"

"Yes. Before we left." Gabby glanced up from her phone. "Are you trying to get rid of me?"

"Yes." Laurel shooed her into the apartment, no doubt wanting to say something to Ashley or Wyatt or both.

Like Ashley needed a reminder of the dangers of Wyatt up close and personal. "I'm headed for bed. Early morning and all." She tugged a bit harder.

And her twin was right to be worried, because Wyatt still didn't let Ashley go. He held on and caressed her hand with his thumb as he led her upstairs. And Ashley didn't protest because that might upset Wyatt, who'd actually seemed like he got along with people tonight, even Mitch. And wasn't that part of the reason he was here, and Ashley was pretending to be his wedding date? To help unravel the knots tangling them all together?

CHAPTER NINE

THE MORNING AFTER the baby shower, Ashley hadn't even gotten her tea from Cam when Wyatt entered the diner, beautifully sweaty.

That shouldn't be a thing.

She'd spent much of the night tossing and turning, thinking about Wyatt and things she'd said—too much—and how he made her feel—too much—and vows she'd made to her sister. She'd wanted to go downstairs for a cup of tea in the middle of the night, but what if Wyatt was down there? She'd tossed some more, until Mom had poked her and commanded her to lie still so one of them could get her beauty sleep.

Ashley had welcomed the chance to dive into the distraction of work this morning. And then what had happened? Her biggest distraction had walked through that door.

She felt like slouching and hunching her shoulders in an attempt to be invisible. Instead, she rolled them back and reached for a smile that conveyed disdain for sweaty men who didn't kiss women good-night.

"Good morning." Wyatt sauntered behind the lunch counter and washed his hands as if he was a long-term resident and customer. "I'll get my own water. I know you're busy, Chef."

Cam tossed him a towel via the pass-through. "Thanks, man. Where have you been eating? I haven't seen you in the diner."

"He's eating clean," Ashley said, a little unnerved by the ease with which Wyatt suddenly fit in to what should have been her world. "Nonprocessed foods he buys from the general store." Mack had told her that when Ashley had stopped by yesterday to check out the Mike Moody merchandise displayed in the store window.

"Does nothing I do go unnoticed in Second Chance?" Wyatt shook his head, but he was smiling.

Just not at her.

Which was good. It meant she could refuse to feel guilty that the pictures Second Chance residents had posted on social media were trending in popularity. Not that she should feel guilty. He'd posted a picture of her walking through the meadow and the one Gabby had taken of them yesterday during her homework interview. They were both doing their part to avert disaster. If only he'd agree to forgoing his rights to those babies, they'd be free and clear to go their separate ways. Instead, it felt like half of Hollywood was coming to witness what could be their career demise if things didn't go smoothly.

"Eating keto doesn't mean he has to eat plain." Cam diced something with a series of quick chop-chop-chops.

"What's on the agenda today?" Wyatt sat down across from Ashley, scrubbing at his face and neck with the towel, removing all that sweat, just not any of his beauty.

"I'm very busy."

"And I'm very bad at taking a hint." But he said it with a smile that softened his words and threatened to soften her resolve. "It's a skill I learned from having two older sisters."

She didn't want to imagine him as a precocious young boy who followed his sisters around. Had he been an angel like little Adam Clark? Or more of a mischief-maker like the middle Clark boy, Charlie?

"I'm very busy with boring preproduction work." She had to review the portfolios of set directors and their pitches to dress Second Chance for the film. "And then I have to squeeze in a special project for Shane." She was directing the street production of *The*

Legend of Mike Moody for his Old West Festival on Sunday.

"Yes, where is Shane?" Wyatt set his elbows on the table and leaned forward. "I have a bone to pick with him, not to mention he owes me a set of spark plugs."

"I thought you went to the Bucking Bull yesterday." Cam butted into their conversation as if he'd been invited. "Shane lives there now. He's getting married to Franny on New Year's Eve."

"Thank you, Cam." Cousin Blabbermouth. She gave him a dirty look.

Wyatt's expression darkened.

"I don't expect to see Shane today," Ashley barreled on, still intent upon trying to shake Wyatt loose. "I've got wedding details to go over. It's all boring stuff." But it wouldn't be if Wyatt were along, of that she was certain.

"Is Wyatt coming to dinner?" Cam wasn't much good at reading Ashley's hints. "I'm making vegetarian surprise."

"What's the surprise?" Wyatt asked.

Cam shrugged. "Whatever comes in my food delivery today. It's hard to predict."

"I'll be Ashley's plus-one for dinner," Wyatt said, flashing her a grin. "Wouldn't want to miss vegetarian surprise."

"Then your day is free until about seven." She tried not to sound too relieved.

"Yeah, I like yesterday's work better." Wyatt took a draft of water. "Tell me when you go back to the Bucking Bull to practice stunt work. I'll enjoy that and *requesting* Shane return my stolen property. An actor can never let his skills get rusty, be they riding or using his fists."

Oh, come on. Ashley was about to reiterate that she didn't think Wyatt needed to join her because he wasn't right for the part of Mike Moody when the front door of the diner was flung open.

"I raced all the way over here for fear of running into that bear." Gabby hurried inside, wearing a hoodie and toting a backpack. "I need to do my online homework without distractions, so I'm knuckling down over here for a few hours. There were too many early risers at the inn." She sat on a stool at the lunch counter. "Cam, can I have a breakfast special? Whatever the special is today, anyway."

"You're my kind of customer, kid." Cam poured a yellow mixture into something Ashley couldn't see. "The kind who doesn't ask what the special is but just orders it anyway. I'm making bacon-and-red-pepper egg cups."

Cam slid a tray into the oven. "One special, coming right up."

"I thought you weren't open." Wyatt sat up, looking toward the kitchen and Ashley's cousin. "Egg cups? Is that keto?"

"It is keto. If you'd bother to look, we have a diverse breakfast menu." Cam sounded annoyed. "But we're closed for all but our hometown heroes. Gabby once saved my fiancée's life."

"I heard about that," Ashley said gently, because Laurel had told her it had been harrowing not just for Ivy, but for Gabby. "Do you need a hug, Gabby?"

"No." But Gabby squirmed in her seat as if she were uncomfortable.

Ashley got up and gave her a hug anyway.

"I save people on the big screen." Wyatt grinned at Ashley and held out his arms as if he, too, needed a hug. When she gave him a scowl instead, he said, "And, Cam, I could do with anything you whip up if you aren't going to offer me your egg cups. Surprise me."

Roy tottered in, wearing his faded blue coveralls. "I saw folks coming inside." He lived in a small cabin across the road next to the medical clinic. "Thought I'd mosey over since you were open early, Cam." He sat next to Gabby. "How's my girl?"

"Overloaded with homework." Gabby opened her laptop, a cue that Ashley should do the same. "So much for summer vacation."

"Want a special, Roy?" Cam was chopping again.

"Sure do. Need me to make the community coffeepot?"

"Sure do." Cam grinned.

Roy got back to his feet and moved to the table with the big metal cistern that allowed residents to serve themselves a cup of coffee without disrupting the workflow in the short-staffed diner.

Wyatt's stomach growled loud enough that Ashley heard. He frowned at everyone, but only Ashley seemed to notice. "Why does Roy get a special?"

"The diner adopted Roy after his heart attack." Cam was in chef mode, darting to and fro in the kitchen.

Without removing her gaze from her laptop, Gabby raised her hand. "I was there to help save Roy, too."

"You know those things always happen in threes," Wyatt grumbled.

Gabby paled, whipping around to stare at Wyatt as if he was a teacher who'd given out an impossible assignment.

"You shouldn't say that to her," Ashley said quickly.

"My mom said it all the time." Wyatt shrugged. "Bad luck comes in threes. It's just an old wives' tale."

"Hush." Ashley kept her voice down. "Gabby's worried something's going to happen to Laurel and the babies."

"Actually, I'm worried I'm going to end up delivering those babies," Gabby said, proving sounds carried in the near-empty diner. "Because that's the kind of streak I'm on. And preemies need doctors."

"Delivering babies is my job." Dr. Carlisle entered the diner, looking fully rested despite last night's bear alert. "Never fear. I took a few days off to attend the wedding and watch out for Laurel." She sat down next to Gabby. "I didn't expect to see you up so early." She glanced around. "I didn't expect the diner to be open so early either."

"Do you want a special, Doc?" Cam called from the kitchen.

"I do." Wyatt raised his hand, schooling his features to look pitiful. "Honestly, I know CPR, and I once played an army medic. I can be heroic." His stomach growled loud enough for everyone to hear.

And hear they did. Everyone turned to stare.

Ashley rolled her eyes. "Honestly, Wyatt. If I didn't know better, I'd think you were using ventriloquism to make that noise."

He drew himself up and tapped his hands on his abs. "I'm starving and you make jokes?"

"All right. Four specials coming up." Cam banged around in the kitchen.

Gabby got off her stool. "Unless someone wants to do my geometry homework, I'm going to be in the corner powering through this stuff."

Ashley was tempted to join her. She couldn't get work done with Wyatt sitting across from her. She tapped her fingers on her stack of folders, gathering her courage to join Gabby.

"Don't do it." Wyatt shook his head. "I'd just follow you over."

"And now you're a mind reader?" Ashley scoffed.

"It's entirely possible." He gave her a cheeky grin. "You and I both know actors pick up random knowledge when studying for a role."

Gabby snorted. "I bet that doesn't include anything useful, like geometry."

"I'M TELLING YOU, Wyatt, this is a good deal."
Wyatt's agent let his impatience show. "If you
sign now, when you see Jess Watanabe on
Saturday, the two of you will be able to toast
to the project."

"And I'm telling you it's not the deal I
want." Wyatt wasn't agreeing with his agent's
opinions or his attitude. It was late morning.
His egg-cup breakfast was fast becoming but
a memory. And Wyatt was getting hungry
for more than food. He hadn't seen or heard
Ashley since breakfast.

Brandon fretted. "If we press them any
more, Wyatt, they'll find someone else to
play Captain Doohoon." In that sci-fi thriller
film with an option for two additional install-
ments.

Wyatt didn't think twice about defending his position. "I've got another Ian Bradford film coming out at the end of summer.
You and I both know it's going to break box-
office records."

"You and I both know there is no guarantee
of anything anymore." Brandon had taken his
difficult pill today. All he wanted to do was
argue. "Great job at trending on social media,
though. Make sure to forward any more pictures you have. You and Ashley Monroe look
like you're getting along."

Wyatt brought the conversation back around to money. "Listen, Brandon, if we don't press for a record-breaking deal now, we'll miss our window." And someone else would command a price higher than Wyatt. "I need this deal. Now." Preferably before Jess Watanabe showed up for Laurel's wedding on Saturday.

"Have you been spending money I don't know about?" Brandon demanded.

"No." Wyatt wasn't ready to tell Brandon that the public relations fire they'd worked so hard to put out could potentially spark to life again. He was circling the idea of fatherhood at his own pace, thank you very much. Just like he seemed to be circling something more than being a convenient wedding date for Ashley. "Just counter."

"I'll counter if you agree this is the last time."

"Last time." Wyatt disconnected the call and stared out his window, knowing Brandon considered him greedy. But Wyatt wanted that contract signed before bad press gave the producer something to negotiate with. He couldn't predict how bankable he'd be if word of Laurel's pregnancy got out again.

Like babies should ever be bad press.

His father would get a good chuckle if he

ever heard Wyatt say that out loud. But his father was old-school. He'd never told Wyatt he loved him. Never said he was proud of his accomplishments. Never really thanked him for buying him a house and paying for its upkeep.

And yet Wyatt knew he'd do anything to hear those words from his father, even if it meant putting off making a decision about Laurel's children. Would he ever have a chance to say he loved those girls? Would they want his love if they knew he was hesitant to take an active role in their lives?

Someone knocked on the door.

It was Mitch. The inn's manager glanced around, taking in the bed Wyatt slept on pushed to one side and Jeremy's mattress and box spring leaning against a wall.

Wyatt waited for a blowup. But it didn't come.

Mitch sighed. "All right, Halford. I'll make you a deal. I'll help you carry whatever you wanted moved in here if you help me put together the baby stroller."

"You need help with that?" Wyatt raised his brows. "It can't be that hard."

"Oh, it can. The instructions are half-missing. And the pages I do have? They're in Swedish."

"WHAT HAVE YOU done to Mom? She's been hiding in her room all morning."

Ashley finished logging call notes in her phone before glancing up at Laurel. "Are you asking because you want to know how it's done?"

They sat on the front porch of the Lodgepole Inn, waiting to greet Monroes as they arrived. Laurel wore a lime-green maternity dress and flip-flops and still complained about the heat. Across the highway, the tall pines swayed in the gentle breeze. It was a beautiful morning and not as hot as Laurel seemed to think. Ashley was comfortable in her jeans and lightweight sweater. Gabby sat on the far end of the porch, bent over her laptop, typing like crazy.

"You know what I mean." Laurel contorted in her chair. "Gah. *Practice contraction.*" She held her breath. Almost immediately, her face turned red.

Gabby stopped typing. "Aren't you supposed to breathe, even if it's only practice?"

"Thanks. I. Forgot." Laurel groaned and began taking shallow breaths. "Don't think I'm…letting you…off the hook…about Mom."

"All I did was threaten to fire her. It can't all be laid at my door. She's been drinking since we got here." Ashley caught Gabby's eye. "Is Laurel supposed to be this uncomfortable when she practices contractions?"

"Yes." Laurel collapsed into the chair and drew a deep breath. "It's not like practicing a golf swing. It's like the body is preparing for Armageddon. Braxton Hicks contractions are the boot camp of pregnancy."

"I'm never having babies." Gabby bent over her laptop.

A car slowed as it made the turn from Boise and headed toward town. It looked like two women were in the front seat.

"Is this Olivia and Kendall?" Ashley got up and waved, welcoming two of her Monroe cousins.

The car didn't stop. But the two women inside did gawk at Ashley as they passed.

Laurel dissolved into laughter. "Those women are going to argue for the next hour about whether or not Ashley Monroe was waving at them. Don't you recognize your own cousins?"

"There was glare on the windshield." Ashley sat back down. She had more calls to make, more emails to send. And yet she didn't want to work. She could hear the rumble of Mitch's and Wyatt's voices inside as they assembled the baby stroller. Inappropriate as it was, her attention kept drifting that way.

"You need to make up with Mom." Laurel wasn't asking. She'd been feisty all morning. "I'm not kidding."

"Why?" Mom hadn't tried to tell Ashley what to do all day. She hadn't pointed out Ashley's weaknesses or warned of the financial pitfalls of trying to start her own business. "You, of all people, know how she can get." For years, Laurel had been Mom's favorite target.

"Because she's miserable. And so am I." Laurel covered her face with her hands. "This must be a hormone swing. I feel so on edge. Keep me away from Mitch. He's been so sensitive lately."

Mitch had been walking on a tightrope, trying to keep Laurel happy and comfortable. Earlier, he'd asked Laurel, *Why are we putting the stroller together today? I still need to assemble the cribs.*

She'd snapped back a tried-and-true parental phrase: *Because I said so.* Ashley had taken pity on him and ushered Laurel outside.

And now Wyatt was helping Mitch with all the baby gear. And Ashley had become half-hearted in her hope that he'd sign away all claim to Laurel's girls. It had been adorable to watch him with Adam Clark at the Bucking Bull. Despite his doubts, Wyatt would make a good dad. If only he wouldn't complicate this situation for them all, especially Laurel.

A big, boxy motor home pulled into a parking space in front of them. The sun bounced off the windshield, practically blinding her.

"Who's that?" Laurel squinted and shaded her eyes.

"It's Holden," Gabby said from the corner, where the glare might not have been so bad. Not being a Holden fan, she hunkered down over her computer.

"That can't be Holden." Laurel tried to lean forward for a better look, but she was deep in her seat and not going anywhere without a helping hand.

Cousin Holden stepped out of the side door, stretching his tall body, streaks of gray catching the sunlight in his short brown hair. "Take note, Dev. This is how your Hollywood cousins treat East Coast Monroes. We wave, and they completely snub us."

"Who could see you with all that *glare* on your windshield?" Laurel poked Ashley's shoulder. "You could have been two strange women, for all we could see."

"Hardy-har," Ashley said, picking up on

the reminder of her misidentification of the earlier passing car.

Holden's son, Devin, dropped to the ground from the side door. He'd just graduated high school and looked as handsome as Holden had when he was seventeen. Thankfully, he was more interested in studying science than studying girls.

Gabby shot up in her seat as if she'd been electrocuted. "Who is that?" she whispered.

Laurel and Ashley exchanged looks and mischievous smiles. Ashley didn't need twin speak to know what her hormonal sister was thinking.

Gabby, Gabby, Gabby.

Ashley rubbed her hands together. Soon, Gabby would officially be family. As such, she needed to get used to Monroe teasing.

"Devin, come up here so I can give you a hug." With effort, Laurel pushed herself out of the chair, stomach first. "And so I can warn you away from my stepdaughter."

Gabby gasped.

"Don't you mean introduce Dev to Gabby, his new cousin by marriage?" Ashley got up and tugged Gabby to her feet. "He's too old for you," she whispered. "Besides, what would Wyatt think if you start mooning over someone else?"

"Uh…" Gabby's already flushing cheeks turned a deep red.

Laurel finished mugging Devin. "I want you to meet Mitch's daughter, Gabby. Now, you're the first boy her age to stay more than a day in Second Chance all year, so make sure you treat her like a nonkissing cousin."

Devin's cheeks turned ruddy. "Whatever you say." He was somewhat used to the teasing of his second cousins.

"You've trained him well, Holden." Ashley took a turn giving Devin a hug.

Gabby and Devin stared at each other and made awkward gestures of greeting.

Holden stared at the diner parking lot as he walked up the stairs. "Is that Bernadette's car?"

"You mean Dr. Carlisle?" Laurel frowned. And then slugged his shoulder. "You did not."

"Am I missing something here?" Anytime Holden was being punished, Ashley wanted to be involved. He was the oldest Monroe of their generation and something of a stick-in-the-mud.

"You dated my doctor?" Laurel slugged his shoulder again. "When?"

"Is no woman safe from you?" Ashley looked her cousin up and down. For such a stuffed shirt, Holden was always the popular one.

"Hey, keep it down. My personal life is none of your business." Holden stepped quickly out of Laurel's reach.

"You keep telling yourself that, bub." Laurel jabbed her finger toward Holden. "But if you break her heart and I hear about it, you're toast."

Holden scoffed.

"You think I can't make you squirm?" Laurel rolled her shoulders back as if she was going to raise her fists and duke it out. "I can tell Devin stories about you. Don't think I won't. My doctor is off-limits. Do you hear me?"

"I thought you were the nice twin," Holden said, edging toward the inn's door until he was close enough to dart in.

"Are you running away from me?" Laurel followed him, pausing in the doorway to turn to Devin. "You let me know if you need anything during your stay, Dev. Or if Gabby tries to hit on you. She just got her braces off, so you know she's on the lookout for a first kiss." Laurel froze, face reddening. "Somebody stop me from talking."

"Stop talking, Laurel," Ashley and Dev said in unison.

"I was teasing, but… I need a time-out." Laurel went inside.

After a moment of awkward silence, Dev shrugged and followed her in.

Gabby hung her head. "This is worse than the time I left my training bra in the changing room of the department store, and she made me go back and ask for it at the lost and found. Is Laurel going to say stuff like that the entire time Devin's here?"

"Yup." Ashley slung her arm over Gabby's shoulders. "Isn't family grand?"

CHAPTER TEN

"THE BRAKES STICK." Wyatt sat back on his heels.

He and Mitch had moved his inversion machine up to his room. And since then, they'd spent over an hour trying to put together the stroller.

"I told you the diagram was wrong." Mitch turned the instructions around. And around. And around. He let the paper drift to the floor. "It's time to call in the expert."

"The customer support line?" Wyatt shook his head. "I'm out. I don't do well with automated phone trees. *Press one if I've annoyed you.*"

"I meant Roy."

"The old man?" The guy who'd thought Wyatt's biceps were photoshopped? "You're joking."

"I'm not." Mitch checked the time on his phone. "He should be on his morning coffee break at the Bent Nickel about now. Let's go see if he has time to help. At the very least, we'll grab a cup of coffee before making a second attempt."

They got to their feet and nearly made it to the door before they were stopped by a cool voice.

"Where are you two going?" It was Laurel. She'd just given her cousin and his teenage son a room key and was glancing from the two men to the scattering of parts across the floor in the lobby. "It looks like Santa couldn't put Christmas together again."

The apartment door was open behind her. Gifts from the baby shower were stacked on the floor and the table, making the small living space seem more like a storage closet.

Wyatt's neck twinged. Laurel's living situation was untenable. A responsible father would make sure his children had a safe home with room to move.

Unaware of Wyatt's train of thought, Mitch quickly reassured Laurel. "Never fear, honey. We'll be right back to fix this mess." He hurried over to give her a loving embrace. "We're going to find Roy. He'll have this thing together in no time."

They went out the door and into the sunshine, passing Ashley sitting in a chair on a phone call and Gabby sitting on the porch steps writing a paper on her laptop.

Mitch matched Wyatt's long stride with one of his own. "Would now be a good time to ask you to sign those paternity papers?"

"No." Wyatt tossed whatever camaraderie they'd had under the passing semitruck.

"If you'd sign, I'd get Roy to help me put together the cribs and baby swings," Mitch added, as if being released from baby paraphernalia construction was a bargaining chip.

"No deal. But tell me… Why are we putting this stuff together now?" Wyatt's frown felt like it was etching itself into his forehead. Perhaps it had been since he'd arrived. "Unless your bedroom is humongous, there's no way you're going to fit all that furniture into your apartment."

"Because Laurel wants it done now. Because she doesn't think we'll have the time or energy to do it after the babies are born." Mitch blocked Wyatt's entrance into the Bent Nickel. "Laurel is compartmentalizing. Do you know what that means?"

Wyatt surrendered with a shrug. "I got nothing."

"The road ahead is unclear, partly because of you." Mitch's tone swung from demoral-

ized to accusatory. "She can't control any out-
come. Not your involvement. Not when the
babies will be born. So, she creates a one-
step-at-a-time plan forward. She wants to get
through the wedding and give birth before we
try to figure out where we're going to live."

Wyatt shouldn't find fault with that when
he was slow to make a decision about fatherhood, but he did.

"It's how she deals with stress. She looks
at first things first." Mitch didn't look happy
about it either. "It's not like I haven't tried to
leapfrog ahead. Roy is fixing up all these cabins around town for the Monroes, but Laurel
refuses to look at them."

"Maybe Ashley can persuade her to consider one." After Wyatt screened her choices.

"I can't ask Ashley to put more on her plate."
Mitch held the diner door open for Wyatt to
pass through.

Immediately, someone called out, "Wyatt
Halford!"

Immediately after that, people began whipping out cell phones and taking pictures. Some
folks asked him to autograph their napkins.

"Sorry, man." Mitch left him to his fans
and went to talk to Roy.

Roy, who knew how large and what state
of repair available cabins were in.

OF COURSE, AFTER Laurel embarrassed Gabby, she'd sent her upstairs to put fresh towels in rooms.

Gah, because she had to complete the chore just down the hall from Devin, who was supercute. And if he came out of his room and saw her carrying two laundry baskets, she'd die. Which wouldn't be the worst of it, because Ashley and Laurel were probably going to tease her about Devin all through his stay.

Welcome to the family.

It was the first time she'd thought being a Monroe sucked.

Gabby knocked on Ashley and Grandma Gen's door hard enough to sting her knuckles. "It's Gabby. Can I come in?"

Grandma Gen made a noise. It had to be her. Ashley was downstairs making lunch. And because Gabby heard a doorknob rattle down the hall near where Devin's room was, she took that Grandma Gen noise for permission and darted inside.

Grandma Gen sat in a small ladder-back chair beneath the room's only window. She'd squeezed it between the bed and the wall. There was no room to walk around it.

"I'd like to be alone," she told Gabby without facing her.

"I'd like to be alone, too," Gabby griped, taking a page from Grandma Gen's sour book. She changed out the towels, and as she was stacking one laundry basket on top of the other, she realized that Grandma Gen hadn't moved, not even a chair-creaking shift in her seat. Her bright red hair wasn't combed smooth. She was still in her bathrobe. She wore no makeup. And most telling of all, she wasn't snapping out the witty sarcastic remarks. "Are you okay?"

"I just—"

"Want to be alone." Gabby stomped toward the door, hugging the bulky baskets to her chest. "I get it. I want to put some distance between me and the Monroes, too."

Grandma Gen turned. "What's wrong with you?"

"Nothing." But Gabby didn't barge off. "Laurel and Ashley were teasing me about Devin." She raised her voice to the ceiling and groaned. "And now I sound like a little kid."

"You're an only child." Grandma Gen looked her up and down. "You haven't been subjected to family teasing before."

"No. And Laurel doesn't usually tease me either." Gabby moved to sit on the corner of the bed, resting the baskets in her lap.

"The dynamic changes when families get together." Grandma Gen gingerly touched her frizzy red hair, as if only now realizing how it must look. "There's more energy, which leads to more frivolity, which means you have to toughen up."

"Right. Of course." Gabby dropped the baskets on the carpet. "And all of a sudden I'm being dropped into a big family."

"You're feeling sorry for yourself."

"As if you're not?" Gabby didn't even care that Grandma Gen had regained some of her superior attitude. "I heard you and Ashley had a fight."

They stared at each other. And it was the first time Gabby could remember Laurel and Ashley's mother give her an approving nod.

"You don't want to be an actress, do you?" Grandma Gen smiled weakly. "I'm quite good at building the careers of young talent. And I might be taking on new clients soon."

"I'm either going to be a doctor or a lawyer."

"If you want to become a doctor, make sure you choose one of the higher-income professions, like brain surgeon or cardiologist."

"I'm not interested in making a lot of money." The statement only made her realize how different she was from the Monroes, who seemed to like both teasing and lots of money.

Grandma Gen made a disapproving noise. "If you go to school to be a doctor or a lawyer, you're going to need to make a lot of money to pay six or seven years of tuition." And then she shook her head. "If you become a lawyer, you'll have to learn how to keep people's confidences."

"Lucky me. I have you to keep reminding me of that." Gabby plucked at a seam in the quilt. "Maybe you should consider a career change. My dad used to be a lawyer and now he's an innkeeper."

Grandma Gen turned up her nose. "He went from a man of power to a man running all this." She tapped the round log wall.

"He went from helping people in the courtroom to helping people in Second Chance." Gabby stood, picking up the laundry baskets. She didn't like anyone picking on her father. "And Ashley's reinventing herself, too."

"Against my wishes."

"I'm a kid, and even I know you can't say that to your adult children." Gabby headed for the door.

"Thank you for the clean towels, darling, but if you were sent here to cheer me up—"

"I did a lousy job." Gabby opened the door. "But, hey, ditto."

"I NEED YOU to come with me." The deep words. The intense look in Wyatt's eyes.

What woman wouldn't melt the moment Wyatt Halford spoke those words to her?

A reinvigorated Ashley Monroe, that was who. She was immune to his charm. Or at least, she had been today without him always at her side. She was camped out in a chair on the back porch of the inn, an empty lunch plate on the small side table. It was calming. The Salmon River ambled by. The moose in the meadow ambled by.

And then Wyatt ambled by, looking like several million bucks and smelling like the lush green forest.

"Come on, Ash." He held out his hand. Oh, so tempting.

She shook her head. "Do you know how many little details go into preproduction of a movie, Wyatt?" She had dozens of emails to respond to, and that didn't count the messages from her social groups.

"Do you know how five people are going to fit into Laurel's cramped apartment?" he countered. "If you won't come with me, maybe you should step inside and look at the amount of baby furniture Laurel's accumulated. Mitch and I spent considerable time putting things together with the help of Roy."

He opened the door that led to the inn's hallway, gesturing she follow.

"If this is about the double stroller, I think
it can be stored in Mitch's garage." In the rafters, though, since it was already crammed
with stuff. But she dutifully stepped into the
lobby. And she obediently surveyed the two
cribs, bassinet swing, double stroller, play-
pen, changing table and a stack of baby toys
that had yet to be brought out of their boxes.
He was right. Where were Laurel, Mitch and
the kids going to live?

"I can fix this," Ashley said, although she
wondered how.

"I have a solution," Wyatt countered.

Ashley faced him, staring directly into
those dark, intense eyes. "If your solution in-
volves moving Laurel to Hollywood, that's
a no."

"Ye of little faith. Come on." Wyatt headed
for the door.

There was no handclasp. He didn't take her
arm. He simply marched ahead, across the
two-lane highway and up the path toward the
clinic. There was no audience to witness their
fake relationship, after all. It was alarming
how Ashley longed for an audience. Was this
how Letty had felt with the town blacksmith?

Knowing they were wrong for each other but drawn to him anyway?

"Where are we going?" Ashley hurried after him, although at a slower pace. She studied the trees ahead, the trees to either side, and cast nervous glances behind her, looking for bears.

"We're going in search of suitable alternative housing." He paused on a rise to let her catch up. "Roy should get his real-estate license. When I told him what Mitch and Laurel needed, he pointed me in two specific directions."

"You want to screen houses for them. That's nice of you." Ashley pondered that for a moment, following when he pressed on. "If you're intent upon finding Laurel a workable home in Second Chance, does that mean you aren't going to press for custody?" If that were true, yay for Laurel! But also, boo for Wyatt and the babies. They'd each be missing out on something wonderful.

Instead of answering, Wyatt pushed through a pair of bushes and stopped in front of a cabin. "This hidden gem has two bedrooms and a loft."

"Really? It looks very rustic." Not like Laurel at all.

"Welcome to what could be Laurel's new

home." Wyatt led her inside. "It's only got one bath, but it's just a five-minute walk from the inn, a little bit longer if they drive since the dirt road originates north of town."

"It's cozy." There was a large stone fireplace with a chunky wood mantel, perfect for hanging Christmas stockings. The kitchen was nearly open. If cabinets hanging above the peninsula were removed, anyone in the kitchen would have a clear sight line of the dining and living spaces. There ended the positives. The surrounding pine trees blocked some of the light. And it was a hike up the path, not exactly a smooth sidewalk in Beverly Hills. But still. Ashley approved. "It's not as tight as their current apartment."

Wyatt took her hand and led her to the back of the cabin. "Look at this bedroom. It's big enough to fit two dressers and two bassinets." And then he pivoted, hauling her back to the loft ladder. "And from upstairs, Gabby can hear everything."

It warmed Ashley's heart that he hadn't forgotten Gabby.

"She likes to be in the know." Ashley liked to be in the know, as well. "What does this mean? For you, I mean."

Wyatt gazed down at her. The longer he stayed in Second Chance, the more untamed his cowlick became. Ashley couldn't resist reaching up and trying to smooth it. She should have known that nothing about Wyatt was smooth or tamable.

"It means…" He seemed at a loss to put it into words. "It means that everyone in Second Chance has been lending Laurel a hand and I didn't want to be the only one who hadn't."

Had Ashley thought she was immune to Wyatt's charm? More like, he was her kind of charming. "So your housing search has nothing to do with a decision about fatherhood?"

Wyatt shook his head slowly. "Does that disappoint you?"

"The clock is ticking, Wyatt. Once those babies are born, there needs to be only one name listed as their father."

"Whoever is listed as their father contributes to their identity for the rest of their lives." His voice took on a rare, grave quality. "Since I've been here, I've had a lot of time to think about family and what it means to do the right thing." His gaze took in the shabby cabin.

Ashley didn't know what he was seeing. She only knew what she saw—a handsome man who normally had the world at his feet; a man's man who'd fought his way to the top of a highly competitive field; an intelligent man who must know that no one stayed on top for long; a man who—

His gaze turned her way and the complexity of emotion in his dark eyes surprised her. Anger, pain, remorse.

"My parents met at a church dance. My mother used to say it was love at first sight." Anger burned down the other emotions in his eyes.

"In the midst of one of their arguments, my father would accuse her of trapping him into marriage. Dad had dreams of going to college, but instead, he took a job in a coal mine because he always did the right thing." And there was pain.

"That resentment ate him up inside almost as efficiently as cancer devoured my mother's lungs." A dimming flash of remorse.

All subtle emotion that she couldn't remember seeing him convey on camera.

"I don't want to make a choice that eats away at me, Ash. Or at Laurel. Or Mitch. Or…anyone." He ran his fingers over her hair, as light as the ripple she imagined he hoped his final decision regarding paternity would cause.

"Come on." He tugged her toward the door. "Let's go see the other cabin. It's a bit bigger, more modern and farther away." He led her confidently through the forest, as if he'd been hiking these woods all his life.

Ashley was still on bear watch, alternating between surveying where she placed her feet and scanning the slopes for grizzlies. Until something unexpected caught her eye, and she pulled Wyatt to a stop.

"Look at this." She pointed at the trunk of a thick, tall pine tree. About six feet up, someone had dug a rectangle in the bark, inserted an old photograph and then covered it with a sheet of clear plastic. The tree had since grown around it, closing in on the three men in the photograph. "It's my grandpa Harlan, his twin brother, Hobart, and Percy Clark of the Bucking Bull." She couldn't keep the excitement out of her voice. "Shane and Jonah told me these were scattered around Second Chance, but other than the one at the Bucking Bull, I've never seen one."

Wyatt stared at the yellowed photograph. "Why would they do this?"

"I'm not exactly sure, but it had something to do with their hunt for Mike Moody's gold, like trail markers or something." Ashley reached up to run her fingers over her grandfather's familiar face. "The thing about Grandpa Harlan I admired most was that he always seemed to know who he was and where he was going."

"Now, there's an actor's job hazard, not knowing where you end and a character begins."

Ashley allowed her gaze to go where it was constantly drawn—to Wyatt. She didn't think she raised so much as an eyebrow—he had, after all, played a certain type of character repeatedly; who was he to be talking about a lack of character identity?

Wyatt held up his hands, much like one of Mike and Letty Moody's victims at the beginning of a holdup. "Busted." There was no tease in his tone. None of that bravado either. "I don't like taking a good long look inside to dredge up my messy emotions, much less use them take after take. I keep my characters as separate from myself as we keep our friends."

"I'm not surprised that you take the easy way out in a role." She softened her words with a slight smile. "But I am surprised you admit it. Like you, I've been typecast." She ignored his rumbles of dissent. "From the age of five, I've been asked to play a variation of the same role. I laugh. I cry. I'm the sweet, open sister and the delicate, slightly crushed flower of a daughter that everyone wants to protect. Audiences love to see me put through the emotional wringer and triumph over adversity with love beneath my wings. And what they don't know, what not even my family seems to guess, is that I draw inspiration from Laurel."

Wyatt's eyes widened slightly.

"Yes. America's Sweetheart should have been her. From the innocent way she looks at the world, taking it at face value, trusting what she sees is true." Ashley's words thickened, as if her confession had been stuck too long in her throat. "Her joy. Her disappointment. Her...betrayals." She'd been the cause of too many of those.

And then the words stopped, and the simple peace of the forest tried to envelop her. The rustle of wind in the pines. The chattering of a blue jay. The dappling of sunlight on their feet. But nature's beauty couldn't settle the lump of guilt and shame she was unable to swallow.

Wyatt cleared his throat. "You told Gabby you were discovered because you used to act out scenes from TV and movies for Laurel. To please Laurel."

Ashley nodded, unable to look at him, afraid of what she'd see. Now he knew her truth. She wasn't the best person on the planet. "And there's irony. I started out genuinely trying to please her, and I ended up needing her authenticity to please the world."

His fingers traced the line of her jaw, gently lifting until their gazes met. "It sounds like you know exactly who you are."

He recognized this? Why, then, was his gaze so accepting?

"But what if I don't like that person?" Her words, just a whisper, were immediately stolen by the wind.

And like her words, the touch of his lips was also here and gone, featherlight on hers. "Then you make amends, as you seem to be doing now. And you forgive yourself." But a shadow crossed his features when he spoke of forgiveness, as if he hadn't found a way to forgive himself some offense.

Ashley wished she were normal, not an actor trained to detect subtleties, not a professional drawn to gradations of character. She wished she could take Wyatt's words and his kiss as a balm to her soul and not worry about his wounds or his burdens. She had enough of her own.

He stared at the picture framed in the bark. "Someone should do a documentary on your grandfather. He sounds like an interesting man."

"He was." And she should consider it. But

just now, she was considering the man standing before her.

Wyatt took her hand, turning his attention forward, not back. "Come on. The next place is just over the rise. They'd have to drive to the inn every day."

He left her no choice but to shift gears and move on. "Good, because I can't imagine walking that far with babies and bears."

They came over the rise to the front yard of an A-frame.

Immediately, Ashley was lovestruck.

Or maybe that was because Wyatt draped his arm over her shoulders and gave her a side hug. "Isn't it great?"

"It is." A flat area in front for a place kids could play. The porch was wide and had enough room to decorate with planters. The front of the house was a wall of gleaming windows.

They hurried inside.

The kitchen looked as if Roy had been working on it. There was a new faucet, but the appliances were dated, and the cabinets... Ick.

"This one has three bedrooms and two baths." Wyatt led her down the hallway. "There's a detached garage out the back and a small barn in

case they want to raise those kids as cowgirls."
He glanced over his shoulder.

She recognized longing in his gaze. He'd
buy those girls ponies. And later, horses. But
would he teach them how to ride?

The bathrooms also looked as if they'd
been given new plumbing fixtures, but the
flooring was peel-and-stick tiles that were no
longer sticking. And those cabinets... Ashley
couldn't get over the thin wood and its cracking paint.

"This isn't exactly move-in ready." Ashley
couldn't contain her disappointment. "And
I want my sister to have a home where she
feels spoiled."

"In Second Chance? Because she's not exactly living in the lap of luxury now." Wyatt
glanced around. "Look again, Ashley. The
fixes here are cosmetic. But the energy here
is fantastic, a place where you can regroup
from the day."

"A place where memories can be made,"
she murmured, envious of her sister once
more, wishing for a home like the one he
described and a man like the one he gave
her glimpses of. "I can talk to her about this
place."

"Good."

They stepped out on the porch, which had

a lovely view of the southern side of the valley. It would have the morning sun and afternoon shade.

Ashley leaned on the porch rail. "I could get used to this view."

"Me, too." Wyatt's arms came slowly around her, so gently that she could have moved away.

He gave her space. And yet he'd welcome her closer. And not just in the physical sense. To engage in verbal sparring matches. To defend her choices and to challenge his, in turn.

Eleven years ago, when she'd been crushed by Caleb's overdose, she'd vowed never to trust a man again, certainly not one in the entertainment industry, where buzz and public adoration could trump talent and reason. And then when Mikhala had tried to end her life, Ashley had put a bubble into place regarding all relationships. With Laurel's help stepping in as her double, she had been able to keep her distance from the world.

She didn't have Laurel as a buffer anymore. And she could feel herself falling in love with this talented, charming man who hid the sweeter side of himself from the public. But not from her. There was nothing pretend about it.

"Where have you been hiding, Ashley Monroe?" It was a tenderly spoken question and he didn't seem to require an answer, because he closed the distance between them and kissed her.

And while she enjoyed that kiss, she wondered if he was asking the wrong question.

It wasn't where had she been hiding.

It was where would she hide when he broke her heart.

"I NEED TO HURRY. We've got dress rehearsal in five." Ashley bounded up the stairs. "See you later."

Wyatt watched her go. Had he thought their attraction was simple? He'd been wrong.

They'd walked back from the A-frame house, not hand in hand as some women might expect after a few kisses, but side by side. He'd always considered himself standoffish, but Ashley was proving to be more so. Or maybe she was being careful. There was still the issue of paternity claims to settle. Or perhaps Genevieve was right: the actress with the biggest heart in Hollywood was afraid to fall in love.

He spotted Laurel in the manager's apartment behind the front desk and unabashedly wandered in. "How are you feeling?"

"Like I'm carrying a bus." Laurel was hand sewing a seam on something pink. "And the bus is taking the mountain pass too fast." She sucked in a breath and shifted. "I suppose you might feel the same way given your impending fatherhood. A little off-balance. A little like you should have seen this coming."

Before Wyatt could decide how to answer, Laurel gasped again. She snagged his wrist and pressed his hand to her mighty belly bump.

Something kicked his hand.

A baby.

He got chills, the way he did when he read a good script. His brain jolted, the way it did when he drank a double shot of espresso. And his heart... His heart nearly stopped beating, the way it was supposed to in that all-confusing moment when a man fell in love.

A baby kicked him a second time.

"So strong," he murmured.

Ashley appeared behind him. The sisters exchanged a glance, a look of endearment. If Ashley carried regrets, she didn't let it stand in the way of her love for Laurel.

Wyatt withdrew his hand slowly, reluctantly, while Laurel finished knotting her thread. She got to her feet, shook out the material—a western-style dress—and handed it to Ashley, who wore... "Is that a man's suit?" Also old-west themed.

Ashley nodded. "Here." She handed him a black parasol and a beaded handbag that was heavy.

"Is this filled with gold coins?" He opened it. "I should have known. It's a pistol. Are you playing Mike Moody?"

"I'm his sister Letty, remember?"

Laurel was fastening the dress over Ashley's suit like a big apron. "Wyatt, can you bind it in back? It's Velcro. I'd rather not bend over for fear of a bus crash, if you know what I mean."

"Laurel, I have no idea what you're talking about, but it doesn't sound good," Ashley chided.

Wyatt and Laurel exchanged a glance, and a friendship of sorts was forged. One that would forevermore be defined by bus references only the two of them would understand. He handed Ashley her parasol and purse, and fastened the dress in the back so that no one could see she was wearing a suit.

As soon as he was done, Ashley hurried out the door.

Wyatt followed her to the porch. "Why does Letty need a man's suit?"

"If you want to know, you'd have to sign a nondisclosure agreement to keep you from giving away the ending." She lifted her skirt in front and ran down the porch steps, bustle swaying behind her like a wedding dress.

"I'm not signing an agreement. And I'm not playing Mike Moody."

"Then you'll just have to wait a few days to watch it in the Old West Festival on Sunday or on the big screen someday." Ashley whirled on him, sending her skirts in a wide swath that brushed his legs like a slap. And then her palm pressed against his chest. "You're not allowed to watch rehearsal. It's closed. Cast members only."

She was fire and brimstone, a complete reversal of her mood in the woods, and yet he wanted to kiss her anyway.

Ashley withdrew her hand and held up a finger. "You can't have life both ways."

"Both ways? What are you talking about?"

"You can't kiss me one minute and expect me to forget my production values the next. The film has a twist and I'd rather the world didn't know it. And you can't go all moony-eyed over Laurel's twins one minute and pretend you've never met her the next. Get over it, and appreciate her for who she is. And—"

He kissed her. Right there on the top porch step, out of sight of the front desk. It was either that or listen to her snipe at him some more, and he was rather tired of the sniping, mostly because she'd made good points.

WHEN WYATT STOPPED kissing her...

When his lips left hers...

Ashley felt like she was still floating. She didn't move, not even to open her eyes. "'Licensed to thrill.'" That was the tagline for Ian Bradford films. "They got that right."

Footsteps sounded. Retreating footsteps.

Ashley opened her eyes.

Wyatt was walking away from her. "Have a great rehearsal. Break a leg." He went into the general store.

I am in big, big trouble.

Laughter drifted to her from down the road. The cast was waiting for her in front of the smithy. They'd picked up their costumes from Laurel before she had.

Ashley hurried down the stairs.

Jonah came out of the diner. He gestured toward the way she'd come. "That was a show unto itself."

"Can't you be like normal brothers and threaten to go slug the guy who stole a kiss from me?"

"Look at me." Jonah held up his slender arms. He had Crohn's disease and managed it well, which meant he had hardly an ounce of fat on him. "I couldn't take Wyatt Halford in a chess match, much less a punchfest."

It was true. And arguing with Jonah was much like leaping on a hamster wheel. He was good at arguing and comebacks and could keep going forever. Ashley chose a change of subject. "I should have done my hair." Several of the women in the cast had their hair swept up. "I'm a horrible example of leadership."

"You're not. You're just half in love with a hot actor."

"Don't even joke about it, Jonah."

He darted in front of her, bringing her to a halt. "I'm not joking. You're falling for Wyatt. You were in a daze after that kiss. If anything needs adjusting to set a good example, it's my little sister's heart."

"I'm not in love with...the sexiest man alive." She'd inserted Wyatt's title because it gave her emotional distance. That was what was called for. She couldn't afford to fall in love with him, much as her heart was increasingly pining to do so.

"Tell yourself whatever you need, Ashley, just don't fall for that guy. You know his reputation. The last thing you need when you launch your own production company is for gossip to be more prominent than your business skill."

CHAPTER ELEVEN

"So, THIS IS your afternoon snack?" Mack, who ran the general store, rang up Wyatt's purchase of a package of olives, almonds and water.

Wyatt smiled, the same way he'd smiled at Roy a few minutes earlier when he'd tried to convince him to finance the renovation of the A-frame. "How's that T-shirt project coming along?"

"I decided to respect your privacy." Mack shrugged. "Or rather Laurel's privacy, since it looks like we'll be having a lot of tourism based on Mike Moody alone."

He took a step back. No one but Laurel's immediate family was supposed to know about his relationship with those babies.

Mack held up her hands. "Your secret is safe with me."

But who wasn't it safe with? "Who told you?" Anger bunched his shoulders. He'd bet anything it was the person who'd posted on the website a few weeks back—Shane. Everything went downhill after they met. And now he was nowhere to be found.

Mack gestured out the open back door, which led to a small porch for guests. "I don't think she meant to do it. But she's having a bad day and she's twelve."

Gabby. Of course.

Wyatt drew a calming breath, collected his purchases and went to seek her out.

She sat at a table eating an ice-cream sandwich. When she saw him, she immediately ducked her head, as if that would make her invisible. She was the only customer on the porch.

Wyatt hesitated in the doorway.

The family of moose were working their way slowly across the meadow. A bee buzzed past. In the distance, someone laughed. It was all so normal, as if he were back home. As if he were sitting with one of his sisters in the backyard after an argument, because that was where his mother used to send them after they'd had a disagreement.

"Work it out," she'd say, pointing toward the kitchen door, even if it was snowing outside.

And they would, because what else were they going to do? They'd want to be inside eventually. Was that why they hadn't worked out their last disagreement?

Wyatt sat down next to Gabby and began eating.

Laughter drifted in the air again. He assumed it came from Ashley's dress rehearsal. He felt a familiar tug, the likes of which he thought of as his acting bug.

"Am I in trouble?" Gabby asked, staring at her ice cream, strawberry blond hair blowing in the breeze.

"Why would you ask that?"

"Because...I told someone something I shouldn't."

People fascinated Wyatt. Not because he was a people person, but because, as an actor, he was curious about their layers of character. Gabby, the much-beloved preteen, was a good person. And good people didn't always make the right choices, especially growing up. How they handled adversity said a lot about their character.

The first few days he'd been in Second Chance, he'd assumed Laurel and Ashley were trying to put something over on him. He'd expected them to hit him up with an unrealistic child support proposition. But the reality was that their intentions were as originally stated. He, Laurel and Ashley were in an unusual situation and, for the most part, the way they'd handled themselves was to be admired. They could have used his reputation for gain, but they hadn't. They were good people.

Just like Gabby.

"I'm sorry," Gabby said, getting to her feet.

Wyatt stayed her with his hand. "Your father raised you right." He'd do a good job raising Laurel's babies, too. Maybe it was time to look at those paternity papers.

"Dad probably wouldn't agree with you right now." But Gabby sat back down, wiping at an ice-cream drip with her napkin. "Twelve has been a difficult year for me."

Laughter cascaded through the air once more.

And Ashley had said it wasn't a comedy.

Wyatt turned to Gabby, the girl who spent most days at the inn's check-in desk, the girl who, by Laurel's admission, had heard more than her share of confidences.

"You said you know the facts about Mike Moody."

"Yep." She gave him a big smile. "Well, most of them, anyway. Jonah didn't give me all the notes he used to write Ashley's script."

But Wyatt bet it was enough for him to get up to speed on the infamous bandit. "Tell me."

ASHLEY ENTERED THE INN with a smile on her face and her arms filled with Letty's dress.

Her wool suit itched, but all in all, rehearsal had gone well. She'd called for another one tomorrow because this one had too much laughter. She might have skills in organizing, but she was being tested as a director, at least with the amateur troupe she'd assembled. While they'd turned in their costumes to Laurel, Egbert had given Ashley and Jonah notes on the performance. He may run the fly-fishing business, but he also considered himself an expert on Mike Moody, and they hadn't gotten the street play to his liking.

"Ashley, can we talk to you?" Laurel sat behind the check-in desk normally occupied by Gabby.

Mom stood next to the rack of costumes, looking like the end of the world was looming.

And then they both turned and went into the apartment.

Ashley followed them inside, closing the door behind her. "What's wrong? Where's Mitch? Is it time to go to the hospital?" She draped Letty's dress on a kitchen chair. "What do you need me to do?"

"Listen, Ashley. Just listen." Mom crossed her arms over her conservative navy pantsuit.

"Okay."

Laurel sat in her usual chair and drew her sketchbook in front of her. "Have you been looking at cabins in town?"

"Yes. There's this cute little A-frame and—"

"Cabins for me?" Laurel's voice escalated.

"Yes. How did you know?" Ashley rushed on. "I'm sorry if I overstepped."

"I knew it," Mom muttered. She never muttered.

Ashley felt the hair rise on the back of her neck.

"Roy told me." Laurel pressed her lips together, as if she couldn't trust herself to say more.

Ashley sat down in the chair with the dress on the back. "Is something wrong?" Something horrible must have happened. "Is Roy okay?"

"Yes and yes." Laurel gripped her sketchbook. "Roy saw you kissing Wyatt at this cute little A-frame you found for me and my family." That was snarky. Laurel was rarely snarky.

"I can explain." Not really. Ashley floundered. "It seemed like the right thing to do, given the mess we're in."

"No." Laurel pounded the sketch pad on

the table. "It's my mess, Ashley. My mess. My wedding. My family."

"I've been trying to help," Ashley whispered, because Laurel rarely lost her cool.

"I've said from the beginning that you don't have control of this situation." Mom lorded over the kitchen. "Falling for Wyatt Halford is not going to help."

"I'm not…" She was. "I just…" Ashley reached for a defense. "This is like being on location and letting the chemistry do its job. It means nothing. Nothing long-term." But her words didn't hit the right note.

"There's chemistry and Wyatt understands you," Mom said as flatly as if explaining terms of a contract.

"Yes." Ashley nodded.

"He's like you in so many ways," Mom said.

"Yes."

"Open your eyes, Ashley." Mom's voice was as somber as an undertaker's. "That doesn't mean he'll fall in love with you."

Ashley nodded. "I don't expect him to. I mean, he's Wyatt Halford. His name has never been linked to anyone for more than a week or two. And, you know—" *stop babbling* "—I suck at relationships. At this rate, I'll never have someone of my own. Which is fine," she rushed on to say. "I'll have my work and…and…a little dog to fill those empty spaces. Right, Mom?"

Laurel and Mom exchanged glances.

"I want you to achieve all your dreams." Tone softened, Laurel pushed her sketch pad toward the middle of the table. "But first, we have to get through this."

"Yes." Ashley couldn't agree more.

"You've spent a lot of time with Wyatt," Mom said, losing the undertaker voice. "Why hasn't he made a decision about the babies?"

"He wants to do the right thing, same as we all do." Ashley's fingers sank into a pink flounce on Letty's dress. "But he doesn't know what that is."

"And so he spends time debating this extremely important issue by kissing you?" Mom raised her finely shaped brows.

"No." Yes. Man, this looked bad.

"You think you're falling for Wyatt. And maybe he's falling for you, too." Mom was being unusually kind, as if she'd drunk too much spiked tea to state more than the hard truths. "But more likely, you're just two celebrities circling a situation, each trying to come out on top in the press."

"It's not like that. Wyatt's not like that." Ashley's heart was sinking. How often had she played a scene like this, where she defended herself when she knew she should be agreeing with everything being said to her? "Wyatt went to Roy because he didn't want you and the babies to be cramped in this space."

"In our home, you mean." Laurel rested a hand on her belly. "That's not his decision to make. Or yours."

"You're right. I crossed a line. I'm sorry."

"There's more," Mom said. "And it's not pretty."

Was any of this? It had been ugly from the get-go.

Laurel nodded. "Last week, Cam and Ivy bought Roy a phone from this century, hoping he could use some of the apps to monitor his health. Roy took a picture of you at that A-frame you toured."

That explained how they'd known about the kiss.

"Only Roy is better with a set of power tools than a smartphone app," Laurel continued. "He doesn't know how to look at the photos he's taken. So, he stopped by here. I pulled up the photo. And before I showed it to him, I deleted it."

"What? Why? I was fully clothed. I swear."

And there had been no inappropriate groping either.

Laurel grimaced. "You were, but—"

"Hang on." Ashley laid a cold hand on Laurel's forearm. "Roy's not part of the Snaparazzi."

"He's not," Mom said, using her undertaker voice once more.

"I sent the picture to myself before I deleted it, but only so you could see it." Laurel picked up her phone. "I feel horrible lying to Roy about it, but he wanted to send the picture to Wyatt. You're both posting pictures, but this…"

"Show me," Ashley demanded.

Laurel tapped her screen but kept it averted. "You may think you've got this under control. After all, as an actress you've had to kiss a lot of guys."

"Not a lot."

Mom's sharp gaze challenged that statement.

"Okay, an average amount for an actress my age," Ashley allowed.

Mom didn't challenge that.

Laurel continued to keep her screen averted. "I've seen your on-screen kisses, Ash. There's distance. We all know why."

"You're afraid of losing people," Mom said,

with that rare maternal note to her voice. "But in this case, how you handle this relationship with Wyatt might just influence the future of Laurel's little girls."

"Reminder. Check." Ashley held out her hand for the cell phone, and this time, Laurel showed it to her.

Ashley leaned forward. There was the A-frame, the porch, she and Wyatt locked in a heated embrace as if that kiss shut everyone else in the world out.

Except Wyatt had his arm raised toward the camera. And his thumb up.

Ashley grew cold. "He knew Roy was there."

"He probably asked him to take the shot. You know how gullible Roy can be sometimes." Laurel toggled through her phone screen. "And if he set this up, he could be setting us up."

"Maybe he wants our little girls all to himself." Mom was fully embracing the glass half-empty now. "I've said that all along. He plays his cards too close to the vest for me to trust him." She stomped out, taking a mug with her, leaving Ashley alone with Laurel, the consequences of a walk through the woods and a few kisses weighing heavily on her shoulders.

"I'm sorry," Ashley said again. "We need him to sign those paternity papers."

"I know I shouldn't want to cut him out of the girls' lives," Laurel said, making little circles around her baby bump. "A man deserves to know his children if he wants to. It's just... Are you falling for him, Ash?" Laurel's voice was small. "Because I get it if you are. It's just..." Her blue eyes, so like Ashley's own, clouded over with worry. "If you're a couple for real, he's going to be around more than any of us thought. Wouldn't that make it harder for us to coparent? He's already butting into our lives, trying to manipulate where we live. He stopped by a few minutes ago to say he'd ordered a pair of high chairs. What if he wants to tell us how to raise them?"

Ashley brushed Laurel's hair from her shoulder. "It's more likely that he's just trying to compete with that stroller I gave you and put Ashley Monroe in her place before he waives his rights to the girls."

Regardless, those papers would be signed.

CHAPTER TWELVE

"HEY, ASHLEY." WYATT wove his way through the horses, Clarks and Monroes assembling for a trail ride to Mike Moody's hideout.

Ashley sat in a saddle on Missy. The demon seed swung that big equine head of hers around when Wyatt approached and reached out as if about to give him another love bite.

Wyatt leaped back. "I missed you this morning at breakfast. Did you sleep in?"

"I had a lot of calls to make that required privacy." Ashley glanced down at him without any of the warmth she'd shown him in previous days.

Her reaction triggered a warning in his head. He needed to proceed carefully.

"I wanted to talk to you about—" Wyatt checked to make sure no one was listening "—playing Mike Moody." And about those kisses, and his jumbled feelings about fatherhood, and those kisses.

"You want..." He'd clearly broadsided her.

"Yes. I've been reading up on him." Perusing the fairly thorough notes Gabby had given him.

"I can't have this conversation with you. Not now." Ashley backed Missy up with barely a move of her hands on the reins. She wore a cowboy hat today and her hair plaited over both shoulders. "You shouldn't even be here. This ride is for family only."

"Adam invited me. And Shane sent someone to pick me up." That friendly horse wrangler Zeke. But only after Mitch had called over to the Bucking Bull when Wyatt couldn't find Ashley or any of the visiting Monroes. And only after Wyatt had offered to read a copy of the paternity papers later. And since he'd arrived at the ranch, there was no sign of Shane, whom he'd wanted to thank before he took him to task for things like stolen spark plugs.

"Shane." Ashley shook her head.

"Have your people send over a nondisclosure agreement to my people," Wyatt said, not sure if he should be annoyed that she was pushing him away or worried that something deeper had changed between them. "I want to read the script."

Ashley opened her mouth, hesitating. And

then she squared her shoulders. "I'm still not sure you're right for the part."

"But I check so many boxes." Gabby had also shared the history of Mike Moody with him yesterday. He was interested. And if Wyatt Halford was interested in a role, people scheduled a meeting and let him read the script. Kisses or no!

"Wyatt!" Emily rode up on a big gray horse, leading a big black horse. "We need to get this show on the road." She handed him Bumblebee's reins. And then she stood in her stirrups to announce, "We're about to get going, folks. We'll be heading through that gate over there. If you're a nervous rider, never fear. We've taken the horses on this route a time or two. They know the way, and most of them will follow the tail in front of them."

Zeke opened the gate and led his strawberry roan through. "Our attraction is now open for business."

The Monroes headed their horses in that direction. There were at least ten of them. Most were about Wyatt's age or younger and looked as if they had some skill on horseback. The Clark boys lingered at the end of the line with Emily and Wyatt.

"Mr. Wyatt, I told Papa Shane you had to

come along." Adam sat on a brown pony and stared up at Wyatt with a proud grin. "'Cause you have to see Merc'less Mike's hiding spot. It's safe now that the new Buttercup is at the rodeo."

"There used to be a wild bull guarding Mike's hideout," Emily explained.

"But we caught him," Davey said, as if it was no big deal.

"And now we call him Buttercup," Charlie added, most likely grinning because it had been a big deal.

"That was all after he tried to kill us," Adam said, straight-faced. "He smashed our work truck and Papa Shane's big black SUV." He created his own sound effects of crashing, none of which fazed his pony.

"Time to go, boys." Emily rode forward, followed by Davey and Charlie.

"I got something to show you. My mom said I couldn't, but later Papa Shane said I could." Adam reached toward Wyatt. "Go on. Take it."

Wyatt held out his hand. Adam dropped a rock in it. Except it wasn't a rock. It was a small gold nugget! Gold like Mike and Letty Moody might have stolen. "You found this?"

"Adam, no straggling," Emily called from the gate. "That goes for you, too, Wyatt."

"Don't lose it, Mr. Wyatt." Adam kicked his pony into a trot, leaving Wyatt no choice but to tuck the nugget into his pocket and follow.

Emily closed the gate behind him. "All set, Zeke."

"May I have your attention, please." Zeke held up his cowboy hat at the front of the straggling line of horses. "Welcome to the inaugural ride of the official Mike Moody Escape Trail Tour. I'm Zeke, and I'll be your tour guide today." He settled his hat back on his head and leaned one forearm on his saddle horn. "Most of you are aware of the legend of Mike Moody. He was a fearsome hombre in these parts for several years. Stagecoaches were his favorite target, but he also robbed trains and the occasional wandering traveler."

Behind Zeke, a tall man wearing an old-timey suit sauntered out of the tree line. He wore a burlap sack over his head with eye-holes cut out and held a six-shooter, aiming it at the tourists. "Hold them hands up high. Come on." He waved his pistol. "Stick 'em up."

A few Monroes chuckled.

Zeke stood tall in the saddle and made a show of peering into the trees. "But a posse was always on Merciless Mike's tail."

Adam giggled. "They're doin' better than at practice."

Merciless Mike slipped into the trees.

"You are now all deputized into Second Chance's posse." Zeke flashed a star badge attached to the lining of his vest. "Be on the lookout for Merciless Mike as we track him into the woods." Zeke turned his horse around and led them up the hill.

Emily and Wyatt brought up the rear of the line, waiting for horses and riders to mosey up the trail.

"You guys are creating an entire experience around Mike Moody?" Wyatt asked.

"Yeah." Emily shrugged. "Shane seems to think it'll bring in tourists. I hope he's right. We bought a lot of horses in anticipation of the summer tour season."

Wyatt's mind hummed around the concept. "Does this tour match the movie script?"

"No." Emily gave him a sly look. "Maybe you should just experience it before you ask all your questions."

The trail opened up. In the lead, Zeke turned in the saddle and reviewed his posse. As he turned back around, he whistled.

The hooded Merciless Mike emerged from the tree line on a tan horse farther up the trail and then disappeared into the woods on the other side.

Zeke leaned over as if looking at the ground. "Fresh tracks. We're on to him."

Adam squealed. "Hurry up. Hurry up. We can catch him." He motioned to his pony but went no faster.

"Didn't Mike die in a rock slide?" Wyatt asked.

"The tour takes a different timeline," Emily explained. "Before Mike's fateful end."

Adam twisted in his saddle to glance at Wyatt, looking intrigued. "Here he comes again."

Sure enough, as they rounded a bend, the bad dude crossed their path once more.

"We've got to catch him before dark!" Zeke swept his arm forward, as if they were going to charge ahead.

The horses continued their leisurely walk up the hill.

The Monroes were laughing and having a good time. It was a great idea and would no doubt be popular once Ashley's movie released.

There was one more Mike Moody sighting before they reached what Zeke called Lookout Ridge.

Once they arrived, Zeke and the Clark boys

tied up everyone's horses to a long hitching post, and the party was encouraged to dismount. There was an outcropping of rock on the far side that served as a backdrop for a small cemetery.

"Gather round, Deputies." Zeke rubbed his hands together. "This is where the tale of Mike Moody gets real. For more than a century, Mike Moody's stash remained a mystery. A secret guarded by the family of Jebediah Clark, a location marked by their family cemetery. But are only Clarks buried up here? Or could there be a mystery woman?"

"There is!" Adam started to march on his short legs toward the small cemetery and its uneven headstones.

Zeke held him back. "This is where the new deputies get a chance to do some sleuthing of their own, little buddy."

While the rest of the Monroes walked through the cemetery reading headstones, Ashley remained and raised her cell phone into the air. "No signal."

Wyatt moved to stand beside her. "I take it you've been here before."

She nodded and smiled, finally showing some of her characteristic warmth and enthusiasm. "Go on. They'll find her in a minute."

Her. Letty.

Jonah emerged from the woods wearing the Mike Moody costume and carrying a burlap mask. He stood near a fissure in the rock. A fissure large enough for a man to walk through.

And Adam had called it Mike's hiding spot.

Wyatt joined the Monroes in the cemetery.

"Jebediah Clark." Holden brushed pine needles from a headstone. "He was the smithy?"

"Yep," Jonah said, with pride.

Adam managed to break free of Zeke's hold. He hurried through the field of headstones on his short legs. "Clark. Clark. Clark," he said, as if he was playing Duck, Duck, Goose. He grinned up at Wyatt and pointed to a small headstone. "Not Clark."

Wyatt bent down, pushing dirt and debris from the small headstone. "Letty." No last name. He got chills.

He turned his gaze back to Ashley. There was a twist to her plot, all right. Something that even Gabby didn't know about.

He had to read that script.

"YOUR FAMILY FOUND the gold," Wyatt said to Ashley on the ride down from Lookout Ridge. He'd guided Bumblebee next to Missy.

"With the help of the Clarks." Ashley gave

credit where credit was due. But she did so while channeling her mother's clipped voice. How easy it was to push him away now that she couldn't take him at face value.

"So the blacksmith, Jeb Clark, was in on it? Is that it?"

"He wasn't part of the gang." Ashley scowled. "We should be talking about your decision regarding the babies so we can put an end to our public charade. Not to mention that it would ease Laurel's mind."

"But Jeb buried Letty up here and knew where the gold was." Wyatt wouldn't take the hint, wouldn't stop looking at her, couldn't even keep his horse from veering closer and practically forcing Ashley into a ditch. "Is it all explained in the script? I won't bug you with questions if you let me read it."

Ashley brought her horse to a halt, feeling like she wanted to nip someone the way Missy sometimes did. "What's going on here, Wyatt? You told me you didn't want anything to do with the film."

He pulled Bumblebee to a stop. "Someone in town told me some of the history."

"History," Ashley huffed. "Gabby."

"For being a beloved daughter of the town, everyone seems to know she is the weakest link when it comes to keeping a secret." But he smiled when he said it, sobering to add, "I can help you get this film made. My name carries a lot of weight in the industry."

Like hers didn't? Granted, his name opened an entirely different set of doors, but still. "At what cost? If I say yes, you can have a role in this film, will you sign those paternity papers?" Had she just said that out loud? The bargain sickened her.

He didn't look happy to hear those words either. "Are those your terms? Really?"

"They should be." She stared ahead, at the ground, up at the mountains, anywhere except at him. She adjusted her fingers around Missy's slim reins. "It doesn't have to be. We can talk this through. If you trust me." Which he shouldn't. She didn't trust him. Not in her head, where it mattered.

"Giving the girls my name implies responsibility. Not just me to them but them to me. Do I want to give them the burden of being Wyatt Halford's daughters? His heirs?"

Ashley wasn't naive enough to believe he could acknowledge them as his without bringing all the baggage of celebrity and wealth along. "You think they'll be spoiled? I doubt Mitch or Laurel would allow that."

"The truth…" He removed his cowboy hat and ran his fingers through that cowlick.

"The truth is I don't know. It's like the decision is there in my head. I can feel it. But I don't know what it is. And maybe I'll know when the babies are born. Maybe I won't feel an attachment and it'll be easy to sign. But I just don't know."

When Laurel had first told the family she was pregnant, the solution had appeared so cut-and-dried. Laurel wanted the babies. Wyatt was a world-renowned playboy who wouldn't. And now nothing was simple.

"You don't really mean to hold the role ransom in exchange for my paternity rights, do you?"

Ashley swallowed thickly. "I need to protect my sister." She couldn't give voice to the bargain again. But she could look into Wyatt's eyes and let him see her turmoil.

He swore.

"Why did you kiss me?" she demanded. "Yesterday. At the A-frame. Why there?"

"My impression was that kiss was mutual." Wyatt's grin. It had launched a million swooning sighs.

It tried to launch one of Ashley's. "You told Roy to take our picture. Don't deny it. I've seen it." The bitterness of betrayal pushed through her words. "You gave him a thumbs-up."

Wyatt frowned. "I didn't ask him for anything but photos of the two places I planned to take you to. When I heard him crashing through the woods, I gave him a thumbs-up to let him know the A-frame was a winner."

Ashley wasn't sure she believed him. "Roy told Laurel he was going to send it to you, presumably so you could post it online."

"You fault me for that when everyone else in town is posting to some newly created fan page? The reason for the cold shoulder is now clear." Wyatt studied her, shaking his head. "You haven't been kissing me like we're in a performance, Ash. Are you afraid your family sees that, too?"

She wasn't going to tell him they had. "We have to remember who has the most to lose here. It's Laurel and the babies. Until you settle things with her, I can't *pretend* I'm your anything."

"And you can't give me a shot at Mike Moody either." It wasn't a question.

But Missy saved her from answering by giving Wyatt a nip on his thigh.

"WYATT, WHAT ARE you doing?" Emily ducked under Bumblebee's neck and the reins that were tied to the arena's rail. "The others are heading back into town."

Wyatt continued loosening his horse's girth

strap. "I can help put the tack away and brush the horses down."

"I've got hands for that." Em frowned.

"I know what I'm doing and…" He met her inquisitive gaze squarely. "I could use a little honest work right now." To prove to himself that there was more to him than pretending in front of a camera, be it a still photo or a film. Ashley's accusations had hit too close to home. He shouldn't have wanted to post a picture of something as intimate as a kiss.

"Okay," Emily allowed slowly. "But you'll have a supervisor. Or three." She craned her neck. "Boys. Make sure Wyatt does right by Bumblebee."

Adam scampered over as Emily moved on. "Are you going to rope, too?"

"I haven't roped in years." Wyatt spared the kid a glance, digging in his pocket for that gold nugget and then handing it over. "Thanks for showing it to me."

Adam grinned, shoving the nugget in his jeans pocket with hardly any care. "Papa Shane says you find friends in all kinds of places, and that you should be kind to them when you do."

That didn't sound like his version of Shane Monroe, but Wyatt nodded politely before returning his attention to removing Bumble-bee's saddle and pad.

Forty-five minutes later, the horses were all turned out to pasture or put back in their stalls. Zeke dragged a practice roping steer into the arena. It was a simple metal sawhorse with a metal steer's head welded on the front. "Join us for roping practice and then I'll drive you back in town."

It was easy to agree, easy to be with people who didn't treat him as if he was Ian Bradford, superspy, on vacation in the Idaho mountains, just waiting to be photographed with his next fan.

The Clark boys each had a lariat and were bouncing around, waiting for Zeke to give the all clear.

"Take turns practicing." Zeke moved to a safe distance, standing with Wyatt. "I feel the need to confess that every time the boys lasso both horns, they earn the right to throw a lariat at me. But I told them since you were sticking around that they could throw at you, too."

"You set me up." But Wyatt laughed when he said it, reminded of growing up and all the games he and his sisters had invented. Ranch kids were a different breed.

"Well…" Zeke looked him up and down.

"You haven't run away, so you can be up first."

Davey waited his turn, letting his younger brothers have a go. He held the loops of his lariat on his right forearm and fingered the rope with his left hand.

"Nothing stops that kid," Zeke said quietly. "You know, Shane runs a camp for kids with challenges."

"He sounds like a saint," Wyatt grumbled.

"Far from it." Zeke paused to give the boys some pointers. "Shane Monroe might just be the most annoying man I've ever met."

The boys weren't great at roping. Wyatt was beginning to think he wasn't going to have to stand in for that roping steer.

"Where are your own boys today?" he asked Zeke.

"Safely out of trouble, with their mother." Zeke called out more instructions. And then he glanced at Wyatt. "Nervous about fatherhood?"

Wyatt gave the cowhand a hard stare.

Zeke laughed. "I'm married to a Monroe. It's not as if I don't know what's going on. You just look a bit shell-shocked, is all."

Wyatt forced himself to breathe evenly and allowed, "You're good with kids."

"It's a learned art. You're releasing too late,

Davey." Zeke crossed his arms over his chest. "I didn't have the best home life. But these Clark boys, and my little cowpokes, they teach me something about parenting every day. All right, guys, let's get serious. First up, Adam."

Little Adam coiled his stiff rope, thrust his tongue out and began his windup. "If I make this, I'm gonna get a shot at roping Mr. Wyatt."

Not without a miracle. The kid hadn't lassoed the practice steer once.

And then a miracle happened.

"WHAT DO YOU mean you want me to cool my jets on the sci-fi thriller deal?"

Wyatt didn't have to see his agent to read his frustration. Brandon shouted loud enough into the phone to be heard in the next room over.

"I just need a couple of days, Brandon. I have a feeling about the Mike Moody project Ashley Monroe is helming." Yesterday, he'd had a feeling about Ashley Monroe, one of a more personal nature. But she was telling him in no uncertain terms where her priorities lay. Despite a quiet voice in his head repeating there was something else between them than the role of a fake wedding date. All he needed was time. Time to unravel which role was most important to his career and discover if his and Ashley's relationship was worth investing time in.

He'd need time for the rope burn on his bicep to heal. Dang if that little Adam hadn't roped him after snagging that practice steer. And then each of his brothers had done the same thing, until Wyatt had to admit that he'd been duped. They were all competent little cowboys.

"No. No. No." Brandon thumped what sounded like his desk. "This can't be happening. Do you know how much time I've spent working the deal of the century? What is going on with you? Am I supposed to call and tell Jess we're no longer interested?"

"No. Jeez, Brandon. Listen to me." Wyatt paced his hotel room, trying to keep the leg muscle where Missy had bit him a second time from cramping. "Let everything ride until after this weekend."

"Oh, the weekend. The weekend! The weekend where you're going to be at the same wedding as Jess Watanabe?" More desk pounding. "If my cell phone wasn't new, I'd throw it out the window."

"Trust me. When have I ever steered you wrong?"

"When you told me that you wanted to play a villain. When you told me that you needed to go to Idaho to chase down the person who posted that Monroe baby rumor. When you told me to push for a record-breaking payday on a Jess Watanabe movie, which you should be down on your knees begging for since he is an award-winning god."

Wow. Brandon hadn't even hesitated with that list. Wyatt didn't know what to say.

"I'm supposed to be navigating your career because I'm the one with a cool head. While you... You're playing with fire, Wyatt. And in the end, we're both going to get burned."

THE WELCOME PARTY for the out-of-town family wedding guests was held outside the church Thursday night. There were tables and chairs set up. Food and drink everywhere. Guests chattering and laughing.

Laurel had been given a big cushy chair in a circle of seats beneath a white canopy. She seemed happy.

Ashley wasn't happy and Mom knew it.

"You look like you're waiting to hear a rejection for a much-coveted role." Mom smoothed her fingers over Ashley's forehead. "You should be smiling. Wyatt has a copy of the paternity papers."

"And an interest in my film." Talk about good news, bad news. She could no longer see him in the role of Mike Moody. He had the heart of blacksmith Jeb Clark. But since Wyatt had rocketed to fame, he'd only found success in playing action-packed lead roles. He'd never consider the quieter role of Jeb, the heart of the film.

"Speak of the devil," Mom said as Wyatt approached.

Gone were the jeans, cowboy boots and hat. In their place were fine wool slacks, leather loafers and a pressed charcoal button-down. He walked with a confidence Ashley envied. Powerful strides. Head high. And everyone who looked his way knew the world was his oyster.

"It's back to thinking I'm the devil, is it, Genevieve?" Wyatt stepped next to Ashley and put his arm around her as if they were, in fact, dating.

"My family doesn't need to be fooled." Ashley tried to step away, but he twirled her around and dipped her. Strong arms held her body. Mischievous eyes held her gaze. "Oh." She wanted a kiss.

He knew it, too. His smile broadened.

Several family members cooed.

"You're so adorable together," Cousin Kendall said.

Gabby snapped a picture.

And there went the desire to kiss him.

"You think I'm the devil, too." The mischief went out of his eyes. He set her back on her feet.

She gave a little headshake, putting as much space as she could between them.

"Bernadette. Hi." From a few feet away, Holden's voice seemed strained, almost teenage squawky.

Ashley turned to look. Cousin Holden was talking to Dr. Carlisle. Was he blushing?

While his cheeks were pinkening, Laurel's were turning a deep red. "Holden," she warned.

"It's been a long time, Holden." Dr. Carlisle's voice shook, and she adjusted her thick glasses with trembling hands. "And you haven't returned any of my…anything."

"Holden!" Laurel shouted again. "What did I tell you?"

Neither Holden nor Dr. Carlisle acknowledged Laurel's question. But Ashley knew the answer. Laurel had told Holden not to break Dr. Carlisle's heart.

Looked like that bit of instruction came too late.

"This is none of our business." Wyatt began to tug Ashley toward the drinks table.

"That's what makes it so awesome." Ashley tugged back, unwilling to miss a thing.

Holden had a reputation as a ladies' man, and Dr. Carlisle, though pretty, didn't look like his usual high-maintenance, short-term girlfriend. But really... Ashley chuckled. She wasn't normally a witness to the fallout from Holden's relationships. If Dr. Carlisle wasn't so visibly shaken, Ashley might find a chair and toss out a word or two of support for her. The poor doctor just looked about to fall apart.

Wyatt stopped pulling but held on to Ashley's hand.

"I'd like you to meet my son, Devin," Holden was saying to Dr. Carlisle. "He just graduated from high school and he's headed to MIT in the fall."

"A son..." The good doctor paled. "I hadn't realized you had a son. Or a...wife?"

"No wife." Holden seemed perplexed. "My son and I are going on a camping trip together after the wedding. Our last guys-only vacation before he goes off to college and forgets his old man." Holden was babbling. He was never at a loss for words, but he never babbled. And yet here he was. Babbling.

Ashley grinned.

Best. Monroe. Moment. Ever.

Ashley glanced around, trying to locate Shane. He'd enjoy this. The cousins were frenemies. But he had yet to arrive.

Devin rolled his eyes. "Dad."

And there was the rain on Ashley's parade, because Devin didn't need to witness this scene.

Despite her severe case of nerves, Dr. Carlisle was making Holden squirm. "A son? You didn't think that was something you should tell me?"

Holden tugged at the collar of his polo, wrinkling the navy fabric. Honestly, he didn't look like the cock of Wall Street. More like a high school science teacher who'd accidentally set fire to the lab. "We're going to tour Yellowstone and the surrounding areas via motor home. And I… Well, I…I had something come up that precluded me from calling you or…"

"Oh." Dr. Carlisle held up a hand as blood seemed to drain from her face. "Excuse me…" She rushed around the side of the church. And then there was the horrid sound of retching.

Before Ashley could disengage herself from Wyatt's hold, Ivy ran past.

Wyatt whispered, "One witness is probably enough."

Meanwhile, Cam grabbed Holden's arm, towing him toward Dr. Carlisle. "Come on. Time to face the music."

"Why?" Holden looked shell-shocked.

"Because you got her pregnant, you idiot," Cam said bluntly and with little sympathy.

Everyone froze.

"Dad?" Devin's voice was a mixture of incredulity and horror.

Gabby gasped, no doubt thinking this was another one of her precious secrets revealed.

Holden stared from Devin to the direction of the retching and then toward Laurel, who sat glaring at him, very much the unhappy expectant empress.

Wyatt started to chuckle, and then it turned into full-blown laughter, the kind of false frivolity that resulted from too much pressure held in too long. His laughter cascaded across the slope and over the gathering of Monroes.

That was too much for Holden. He launched himself at Wyatt, taking them both to the ground.

"THIS IS GOING to be one heck of a shiner." Ashley gently placed a bag of ice over Wyatt's rapidly swelling right eye.

"You should see the other guy." The cold immediately dulled the throbbing. It had felt pretty darn good to tussle with someone. He lay on his bed with Ashley sitting near. That felt good, too.

Ashley sighed, studying his face. "Why are men so proud of their stupid fights?"

"Fight? Holden tackled me and we rolled down the hill." Until they'd collided with a tree. His fingers found hers, and for the first time in a day, she didn't step out of reach or try to pull away. "I don't think either of us landed a punch." In fact, it was anyone's guess how Wyatt ended up with a shiner. He could have collided with a tree, the earth or Holden's hard head.

Ashley's blue gaze was as tender as her touch. "I see a remake of *Fight Club* in your future."

He liked it when Ashley made fun of him. It made him forget about dates he hadn't had and babies he hadn't expected. "In my defense, I didn't start anything."

"You did. You laughed." She laughed, the melody filling the room and his heart with joy. "Of all the Monroes, you choose to laugh at the man with the biggest ego."

"I thought that was Shane." He would have

raised his eyebrows dubiously if not for the pack of ice on his face.

"Shane used to be first. But then he fell in love with Franny Clark." Ashley stared down at Wyatt with what felt like love in her eyes.

The frequent use of the *L* word should have made Wyatt extremely nervous, but for whatever reason, he wasn't edgy. He was happy.

News flash: Sexiest Man Alive falls for America's Sweetheart. Gets black eye and doesn't care.

"This is nice," he told her, meaning it.

A shadow ruined the shine in her eyes. "Nice?"

"Yes?" Did he have to put that in the form of a question?

Ashley extricated her hand. "You made a spectacle of yourself at Laurel's welcome dinner. The resulting feeling shouldn't be nice."

"Why do I get the feeling that you think this is my fault?"

"Because it is! You laughed." She brushed his hair away from the ice bag, her tender actions at odds with her rebuke. "Holden had just learned he was going to be a father. And you laughed."

"You don't see the irony in this? It's as if I was watching what happened to me in real time. You don't think there's some humor seeing another man blindsided by fatherhood? Not even a little bit?" He removed the ice bag so he could see her more clearly, only his right eye wouldn't focus.

"Maybe there's a little bit of humor in there," she allowed, easing the bag back over his face. "But maybe it's something you laugh about years later. Not in the moment."

"Can I come in?" Dr. Carlisle knocked on the door, which hadn't been closed all the way. She stared at Wyatt's face and then went into his bathroom to wash her hands. "Busy night for ice packs."

Ashley got up to make room for the doc, and it felt as if by doing so she took all the warmth with her.

"Bad joke." The doctor leaned over to examine his eye. "I'm sorry."

"No apology necessary," Wyatt said. And he meant it.

"No. I caused all this. I should have handled things better with Holden." Dr. Carlisle glanced up at Ashley. "He just made me so upset."

"Holden seems to have that effect on people." Ashley smiled gently at Wyatt. "He's stubborn and proud, like someone else I know."

"I want you to ice this off and on for twenty-four hours." Dr. Carlisle stood. "I'll check on you in the morning." She glanced at Ashley. "I'll need someone to come get me if he acts odd or shows any signs of concussion—dizziness, drowsiness, vomiting…" Her hand drifted to her abdomen.

"Can do," Wyatt reassured her, thinking how nice it would be to have Ashley watching over him.

The doctor brushed Wyatt's arm with her hand. "Best not to exercise tomorrow. I've seen you out running every day."

Wyatt removed the bag of ice from his eye. "But—"

"Take a day off. Doctor's orders."

Ashley walked the doctor to the door.

It struck Wyatt that in a few days, he'd be gone from here—gone from the small-town hero worship, gone from the community bustle created by and revolving around the Monroes, gone from Ashley's highly structured, goal-oriented life.

"My mother would have liked you," he said as Ashley closed the door. He put the ice pack on his eye, staring at the ceiling. Why had he said that? It wasn't what he'd been thinking. He tried hard not to think of his mother, not to relive painful memories.

The mattress shifted and creaked as Ashley sat on the bed.

"You never talk about her in the media," she said in a soft voice. And then she continued in a softer one, "It's one of your interview terms, isn't it?" Then instead of asking *"What was your mother like?"* she fell silent, as if respecting his privacy.

Wyatt felt the need to forget about boundaries and say something, because he felt Ashley needed to hear something personal. He just couldn't find the right words about his mother.

"If this was your beloved action-adventure genre, Wyatt, this would be one of those quiet moments when the hero and his heroine weren't tracking down villains or running from the overwhelming enemy forces."

He should change the tone and protest her retreat into the film genre. He should make a joke and draw her into his arms. "You mean a quiet moment for a love scene?" he said gruffly instead, because it was the right answer, the answer that normally fit his real life when alone with a beautiful woman, but this moment felt nothing like that.

"No." Ashley tsked. "This would be a moment of rest from all the action, one destined to be filled with intimate conversation." She could have stopped there. She didn't. "That's what people who are growing close do in the movies. They have intimate conversations and reveal a deep, dark secret they've been carrying around for years."

Wyatt didn't want to be part of her unguarded scene. Not in real life and not in any movie. And suddenly, Wyatt knew why he stuck to the action genre. The character growth was minimal. The unveiling of deep, dark secrets rare. At least in the roles he'd been playing. And for sure in his most hated role—that of a cardboard, clichéd villain. His casting against type might have succeeded if he'd insisted on more character development in the script. His character might have been one of those villains people loved to hate because it was written and played so well.

But then he'd never have gone on a date with Laurel. Or met Ashley in Second Chance.

"Why do you have to pull up these movie examples?" They were killing him inside. He dared look at her. At that warm and colorful woman that was Ashley Monroe, film expert.

She drew a deep breath, gathering her shoulders up toward her ears in an endearing show of nerves.

What did she have to be nervous about?

Then it struck him. The intimate moment.

She was as nervous about baring her deep, dark secrets as he was about keeping his stuffed down in the hidden corners of his soul.

"Movie genres." She drew another breath and pulled herself together, shoulders loosening, like an actor slipping into a role. "It's something I do to focus."

"You're having trouble focusing?" They were in a quiet room in a quiet hotel in a quiet town. "No. What is it? Really."

"When I say focus…" Ashley glanced toward the door as if anticipating someone entering. And then she glanced at Wyatt. At his lips. As if she was considering kissing him again. "I'm using an acting term."

He understood. "Ah, *focus*. You need to rebuild the fourth wall." That imaginary barrier between an actor doing a live performance and the audience. "You're acting with me? *For* me?"

"I am…" She took another deep breath and released it. "I am stepping out of my comfort zone in real life. Not for *you*, but for *me*." She hurried on to explain. "I was raised to listen to those in positions of authority—producers, directors, actors with more experience and cachet than me. You want my line delivered louder? I'll give you louder." She raised her voice. "You want more punch to my dialogue? I. Will. Give. You. Punch." Every one of those words was crisply delivered.

"My programmed response is to get along and behave. Don't make waves." Her shoulders had been creeping up on her. She visibly forced them back down. "Not a lot of successful businesses are built by those who do exactly what everyone else wants them to do, especially not by a woman in a man's world."

Wyatt thought back to the times she'd used movie examples in their conversation. "When you talked horror movies and mysteries, I was angry."

She nodded, glancing toward the door.

He wasn't going to let her escape that easily. He placed a gentle hand over hers, but he had to stretch his arm to do so. She was sitting as far away from him as she possibly could and still be on the bed. "Don't leave yet. Please." Because he was thinking through the nuances of her so-called performances, the times when she'd worn a brave face at odds with the Ashley Monroe he and the public knew so well. "And when we talked westerns, I had assumed you were making a rom-com of Mike Moody's story."

She nodded again, staying on the bed, although her hand seemed to be sliding infinitesimally from beneath his.

He subtly increased his hold. "And just now… We were talking about character reveals."

"So-called bedroom secrets that lovers share." Her words were so low, he almost didn't hear them. And she wouldn't look at him, not even his lips, which would have been nice because it had been more than a day since they'd last kissed.

"You don't have to act with me." He knew immediately they were the right words.

Her shoulders loosened. Her mouth relaxed into a smile. But she continued to move her hand out from under his. "You're louder than I am. Brasher than I am. More confident than I am. Of course, I have to act like the idealized version of Ashley Monroe when we're together."

"Only when I'm upsetting you, it seems." He brushed his thumb over the back of her hand. "You aren't always acting." There were those quiet moments, including that kiss at the A-frame.

"No, but I have my support group here. And distance with business contacts. The phone. Email."

Ah, distance. The fragile Ashley's defense. "Don't forget those message groups of yours."

"Yes."

Silence closed around them. Or around Wyatt. It was a weighty silence, one that pressed in on him, like the deep throb around his eye. He took the ice pack off. He was supposed to say something. It was his turn.

Again, he thought of his mother. *Do the right thing.*

Again, he pushed back the painful memories, allowing the less painful ones to the fore.

"My father sits in the home I bought him, in the recliner I bought him, waiting for me to fail." He'd never said the words out loud before. Not even to his sisters, although they knew and perhaps, given the way they benefited from his status, didn't care. "And when I was younger, it didn't matter how much I contributed to put food on the table and keep a roof over our heads. He'd be the one sitting in the corner saying he'd still have a job when my looks dried up."

"You are more than just your looks." Ashley moved the ice pack back into position. "Although it is the first thing everyone sees."

"And the driver of my ticket sales, if the corporate bean counters are to be believed."

He hated that his looks contributed to his bottom line.

"It's why you came charging into Second Chance," Ashley surmised, still in that gentle voice. "To protect your image and box-office power."

"I can admit I'm shallow. To you," he added, because they were close despite being at odds. "The more money I make, the more records I break, the more it will feel like I'm proving him wrong."

"Somehow I don't think that's what your father needs from you. Maybe you should stop using his approval as the benchmark of your success."

It wasn't success. It was absolution for the circumstances surrounding his mother's death. Nothing he could ever do or buy his father would achieve that. Didn't mean he was going to stop trying.

"There." Wyatt smiled at Ashley. "Intimate scene objective accomplished. We've removed layers and bared our souls."

Ashley didn't think so. She gave away her rejection of his statement with the smallest of flinches. And then she stood.

Wyatt sat up, ignoring the minor head rush, and caught at her hand. "Where are you going? The doc said I need monitoring."

"I'm going to get Mitch." Ashley stared at his hold on her, slowly pulling herself back until she was out of reach. "I can't do this."

"What?"

"We'd make a great *on-screen* couple, Wyatt. Because we have chemistry and we could appear to bare our souls as we read someone else's words. But neither one of us can do this in the real world. You're holding back your truths, and I'm afraid to trust you with more than friendship." She drew her hand free and darted out the door.

Wyatt lay down, turning Ashley's words over, adding them to what he already knew about her. She was right. He wasn't being completely honest with her. And there were complications to a romance, even one as brief as the fling they were projecting to the world. But there was chemistry. And something more, a symmetry to their very beings that called from one to the other.

And wouldn't his father guffaw over that. *I've been in Hollywood too long.*

A few minutes later, Mitch stood in the doorway. He took stock of the room. "For some reason, I expected the bed to be put back in place."

"Why?"

"Because I'm your night nurse." Mitch,

who'd told him he used to be a defense attorney, still had that courtroom stare nailed down.

Wyatt stowed the look away for use at a later date. "Okay, princess, do you need me to put a mattress on the floor for you?" The second antique bed frame hadn't fit with the inversion machine set up.

"No." Mitch wrestled the mattress onto the floor. "Ashley was right."

"About what?"

"You and Holden sharing a room." He straightened out the bed linens with quick, practiced movements. "She said it'd be good for both of your egos. Something about learning to bare your souls?"

CHAPTER THIRTEEN

ASHLEY DRAGGED HERSELF into the Bent Nickel Friday morning, late for once.

Cam was already busy over a hot stove. The smell of bacon and fried potatoes filled the air. "Your tea is waiting at your table."

So was Wyatt. He was the reason she'd slept in. She couldn't stop thinking about him last night. Stubborn man that he was. Unused to sharing his innermost secrets. So like her. But so off-limits.

And now Wyatt was in front of her with a gloriously purple bruise around his eye, and she had no time to get into character.

"I've been thinking…" Wyatt turned in the booth, never taking his gaze from her.

Had he been thinking of the pretty little speech she'd made to him last night? Had he been thinking about her? About them?

Her heart leapfrogged over don'ts and shouldn'ts, because it was Wyatt her heart wanted after all this time alone. That big ego of his that protected his big heart. Being with him shouldn't make her feel stronger and whole. All that noise he made. And his physicality. She couldn't ignore him.

But his heart called to hers. A call of love. A call she was going to ignore for Laurel's sake.

Ashley clung to her folders and laptop, because she could sense his presence wasn't conducive to getting work done.

"Aren't you going to sit?" He had a way of quirking his brows that weakened her knees.

She plunked down in the booth, shoulders sagging. She loved Wyatt.

Why had this happened? She tried to pin-point when she'd fallen for him. But it was no use. What did knowing the exact moment matter? She loved Wyatt.

Wyatt readjusted himself in his seat, lean-ing forward, smile growing. If anything, that black eye made him edgier, sexier, everything America's Sweetheart shouldn't want. "I've been thinking that I should audition for the role of Mike Moody, rather than having to sign those papers."

"No." The word burst out of her before she could even process how heinous the situation had become.

Wyatt frowned. "Did you lock down some-one else?"

"No."

He ran a hand over his freshly shaved jaw while he stared at her. "You've changed your mind and think I'm right for the part?"

"No." She had to say something other than that. Ashley drank some of her tea and tried again. "I mean, I've decided that I'm not the right director for you."

"That's not it. I can see it in your eyes."

Really? She hoped he couldn't see the love she was hiding. Her gaze dropped to her hands.

He sat back in the booth. "Hang on. You're going to direct the movie, too?"

She knew it was beyond her at this point. But she had to run with the statement she'd tossed out on the table as if this was improv. "If I did, you wouldn't take orders from me."

"Oh, come on." The trademark Wyatt Halford intensity was building, like a fire in a blocked furnace that was about to explode.

"You know it's true." And what a relief. Both that she'd rediscovered her vocabulary and that he'd given her an out. "Tone it down, Wyatt. Mike and Letty are siblings who are very close and don't object to being criminals."

He clenched his jaw. "Feed me a line...*sis*."

Ashley took a moment to run through sec-tions of dialogue in her head, trying to find the right one. Ah, yes. "You shouldn't have taken Mrs. Granville's jewelry box."

The fire in Wyatt's eyes banked. Ashley could almost see his brain working, repeating and testing the line with different emphasis, finding the best way to portray Mike Moody and make him Wyatt's. "You shouldn't have taken Mrs. Granville's jewelry box."

"That's too judgy. The follow-up line I say is, 'Or Miss Hillard's hair comb.' Which you counter with, 'Or Miss Jenkin's silver spoon.' Try it again." The lines themselves should have told Wyatt more about the siblings' relationship than she had. And a bit about Letty, chief criminal.

Working the lines should have eased the hold this man had on her heart. He should have become Mike, Letty's brother.

"Ah, they're buddies." His gaze softened, became less reproachful but not an expression that completely absolved Letty of whatever trouble she'd caused. "You shouldn't have taken Mrs. Granville's jewelry box."

Ashley gave him Letty's secretive smile. "Or Miss Hillard's hair comb."

"Or Miss Jenkin's silver spoon." His smile matched hers.

And just like that, Ashley knew she was in

trouble. If Wyatt wanted the role, she'd give it to him. Not because she believed he was the perfect casting choice but because their on-screen chemistry would be riveting. And if he wanted her heart, she was at risk of giving him that, too.

Of the two gifts, casting him as Mike Moody was the safer bet all around.

WYATT'S WORLD WAS upside down.

And it felt fabulous. For his back.

For his heart, his head and his swollen eye, not so much.

The mattress Mitch had slept on was back against the wall. Wyatt's feet were locked into the inversion boots and blood was rushing to his head, pounding around his eye—probably not wise—but gravity was doing its job, giving every vertebra the space it needed.

Ashley needed space, too. It wasn't always easy to make the leap from actor to director or producer. She had a job to do, and he had to be patient and understanding of her creative and business-based choices. He was a popular star with a well-known reputation, and they'd gotten off on the wrong foot. But they were finding common ground. He knew she'd been impressed with their little reading.

He'd seen surprise on her face when he'd met her challenge and delivered those lines.

Ashley also needed space on the personal front. The few times he'd taken her hand, she'd extended her arm, inserting distance between them. He was trying to draw her closer with his winning charm and his tender touch. Even after they'd kissed, she'd found all kinds of excuses to dig in her heels. Not that they weren't legitimate reasons. Work. Dreams. The babies.

But no matter how much she was trying to put him in the friend zone, Wyatt rebelled. He didn't want to be her buddy or an actor on her set. And he for sure didn't want to be someone she added to that cyber circle of friends. He wanted… He felt…

He hadn't been able to put his finger on what he wanted or what his feelings were in Second Chance. Not where those babies were concerned. Not where Ashley was concerned. And, increasingly, not where his career was concerned.

He was hanging upside down with blood rushing to his head twice a day. He should be able to think through every enigma. Instead, his head hurt. And when his head hurt, the memories intruded.

"Why are you wasting your time in a

school play? Do you really need to stand up on a stage and have people applaud how good-looking you are?" His father hadn't lifted his head from shoveling stew in his mouth, hadn't let up his criticism since he'd come in the door after work. "You want something to do after school? Get a job that puts food on this table."

Wyatt's job put food on his father's table and a roof over his head. And still, he was criticized. Still, his love, his effort, his very being, was rejected.

Wyatt rubbed a hand across his forehead, trying to wipe out the painful memory and the nagging need to have his father's love.

Voices drifted to him. Shouted instructions. A half-hearted scream. Laughter.

"Stick 'em up!"

What?

That same half-hearted scream.

"That's right. Hands high."

"Cut." That was Ashley's voice.

Wyatt contorted himself, so his head was pointed toward the ceiling the way it should be. He let the head rush subside before he freed his feet. Only then did he go to the other window, the one facing south. From it, he could see the small white church across the road. Workers were giving it a new coat of paint before the wedding tomorrow.

"Odette, you need to scream like a mouse just ran across your bare foot." Ashley stood near the river, two stories beneath him with a group of people. She had a thin stack of papers in her hand.

If Wyatt had to guess, Ashley held a script. Was this another rehearsal for that festival she'd talked about? The one where she wore both a suit and a dress?

"Take it from the robbery," Ashley instructed.

Wyatt felt a tug of longing. To belong to a cast. To be a cog in the ensemble. To put on the mantle of a character and lose himself in telling a story.

The cast rearranged themselves. One man stood alone to the far side, his face hidden by a burlap bag.

"Action!" Ashley cried.

The solitary man ran up, finger guns drawn. "Stick 'em up!"

Odette screamed more convincingly this time. She and her cast mates thrust their hands in the air.

"That's right. Hands high." The villain in this badly acted drama circled the other participants. "Toss me your coins."

The cast made a show of tugging money out of imaginary pockets and purses, tossing them to the ground.

The bandit knelt to pick their money up, totally without realizing he was making himself vulnerable.

I mean, come on. I can do better than that.

Didn't matter that it was a street-fair performance. He could show this guy how it was done.

"Good. Now make your escape," Ashley directed.

Good? Wyatt shook his head. Her ability to ride and shoot notwithstanding, Ashley knew nothing about directing action films.

Before he knew what was happening, Wyatt had his cowboy hat and boots on and was out the door and headed downstairs.

He passed Gabby at the front desk, barely registering a wheeled rack near her with clothes hanging from it.

"Nice shiner." Gabby reached for her phone, but if it was a picture she was looking for, she was out of luck. "Where are you going?"

"Nowhere." Wyatt's boots pounded across the lobby and out the door.

Summer heat assailed him, along with a feeling of humidity. Since it was nothing like South America heat and humidity, he kept going. Down the porch steps, through the now-crowded parking lot, to the crest of a slope that led down to the Salmon River. A cluster of Monroes stood watching. None of whom were Holden. Wyatt paused behind them.

"He got me." The would-be bandit hunched over, having been shot by another actor's finger gun. He stumbled away in the worst case of overacting Wyatt had seen since his first job in commercials.

The three Clark boys clustered around a woman Wyatt didn't recognize. She pointed at a middle-aged man lying on the ground. "Get the doctor. The blacksmith was stabbed by Mike Moody."

Dr. Carlisle stepped out of the throng of background players and knelt to attend to her patient. Immediately, the Clark boys surrounded the pair.

"Grandpa, you're good at this," Adam told the man with the pretend stab wound.

"Here comes the sheriff!" Odette pointed at the retreating bandit. "Help! We've been robbed."

The sheriff stepped into the midst of the group of actors. "Who's with me? If we hurry, we can catch him."

Ashley was grinning.

Really? This was atrocious! Even for a street performance.

Wyatt pushed past the audience of Monroes, hurried down the slope and joined her as the posse searched for the wounded bandit, who'd exited stage right. "You've got to be kidding me."

"Shhh." Ashley grabbed on to his arm and drew him close. "This is the best part."

And it was. Because she was touching him and the familiar heat she created was making him move closer. He may have let instinct move his body, but his intellect was still working. "This is the worst part ever."

"Shhh." She leaned against his chest.

"Did you hear that?" The sheriff paused in his search.

"Crack. Boom. Boom," the villain intoned in an ominous voice. "Splat."

Wyatt rolled his eyes, which only aggravated the ache in his black eye.

"Rock slide," one of the chorus said in over-amplified horror. "Do you think…?"

"Look! It's his horse," said another, as far overboard as her cast mate.

As one, the posse watched an imaginary horse run past. As one, they inched forward, gazes sweeping the ground. As one, they gasped.

"Look at those boots. It's him," said a third, pointing. "Under that boulder."

"How like the move in *The Wizard of Oz*," Wyatt murmured in Ashley's ear.

She shushed him.

Wyatt refused to be shushed. "Witch flattened by farmhouse. Bandit flattened by boulder."

Ashley subtly elbowed him.

The posse heaved an imaginary boulder from the booted villain.

"But…where's the stolen gold?" The sheriff glanced around, clearly looking for it.

One of the chorus stepped forward, staring at a point above Ashley's head. "For over one hundred years, Merciless Mike Moody's hideout was never found. Many searched for it and his gold, some losing their lives. And now you, too, can chase Mike Moody through the hills to his hideout."

"Cut. Fantastic." Ashley stepped forward, glowing. "And then Shane will offer horseback tours of Mike Moody's infamous hideout. After which, you'll all take a bow."

The troupe did. And as they bent their heads, Wyatt's head began to spin. America's Sweetheart was hawking horseback riding to tourists? This was so far from red carpets and fancy parties.

"Laurel has the wardrobe ready at the inn for one last fitting." Ashley returned to Wyatt's side, keeping a distance between them that said they were friendly, not dating. "See everyone on Sunday."

Wyatt wished he'd grabbed his sunglasses when he'd run out the door, because now the cast was approaching, most chattering excitedly. He snagged Ashley's sunglasses, trying to hide his shiner.

"Hey." Ashley protested but didn't reach for her sunglasses. She smiled at her cast. "Wyatt, this is everyone. Everyone, this is Wyatt. Now go try on your wardrobe. Laurel's waiting."

Most left, but not before Wyatt shook each of their hands in turn. Ashley had a kind word to say for each of them, too, shooing them along.

Jonah had reprised his role as Mike Moody. He approached with his burlap mask off, trailed by the injured blacksmith, the man Adam had called Grandpa.

"Not bad, right?" Jonah asked Wyatt, who nodded and looked to the other man.

The blacksmith wore traditional ranchers' garb—a faded brown T-shirt, blue jeans and boots. And he had a bow to his knees as if he'd spent too much time in the saddle. "This is embarrassing, Ashley. I only signed on to please my grandsons. Didn't think I'd have a speaking role."

"Now, Rich." Ashley rubbed his shoulder encouragingly. "We're short on male actors. You're doing fine."

"I have an idea," Wyatt said, possibly because of all that increased blood flow to his brain. "How about I play Mike Moody, Jonah plays the blacksmith and then Rich can fill out the chorus."

"Hey," Jonah protested. "You can't just take my role."

"Grandpa, come on," Adam called from the slope above. "We're getting ice cream at the general store."

"He can play Jeb," Rich said, moseying up the hill without waiting to see what Ashley had to say about that.

Jonah and Wyatt turned to her.

"It can be my audition for the movie," Wyatt ground out when she didn't make the call herself.

"You can play the blacksmith," Jonah said stubbornly.

Wyatt shook his head. "It's *The Ballad of Mike Moody*, not *The Ballad of the Blacksmith*. People expect me to be in the lead role."

Ashley laughed. "I totally expected you to say that."

Her response confused him. "Don't act like this is a bad thing. If I play Mike, you have my permission to announce my casting for the street fair on social media. People will come to see me, not your no-name brother."

"Hey. People will come to see Ashley," Jonah said hotly. "They already plan to."

Ashley sighed. "But more will come to see Wyatt. And Shane wanted a crowd on Sunday. Sorry, Jonah. I owe you." She hooked her arm through Wyatt's and came in close. "Take a picture of us and post it."

"Good thing I know the lines," Jonah grumbled as he snapped a picture with his cell phone. "And, no, I'm not photoshopping your black eye out." He stomped off.

"Well, you've got your audition." Ashley started up the slope. But instead of heading toward the Lodgepole Inn and wardrobe, she turned south toward the church across the two-lane highway.

Wyatt followed. He was beginning to suspect he'd follow her anywhere. "Can I at least glance at the script? Or do you want me to improv everything on Sunday?"

"Here." She gave him the pages she'd been carrying.

Small font. Two columns on a landscaped page. Even if the sun hadn't been glaring off of the white paper and making him squint, he might have had trouble reading it. But there was no time to read. Ashley was still moving.

"Let me know if you have questions," she said.

"Where are you going?"

"I'm meeting with the wedding decorator at the church." She glanced at her phone and dashed off a message, moving too close to the highway and an approaching truck.

Wyatt grabbed her shoulders and held her back. "Where's your assistant? Or your mother? You need a keeper."

"I don't have an assistant other than Mom, but she's more interested in sipping tea lately than in what I'm up to." She waved to a brunette wearing glasses standing near the church. Her phone pinged. She paused on the orange line dividing the road to read the message.

"Did that dragon of a mother of yours teach you nothing about safety?" Wyatt dragged her to the other side of the road. "You don't check your phone in the middle of a highway."

"It was urgent." Ashley tucked her phone in the back of her jeans pocket.

"And so is living."

"Hey, Sophie." Ashley greeted the brunette. "Wyatt, this is my cousin Sophie. I can't remember if you've met. She's doing double duty as wedding decorator and my set consultant."

After his introduction, the women ignored him and discussed the placement of flowers, chairs and food for the outdoor ceremony. He took another look at the script, but his head hurt and his vision was too wonky.

A few more cars drove past, slowing for the stop sign and taking a good long look in their direction before proceeding. Not that their passing audience bothered Sophie or Ashley. Or the painters finishing their work.

"What about tents for privacy?" Wyatt couldn't stand it anymore. They were just a few hundred feet from the intersection of two mountain highways. "Anybody can park and take photographs." If it were his wedding, he'd want a huge tent and security guards, his privacy protected.

"Hardly anyone drove by when I got married here a few months ago." Sophie adjusted her glasses. "Although there was that one car that honked when the minister said Zeke could kiss the bride." She blushed.

Ashley's cousin Cam, the chef, joined them. The conversation turned to the logistics of food service.

Wyatt drifted inside the church. He'd

grown up attending a church this size in Virginia, but it lacked the grandeur of windows behind the pulpit that allowed the parishioners a view of the Sawtooth Mountains, similar to the view from his hotel room window.

He sat in the back, an unusual place for him. His mother had always made sure their family sat in the front row. Wyatt used to think it was because their family received supplemental groceries from the church every week and Mom wanted them to look pious and grateful. Sure as sunrise, they wouldn't have made their presence known like that if Dad had ever attended church with them.

Two little boys popped up from the front pew, finger guns trained on him. They were identical, with Sophie's shade of brown hair and smiles as mischievous as the Clark boys.

"Stick 'em up, mister," said the boy with the cowlick.

Wyatt dutifully raised his hands in the air, although he was tempted to touch his own misbehaving lock of hair in tribute to the little man. "I didn't think Mike Moody would rob a man in church."

"We're not Mr. Moody." The second boy rolled his eyes. "We're the Merc'less Monroe Twins."

His brother elbowed him. "Merciless Roosevelt Twins."

"The Ruthless Roosevelts." Wyatt provided an edit to the script. Free of charge.

"Ruthless," the two echoed, grinning at each other.

They stood and ran out, cowboy hats in hand instead of on their heads, boots ringing on the church hardwoods.

"Mom, we're ruthless!"

"You certainly are," Sophie agreed happily.

"Can we ride ponies today?"

"Papa Zeke said you can tomorrow," Sophie said.

Smiling, Wyatt turned back to the church window. The light was easier on his eyes. He should try reading the script again, but more memories of his mother leaped to mind. Her laughter. How she made sure her children ate before she did. Her willingness to volunteer for good works. He should start a charity in her name.

"Beautiful, isn't it?" Ashley sat near him. "Shane's looking for a minister in nearby towns, someone who wouldn't mind holding service here weekly or monthly."

"Why would Shane do that?"

"We own this town." Ashley spoke as if she was telling him she owned stock in a shoe company, as if it was no big deal. "We inherited it from our grandfather. Surely someone's told you that by now."

"No. You own this shabby, run-down town?" Wyatt sat back hard; his spine bumped against the church pew. "No one told me. Not even Gabby."

"It's probably not much of a secret for her." Ashley's perfect smile never wavered. "The first time I came here was for Sophie's wedding. And I couldn't wait to leave. And then I heard the story of Mike Moody, and about the gold, and Jonah's version of how it all went wrong with Letty's death." Ashley angled her body to face him, and the excitement in her eyes was almost palpable.

Here comes that twist in the script.

But it didn't seem as important as basking in her enthusiasm. Wyatt couldn't remember when he'd been as excited as she was about a movie project or...well...anything. He bet she woke up every morning eager to face the day, hopping out of bed with the enthusiasm of a child on Christmas morning. Conversely, most days he woke up mentally rehearsing the predictable lines from one of his action films and carefully stretching his battered body before ever extending a toe toward the floor. That was, until he'd come to Second

Chance and discovered Ashley at the diner. Now he had something exciting to roll out of bed for. And if the part was meaty enough and he landed a role in her film, he could feel that way through the entire project.

Ashley stared at Wyatt with stars in her eyes. Unfortunately, he was fairly certain those stars weren't shining for him.

"Wyatt?" she asked in a voice that told him he'd spaced out and misplaced the thread of conversation.

"Feed me that line one more time," he said automatically, as if they were on set.

"I asked you if you brought a tux for the wedding on Saturday."

That wasn't right. She hadn't been talking about his clothes. This was a test of some kind. "We were talking about Mike Moody."

"Past tense." She got to her feet, heading for the door. "I've got to check on the Old West Festival cast to make sure they don't exhaust Laurel."

"Wait."

There was something she wasn't telling him. Something she was holding back. And the only time Ashley seemed to hold back was when the topic was her sister.

Wyatt glanced out the open door at the wildflower-filled meadow and then inside at the crisp white walls. And then his gaze came to rest on Ashley, on her deep red hair, her delicate features, her bright blue eyes. But there was more to her than what the world saw. She wasn't saccharine sweet or a coddled star. She was kind and smart and sexy, and the woman he wanted to grow old with.

Ashley Monroe, America's Sweetheart.

He loved her.

And yet she'd reject that love because of the situation they were in.

He stood and went to her. Instead of telling her his feelings, he ran his fingers through her fine red hair and asked, "Why am I wrong for the role of Mike?"

Her expression flinched, just a quick flash that her focus had been broken. "We've been over this."

"The truth, Ash."

CHAPTER FOURTEEN

THE LODGEPOLE INN was bustling with cast members, all chattering. Gabby kept an eye on them, registering Odette talking about finishing a quilt, Flip discussing the too-pale shade of her dress for the show, and Jonah trying on the blacksmith's apron while telling anyone who'd listen that Wyatt had stolen his role as Mike Moody.

"Sweet," Gabby said to herself.

Dad had put a temporary rod across the kitchen alcove to allow people to change into their costumes. Laurel walked around the lobby, giving a reassuring word and putting pins in where needed. Gabby sat at the check-in desk, head down and screen averted as she searched the fan page for new pictures of Wyatt and Ashley.

"You need to rest," Dad told Laurel. "At least sit down."

Gabby raised her head. Anything that concerned Laurel and the babies concerned her.

Laurel waved him off. "This is the first,

and last, chance to adjust costumes before Sunday. I'll be done in fifteen minutes."

"But you've been on your feet for an hour." Dad paced around Laurel. He looked like he might just march her back to the apartment and put her to bed, the way he used to do with Gabby when she was a kid.

Not that Gabby remembered. But having seen Sophie take care of her toddlers earlier this year, she assumed there had been days where she'd tested her father's patience, just like Laurel was testing it now.

"You should rest, Laurel," Gabby said. "I'll put all the costumes back." Gabby was Team Twin, after all. She'd do whatever she could for those babies. It was why she'd agreed to help Ashley's cousin Shane on Operation Snaparazzi.

Genevieve appeared at Gabby's shoulder. "Laurel's working too hard. She should be resting. Her wedding's tomorrow."

"You try telling her to rest." Gabby nodded toward the lobby, where Laurel and Dad continued to spar.

"Is that part of your operation? Let me see what you've done so far." Genevieve leaned on the check-in desk and peered at Gabby's computer screen. "If there's one thing positive I can say about Second Chance, it's that you all pull together."

"It was Shane's idea." Shane had lots of ideas. "But Wyatt's people are doing it, too."

"That Shane." Genevieve frowned. "Growing up, my nephew was a handful."

Gabby grinned. "That's what Dad says about me."

Genevieve tapped the screen with her manicured fingernail over the photo Jonah had just contributed to promote the Old West Festival. "If you say Wyatt Halford is going to be in the festival, you should also say he's going to be in the film." She angled the laptop toward her and made an edit. "Wyatt Halford and Ashley Monroe will also soon appear in the on-screen version."

"But that's not true." Gabby pointed to a small number beneath a photograph. "And we've got five thousand views already without mentioning the movie."

"I haven't saved it." Genevieve drummed her fingers on the keys as if she was going to type more. "You can play with the truth sometimes. Maybe we could say 'hopefully soon to be seen'?"

"What's that?" Dad leaned in to look at what they were doing. "Are you on social media?"

Uh-oh. When had he sneaked up on them? Dad didn't know about the Snaparazzi.

"Gabby, you promised me the last time I gave you back your phone that you wouldn't go on social media."

"It's for a project I'm working on," Gabby said quickly. "And it's only on my laptop." That might have been a lie.

And while she was fibbing, Grandma Gen closed her laptop.

Her father stepped back.

Had she exited out of edit mode? Had she made changes and saved them? This was déjà vu, just like what had happened a few weeks ago when she'd accidentally posted on that website about Wyatt becoming a dad. Gabby ran her thumb along the lid, desperate to open the laptop and view the post.

Dad scowled. "Why do you always have to bend the rules?"

Uh-oh. Gabby could feel a grounding coming. And this time, Dad might take away more than her phone. She never should have told him she'd posted from her laptop.

"Hand it over." Sure enough, Dad held out a hand toward her laptop.

Since her phone was next to it, Gabby handed him the phone first, still hoping to keep the computer.

Her phone went into his back pocket. "The laptop, too."

"But, Dad, you enrolled me in online classes."

"We'll come up with a schedule for you to do your work. I know you have something due Sunday night, but for now, let's take a break."

That was a relief. She'd be able to check the post later.

"And for the next few weeks, the only time you can use that laptop is if I'm sitting right next to you."

"But, Dad!"

"THE TRUTH, ASH," Wyatt said again. "Why am I miscast for the role of Mike Moody?"

Ashley took his hand from her arm but didn't toss his hold aside. She held each of his hands in that church aisle. She held on to him as if they were standing on the altar taking vows, as if the words she was about to recite were of grave importance. "Your ego is too big."

He wanted to shake himself free, but for once, it was Ashley who held on to him.

"You'll understand once you read the script." She looked as if she was sorry to have put one over on him. "Mike Moody is the sidekick."

"A sidekick?" The legend was about the man. The movie was named after him. "To Letty?" His gut instinct was to reject the role. Back away. Back out. But the door was behind Ashley, and he thought he loved her. And so he swallowed his pride and said, "Please explain."

"All I can say without you signing that nondisclosure agreement is that the heart of the film isn't Mike Moody. That belongs to the character still standing at the end of the movie."

"But that's...Jeb Clark." The blacksmith who buried Letty in his family cemetery at the foot of Mike Moody's hideout.

Ashley nodded. "That's not in the street-fair script. But Wyatt Halford doesn't play second fiddle in a movie. It goes against the very fiber of your being. I can see you struggling with the idea as we speak."

"Yes." He wasn't going to lie to her.

But she wasn't done. "When you enter the stage or screen, you have a larger-than-life presence. It isn't just your ego that demands top billing—it's your very body language."

Body language. It was a tool actors used to play a role. She was telling him that she didn't believe he could modulate his being to the role.

"Wyatt, this is why everyone wonders about your ability to coparent. You took me house hunting without telling Mitch or Laurel, the intended occupants. You ordered high chairs for the girls."

"I hadn't really gotten them anything. That stroller was yours."

"Shane would love to use your name for buzz about the town, and my mom would love to use it for buzz about my movie, but can you honestly say you can play a secondary role as a father who doesn't have custody? That you'll be able to listen to those girls call Mitch *Daddy* instead of you? If you can answer me that, maybe you can answer how you'll approach the role of Mike Moody."

Wyatt felt battered. Ashley wasn't throwing sucker punches. These were blows he saw coming and couldn't deflect. He needed to pull away, step back, rebuild the Wyatt Halford persona from the ground up.

The only question was: Was Wyatt Halford a man who could play a sidekick on-screen and in real life?

His phone had the breakdown Wyatt was trying not to have. Vibrating with a text message. Incoming call ringing. It jangled along with his nerves.

The text overlaid the call screen.

HAVE YOU LOST YOUR MIND?

Brandon. He was calling, too.

Wyatt picked up.

"You can't accept a role in Ashley Monroe's movie. If Jess Watanabe sees this—and he will—your chances at this lottery-winning payday are nil."

Ashley had to have heard every word. Her expression hadn't changed since she'd asked him her multimillion-dollar questions.

"Hang on. Slow down. What happened?"

"There's a post on social media…"

"YOU DID ALL THIS?" Dad stared at her laptop screen after Gabby begged to make one last change to something.

The computer had opened to the social-media page. He scrolled through her fan-page posts.

"You're going to apologize to Wyatt for posting those pictures of him," Dad said in an icy voice. "It's an invasion of privacy."

And he hadn't even read any of the text. He'd scrolled by the latest post so fast, she hadn't been able to either.

"But, Dad! Everyone contributed to the pictures. And Wyatt even posed for a lot of them."

Genevieve took one look at Gabby's face and jumped in to defend her. "Now, Mitch…"

"I was talking to my daughter." Dad's voice had that hard quality he normally reserved for Holden Monroe, the tone he used to use on Shane before they'd worked out their differences, the tone he seldom used on Gabby. "I suspect there's more going on here than just pictures. Am I right?"

Across the room, Laurel was finishing up with wardrobe, dismissing cast members, who scurried toward the makeshift changing room.

Gabby hung her head. "Shane got a bunch of us in town to take Wyatt and Ashley's picture."

"Why?" His frown deepened.

"We're helping spread the word about Mike Moody and—"

"Mike Moody." Dad glared at the cast, who were staring at him in silence. "I'm getting kind of tired of hearing about that guy and his film."

"Are you?" Genevieve asked. "Or are you just angry that my daughter and yours are spending their time furthering his story instead of obeying your every command?"

Shoot. Dad hadn't let Gabby tell him that the pictures were supposed to pressure Wyatt into signing the paternity release papers, too. "Dad, Shane said—"

"I don't want to hear any more about what Shane said." Dad stared across the lobby at Laurel, who sank down on the couch, looking as uncertain as Gabby felt. "Gabby, what have I told you about getting caught up in Shane's plans?"

"Not to." Gabby's shoulders were folding in on her.

"Mitch, I think you're being unfair," Genevieve said.

"You would," Dad snapped. "Come on, Gabby." He grabbed his keys and charged toward the door, expecting Gabby to follow.

"WHO'S BEHIND THE town's social-media page?" Wyatt asked, voice rising loud enough to shake the church's rafters. "You?"

"What? No. Shane thought—"

"I need to see Shane." Wyatt led Ashley out of the church. "Someone just posted that picture Jonah took of us and said I was going to be in your film."

"As if you'd ever consider it now," Ashley muttered.

They were close enough to the inn that he could see Mitch pull out in an older-model

SUV and head north. It looked like Gabby was in the passenger seat.

"Why do you want to see Shane?" Ashley asked.

"Isn't it obvious?" Wyatt marched down the hill. "It was Shane who came to find me. Not you or your mother. It was Shane who stole my spark plugs. And just now, you said it was Shane who wanted to use me for buzz."

"Slow down. The picture Jonah just took?"

"Yes. And the caption is going to cost me millions." It didn't matter that just yesterday he'd been considering walking away from the sci-fi thriller. That had been his choice. But this... Someone was taking the reins out of his hands. "Is Shane at the Bucking Bull? I have to get this straightened out ASAP."

"That's not a good idea, Wyatt." Ashley wasn't keeping up with him. She lagged about twenty feet back. "Not today. And I don't think Shane posted that picture."

Wyatt swung back around, closing the distance between them. "You need to be there, too. Where is he?"

"He's at Davey's Camp for Cowboys and Cowgirls. It's the first day of the new session."

Wyatt gritted his teeth. "Take me to your leader, Ash."

"He's not my leader." Ashley made a half-hearted defense. "And you'll gain nothing by picking a fight with him."

"He's the Monroe leader," Wyatt said with a nod. "And I need to see him. I bet he's the one who posted about Laurel's pregnancy. Does that sound like a trusted family member to you?"

"If it was him, he meant well."

"That remains to be seen." He strode forward, passing the tree he and Holden had crashed into the night before. "When we get to the inn, grab your car keys. Thanks to Shane, I can't drive myself." Not that he knew where this camp was in the first place.

"Oh, yes, you can." Ashley sped ahead of him.

"If that's an offer to take your rental, thanks. But you can't get out of this trip so easily."

As they approached the inn, cast members were spilling out of the place with more urgency than they'd filled it.

She stopped and turned. "Wyatt, I meant you can drive yourself in your own rental." She sighed. "Shane never stole your spark plugs."

"But you said he did." Wyatt had taken her at her word. "Okay, change of plans. Wait for me downstairs while I retrieve my keys. Like it or not, you're coming with me."

"ASHLEY." MOM HELD out a hand when Ashley and Wyatt entered the lobby. She looked pained. "Thank heavens you're here. There was an argument and Mitch stormed out with Gabby."

Similarly, Wyatt stormed up the stairs.

"Mitch and Laurel fought?" Ashley rushed into the apartment, expecting to find Laurel in her bedroom in tears.

She was in tears, just not in her bedroom. Laurel sat in her usual kitchen chair. "He was upset about Gabby, but it was my fault. He wanted me to rest and I wanted to finish the costume fittings. He got frustrated and I think he went to find Shane."

Ashley hugged Laurel. "I'll find them. In the meantime, you should rest."

"She's exhausted," Mom said. "Just look at her. She hasn't gotten any sleep."

"She's not going to get much sleep of any kind once the babies arrive." Ashley knelt next to her sister. "It's official. I'm putting you on maternity leave."

"What? I can sketch with my feet up. You need me." She wiped her wet cheeks, but then her face crumpled.

"Ashley." Wyatt appeared in the door. "Let's go."

"Mr. Halford," Mom said in her most superior tone. "We're having a family crisis here."

"When aren't the Monroes having a crisis?" Wyatt made the come-hither gesture with his hand. "Time's a wasting."

Laurel's gaze took in Ashley and then Wyatt's retreating back. And for the first time in what seemed like forever, it felt like Laurel knew exactly what Ashley was thinking: *he's as upset as Mitch.*

"I didn't want this for you," Laurel said.

"Ashley!" Wyatt called from the inn's outer door.

"I'm going to see this through to the end," Ashley told them.

"This? What this?" Mom looked perplexed.

"Everything."

DAVEY'S CAMP FOR Cowboys and Cowgirls was indeed open for campers.

Wyatt had to drive past the main gates and up the gravel drive toward the Bucking Bull just to find a parking spot. Ashley hadn't said more than six words to him the entire drive.

"Head north."

"Turn left."

"Right there."

If Wyatt had been in a calmer mindset, he'd have appreciated the picturesque small cabins dotted along the edge of a small lake. The camp was teeming with parents carrying luggage and sleeping bags. There was chatter and laughter but no kids racing about. The children coming to camp had metal walking canes and walkers. Some even had electric wheelchairs.

"I told you today isn't the best day for this," Ashley said. "Oh, jeez. There's Mitch."

Laurel's fiancé stood at the main gate, arms crossed. Gabby stood next to him. And standing at the entrance was the man Wyatt was determined to see. Shane Monroe.

He marched toward his goal.

Mitch spotted him and acknowledged him with a one-word greeting. "Wyatt."

"Mitch." Wyatt hit his stride just as he drew up equal with Mitch.

Laurel's fiancé held out an arm to stop him. "If it's Shane you want, you'll have to wait in line. I'm first."

Gabby tried a weak smile.

"If you know anything about Wyatt Halford, you know he always goes to the head of the line." Wyatt pushed Mitch's hand away.

"Not today, Hollywood." Mitch's voice was

as hard as the first day they'd met, when he'd demanded Wyatt forgo his paternal rights.

"Can we at least take this conversation up the road?" Ashley asked, gesturing at the crowd of campers and parents.

"No," both Mitch and Wyatt told her.

Ashley took one look at Gabby and put her arm around her.

"Gentlemen." Shane passed through the gates and into unprotected territory. "Welcome to Davey's Camp. We appreciate the community *and* celebrity support." He had the same galling confidence he'd shown in South America when he'd insisted Wyatt show up in Second Chance.

"Do you have no shame?" Mitch demanded in a low voice. He glanced around at the campers and their parents, who were beginning to take note of Ashley and Wyatt. "I told you we needed to talk in private."

Wyatt thought about calling them on their claim for privacy now. But Ashley laid her hand on his arm, much the same as she had the first day he'd arrived in Second Chance.

Shane's smile never dimmed. But his gaze swung to something behind them. "Welcome to Davey's Camp for Cowboys and Cowgirls." A family bringing campers approached.

"We've got a surprise for you today. Movie stars Wyatt Halford and Ashley Monroe."

Mitch turned to Wyatt with a grin. "Your complaint will have to wait, Mr. Halford. He's all mine now."

Except Shane came up and stood between Wyatt and Ashley. He even had the nerve to drape his arms over their shoulders. "Who wants their photo taken?"

"GABBY, WHY DON'T you and Ashley wait somewhere else?"

That was Mitch, who'd cooled his jets while Wyatt and Ashley had spent thirty minutes having their picture taken with kids.

"They both stay," Wyatt snapped, barely containing his temper. "Let them see Shane's true colors."

The group was following Shane up the gravel drive and away from campers and their parents. When they'd passed the last parked vehicle, Shane turned and crossed his arms. "All right. Hit me. What's this all about?"

"You used my daughter to take pictures of Wyatt!" Mitch accused at the same time that Wyatt snarled, "You posted on the internet that Laurel was pregnant!"

Wyatt had to add, "And you just posted that I was going to star in Ashley's movie."

"Well, you don't have to sound like you didn't want to," Ashley murmured.

Acting must have run in the Monroe family, because Shane's expression didn't shift. Not one iota. "These are serious charges."

"Shane." Mitch took a step forward, but Gabby latched on to his hand.

"No, Dad."

Wyatt gladly took his place. "Shane…"

Gabby grabbed Wyatt's hand. "Don't. Please."

Shane stared at Gabby and his expression softened. "Do you have something you want to say, honey?"

Gabby dropped Mitch's and Wyatt's hands. "It was me."

"I don't understand." Mitch seemed to flounder.

"Operation Snaparazzi was my idea, Dad. Taking pictures of Wyatt and Ashley, and posting them. I asked Shane if we should do it."

"And of course, he said yes." Mitch regained his footing and his scowl.

"You used a little girl in your nefarious plans." Wyatt practically growled the words. "Is there no line you won't cross?"

"Nefarious?" Shane chuckled. "You must

be spending time with Jonah. He's the word-smith in the family."

"This isn't a joke." Wyatt's hands fisted. "You came up with a plot to get me here and ruin my career."

"You mean the invitation so that you could decide whether or not you wanted to be a father?" Shane tsked. "I'll admit to that."

"The pregnancy post…" Gabby stood tall, but her cheeks were flaming. "That was me."

"What?" Wyatt blurted.

"Gabby." Mitch froze.

Even Ashley seemed taken aback.

"It was an accident." Gabby's eyes pleaded for forgiveness. "A few weeks ago, I put the information in, just to see how it looked, and then I closed my laptop, and when I opened it again, it had been added. I never even pushed Save!"

"Gabby," Mitch said again, gentler this time. He put his arm around her and hugged her.

"Go ahead, Dad. Ground me." Gabby swiped at a tear.

Ashley enfolded her into her arms next. "And you haven't told anyone all this time?"

"No-o-o." Gabby's voice shook. "And you know how hard it is for me to keep a secret."

Mitch shook his head. "That doesn't change

the fact that you organized the town to stalk somebody."

"True brilliance," Shane proclaimed, earning a scowl from Mitch.

"But, Gabby—" Ashley knelt in front of her "—who posted the picture of me and Wyatt today?"

"That. Was. Me. Too," Gabby admitted between sobs that grabbed hold of Wyatt's throat and wouldn't let go. "But. Then. Grandma Gen…"

"Say no more." Ashley stood and gave Wyatt a look that said he was going to have to swallow his pride about this, too.

Not yet.

The anger still thrummed in his veins. So much money. It would have been his best role yet. His father would call him a fool for getting involved with anyone in Second Chance. And he'd be right, except…

He'd be wrong, too.

Not yet.

There was damage to be controlled. "Her laptop is back at the inn," Wyatt said. Probably sitting at the check-in desk.

Mitch caught Wyatt's gaze. "Gabby wanted to edit something before we left and I wouldn't let her."

"I'm sorry, Wyatt," Gabby said thickly.

"Do you think Laurel will forgive me for the original post?"

"Of course she will," Mitch reassured her.

"And Wyatt will, too," Ashley said, giving Wyatt a look that said he had to be the bigger man.

But Wyatt stomped away.

CHAPTER FIFTEEN

AFTER THE DRAMA of the day, it was surprising that the wedding rehearsal went off without a hitch.

Ashley shouldn't have been surprised, not when Wyatt and his cowboy hat were nowhere to be seen. Not when her sister took charge as if she'd been a boss her whole life.

Laurel told everyone she was only going to huff and puff up the hill one time, and then they were all going to eat.

As a newly promoted junior bridesmaid, Gabby was self-conscious walking up the grassy hillside. But she did fine, and when Ashley joined her at the top next to Mitch and Shane, they all turned to watch Laurel make her bridal march.

"Slow down, Dad," Laurel had to say twice, because their father wanted to charge up the hill as if he was taking the fort at the top. "Just this once."

And Ashley understood what Laurel

meant. She wanted to be the Monroe twin everyone watched that day.

WHAT A RELIEF to have all her secrets in the open.

Or if not exactly a relief—because Gabby still felt guilty about all the drama she'd caused—at least she was getting what she deserved. A cold shoulder from Wyatt.

She sat next to Dad at the rehearsal dinner, but didn't feel like talking to anyone.

There was an empty seat at the table next to Ashley, and Gabby felt sorry about that, too. Not only had Wyatt not accepted her apology, but apparently he wasn't going to be Ashley's wedding date, either. And just when they'd seemed to be hitting it off.

Gabby noticed her new grandmother kept looking at her new grandfather, who'd brought a young woman as his date. If Gabby was infatuated with Devin, Grandma Gen was in love with her ex-husband. Dinner hadn't even started and she'd already drunk two glasses of wine.

Cam called for everyone's attention and announced the courses and how they paired with the wine. He used a lot of words Gabby had never heard before and talked about notes in food until her eyes glazed over.

Gabby hid a yawn behind her hand and watched Devin, who sat at the opposite end of the table. He was talking to his aunt Kendall, who sat across from him and was a racing boat captain. And who knew that was a valid career path?

Gabby's gaze drifted around the table, barely touching her beet salad before they brought the main course—chicken Kiev.

Holden was talking about interest rates in a voice loud enough that everyone could hear. But suddenly he stopped and stared at Devin. His face grew redder and redder, as if he was mad. But at what?

Gabby had a feeling of uneasiness that had nothing to do with accidental postings on the internet. She took a bite of chicken Kiev. One thing was certain. Cam's food beat Dad's cooking every time. It was worth sitting through a lecture on food notes and nuances.

Holden wiped his face with his napkin. Not his mouth. His entire face.

For whatever reason, Gabby's gaze kept drifting.

Holden pressed a hand to his chest as if he had heartburn or perhaps had accidentally swallowed a bone.

The back of her neck got goose bumps.

Gabby clutched Dad's arm. "Do you have Dr. Carlisle's number?"

"I do," Dad whispered. "But it's not a good idea to invite her over." He glanced toward Holden.

"Dad." Gabby latched on to his arm with both hands without taking her eyes from Holden. "Call her. Now."

Holden gasped for breath.

Gabby ran around the table and squeezed between him and his even stuffier father. She loosened his tie. "Tell me you swallowed a chicken bone." She stared into his cold gray eyes. "Tell me you're not having a heart attack."

"Dad?" Devin rushed to his father's side.

"No bone." Holden gasped. "Can't breathe."

Gabby drew a deep breath, as if she could encourage him to do it with her. "All right." Heart attack. She'd helped Roy through one before, not that she hadn't been scared to death while doing so. "The important thing is not to panic."

"Out of the way, little girl." Holden's father dragged her out from in between their chairs.

Gabby wormed her way back between them, refusing to be treated like a little kid. "I know CPR and first aid. You need to slow down your breathing, Holden. Dad's called Dr. Carlisle. She'll be here any minute."

Fortunately, Dr. Carlisle rushed in carrying her medical backpack. "What happened?" She didn't bat an eye as Gabby related the symptoms she'd seen. Then the doc took over.

No one seemed to notice when Gabby backed away from the table on shaky legs. She made it to the lunch counter and a stool before her legs gave out.

Devin joined her. "That was cool. How'd you know how to do that?"

"I've been studying." More than geometry and language arts. Gabby watched Laurel waddle toward them. "Things tend to happen around here, you know." Medical emergencies, she meant.

"I'm going to study premed." Devin stared over where his dad sat slouched in a booth. "But I didn't see it coming. Thank you."

Which would have really made the scare okay, except Devin patted her on the head before he went back to support his dad.

"You were prepared." Laurel hugged her. "Dr. Carlisle thinks it's just stress, but they're going into Ketchum to run tests at the hospital."

"So it's not that bad?" So this wasn't the third bad thing Wyatt had predicted?

Gabby clung tighter to Laurel.

"I DON'T KNOW how you'll survive in this getup, Ash. I didn't want to make your costume like this. It's too heavy." Laurel moved around Ashley in her small apartment, talking with pins in her mouth while she tugged at fabric. "It's supposed to be close to ninety degrees on Sunday and you're going to do the play twice? All I can say is hydrate."

"I can handle it." Ashley wore the man's thin wool suit under the black-and-pink dress.

"Ashley can handle it." Mom sat at the kitchen table with a mug of *tea* cradled in her hands. "I raised you girls right."

Ashley caught Laurel's eye. Their mother was tipsy and morose tonight.

Mitch came out of the bedroom. "Anyone know why Wyatt didn't come down for dinner?"

"Like I'd invite him when he wouldn't forgive Gabby?" Laurel jabbed a pin too far and stuck Ashley.

"Ow." Ashley pulled away. She might not be able to handle this last fitting. "He's wrestling with a lot of decisions right now, not just about his movie roles." But about who he was as a person.

"I'm going to go up and check on him," Mitch said.

The three Monroe women all turned to stare at him.

"He's a good man, Laurel." And Mitch left it at that.

Nobody said anything for a few minutes after he'd gone.

Laurel huffed. "Do you think he's a good man, Ash?"

"I do." Ashley didn't hesitate to defend the man she loved. "We did more than kiss in the woods, you know?"

"What?" Laurel teased. "I didn't know."

"I'm almost out of tea," Mom said mournfully.

"Talk. We talked," Ashley reassured them. "I've talked more to him than anyone."

"Even me?" Laurel straightened, pressing her hands into the small of her back.

"Even you." Ashley nodded, not without a stab of guilt almost as sharp as her sister's needle.

That brought about another silence, during which time Ashley wished she was a fly on the wall in Wyatt's room, if only to hear what Mitch had to say.

"You don't trust people easily." Laurel came closer, tugged the dress back, and back, and back, until Ashley had to take a step or lose her balance. "And Mitch... Darn hormones. My gut instinct is that Wyatt needs to be involved in these girls' lives."

"Never trust your gut," Mom said. "Always check the figures on the back end."

Laurel and Ashley laughed.

"Maybe you need to give Wyatt a chance to prove himself, Ash." Laurel gathered Ashley's hair and held it off the collar of the dress, presumably to check the seams back there. "Not just as Mike Moody, but as Wyatt Halford. That picture of you two kissing at the A-frame was smoking hot."

"You don't mean that, do you?" Did she? Ashley felt her cheeks heat. "You'll change your mind about him again tomorrow."

"I don't think I will. Not about his being good for you or the babies." Laurel let Ashley's hair down, smoothing the material over her shoulders. "You know…when the people you love put their faith in someone…you should, too."

"Who is that woman your father brought this weekend?" Mom took a swig of her drink.

"Time-out." Making sure she wasn't going to get stuck by a pin, Ashley moved carefully out of Laurel's reach, plucked the mug from her mother's hands and dumped its contents into the sink. "Is that what this bender is all about? Dad?"

"Hey." Mom stared morosely at the sink. "That was the last of my...tea."

"I'm not picking a fight with you, Mom." Ashley gathered up her skirts because they were indeed heavy, weighing almost as heavily as the responsibility for Laurel's future happiness. "Mom, I...*we*...need you to be sober for the wedding."

"And the babies are coming," Laurel said.

Gabby opened her bedroom door. "Not to mention someone has to talk to all those muckety-mucks you invited to the wedding." She closed the door almost immediately.

Something straightened in Genevieve's spine. "Gabby, what did I tell you about keeping secrets?"

"I'm not listening to you," came the reply. "Secrets are bad."

"Go, Gabby," Ashley murmured.

"Your guest list wasn't really a secret, Mom. We have the RSVPs." Laurel sighed. "Honestly, Mitch and I should have eloped."

"Hey, none of that talk." Ashley enfolded Laurel in a hug, although with so many layers of clothes between them, it wasn't quite the sisterly clasp of old. "Everything's going to be fine. Your wedding is going to go perfectly. Cam has everything he needs for catering. Sophie's handling decorations. And Mitch is tackling whatever else comes up. No problemo."

"Easy for you to say." Mom ran her hands over her face. "You aren't competing with a woman who looks half her age."

Ashley released Laurel. "You aren't competing. You're divorced."

"Maybe Wyatt will agree to be my wedding date instead of yours." Mom stood, eyes glittering. "That would give your father pause."

"But it wouldn't make Dad come back," Ashley said gently. She'd forgotten her mother's hard outer shell protected a plethora of vulnerabilities. "And he wouldn't make you happy if he did." Theirs had been a turbulent marriage. "You know what's going to make you happy?"

"What?" Mom's lower lip trembled.

Gabby's door creaked open.

Even Laurel seemed to be waiting for Ashley's next words.

"When those baby girls get here, you're going to be needed again," Ashley said simply. "Laurel and Mitch are going to be stretched to the limit, running this inn and the Mercantile, as well as keeping up with Gabby. They're going to need you, Mom. And much as you hate to hear this, Dad doesn't need you…or me, or Laurel, or Jonah."

Her speech motivated a group hug—both Monroe twins, their mother and Gabby.

"Well." Mom's expression wavered between a brave smile and tears as she stepped back to stand alone. "That's your father's loss, isn't it? Letting his children go?"

"Yes." And Ashley hoped it wasn't going to be Wyatt's.

"CAN I COME IN?" Mitch stood in Wyatt's hotel room doorway.

Wyatt was tempted to close the door in his face. According to his agent, he'd probably already lost the record-breaking payday from Jess. And that wasn't even what he cared about most that he'd lost today.

"I brought whiskey." Mitch produced a bottle from behind his back. "I'm not above bribing my way in. But if you close the door on me, I'll just use my passkey."

Wyatt let him in. He sat on the bed, leaning against the headboard.

Mitch took the glasses from the bathroom and poured them each a drink. He stared at the mattress on the floor, and then claimed a seat next to Wyatt on the bed, also leaning against the headboard, like they were best friends or brothers.

They were something, all right. Tied together by Laurel's babies.

For a few minutes, they sipped their drinks and stared in the direction of the window. All that was visible were the peaks of the Sawtooth Mountains laced with thickening clouds.

Wyatt swirled his whiskey. "I know I owe Gabby an apology."

"It's good for her to wait for forgiveness." Mitch leaned his head back, bumping the headboard. "She needs to learn to think before she acts. Though it helps me to hear that you plan to forgive her, so I'll sleep tonight even if she doesn't."

"You are one tough dad." Fair, but tough. The girls would be in good hands. "I used to think life was fairly simple. Mess up things with your family. Go make a movie. Mess up things with a woman. Go make a movie."

"Learn you're a father. Go make a movie?" Mitch gave him a wry smile. "You can't run from life forever."

"Is that what I was doing?" Wyatt drained his whiskey and held out the glass for more. "Thanks for saving me hours of therapy."

"So?" Mitch poured him another two

fingers. "What is your hesitation regarding parenthood? Is it just the whole mortality thing? Do you need me to reassure you there are no gray hairs on that famous head of yours?" He chuckled, but he would, already being a dad. "Because I can guarantee you will never be tested as much by these girls as you will by some of those stunts I've seen you do on film."

Wyatt didn't believe that for a second. "Would your statement still hold if we were having this conversation before we saw Shane? You were pretty mad."

"At Shane. For good reason. He should have told Gabby she couldn't post pictures of you while you stayed here. And instead, my princess posted pictures and made herself vulnerable to the wicked queen's manipulation." Mitch raised his glass. "I'm allowed one derogatory comment about my soon-to-be mother-in-law after how she behaved today."

"She has been hitting the *tea* quite a bit." Wyatt stared into the shallow depths of his amber whiskey. "I shouldn't judge, seeing as how I'm drinking now."

Somewhere down the hall, a woman laughed. It wasn't Ashley's laughter, but it made Wyatt pine for her all the same.

"But seriously, Halford." Mitch turned to him. "We can do this if you're man enough."

"This?"

"Coparent."

"You come up here and sit in my bed and tell me I might be lacking the nerve to be a father? And yet you still offer me the job?" Wyatt tsked. "If I was Holden, I'd tackle you."

Mitch sipped his whiskey around a smile. "If you were Holden, you'd lecture me to death about my retirement plan first. Parenting is hard but not impossible. You just have to be present. Meaning aware or tuned in."

"Jeez. You do realize I'm only home a few weeks out of the year? The more you talk, the more I realize I'm not father material." Wyatt Halford, actor, playboy, millionaire, wasn't cut out for being a dad. "Seriously."

"You say that now, but I bet that both our fathers had second thoughts when they were told they were going to be a dad. It's all part of the process." Mitch gathered his whiskey and his glass and got to his feet. "I have faith in you, Mr. Halford. You've proved yourself to me and most of Second Chance. The question is, do you have faith in yourself?"

"The right answer is no, because I..." He hated that he hesitated. "I just don't know how this can work without me being Uncle Wyatt."

"You leave that to me and Laurel." Mitch walked around the bed and moved toward the door. At the last minute, he took Wyatt's glass, too.

"Hey, I wasn't done."

"The last thing anyone needs on my wedding day is Wyatt Halford hung over." Mitch drank the remains of Wyatt's whiskey. "You'll get another glass when we toast the birth of our babies."

CHAPTER SIXTEEN

ASHLEY WAS COMING downstairs early on the morning of Laurel's wedding day when she heard someone cry out.

"Laurel?" She ran to the apartment behind the check-in desk. "Laurel?" She pushed open the door.

Mitch was rushing around. "Where's the birthing bag? And my keys. Where are my keys?"

Laurel sat in a kitchen chair. Her cheeks were red. "I have the worst luck. My water broke on my wedding day."

"Are you okay? What can I do?" Ashley set her stack of folders and laptop on the desk and knelt next to her. "And, no, I will not pretend to be the bride so the wedding can go on."

"I hate you right now." Laurel sucked in a breath and pushed her shoulders back, as if she was trying to separate her head from her belly. "But then again, I'm having contractions and I hate everyone. Mark the time. Gabby! Where are you?"

Gabby came through a door carrying a mop and bucket. "I'm on cleanup detail, remember?"

"Ashley can clean up." Laurel was in fine form.

"This is payback for every little thing I've ever done to you, isn't it?" Ashley tried to joke.

"No, Ash. This is labor." Laurel glanced around. "Where is Mitch? Mitch, it stopped. How long was that?"

"I can't find my keys or the hospital go bag." Mitch was bug-eyed.

Wyatt pushed his way inside the small kitchen, cowboy boots ringing with purpose. His black eye was a greenish purple. "I see a set of keys in the fruit bowl beneath the orange. And there's a gym bag under the kitchen table." He pointed to Laurel's feet, which were propped up on it. "Call Dr. Carlisle. Let's get you to the hospital. Forget Mitch's keys. I'm driving."

They all stopped moving.

"I thought you didn't believe these were yours?" Ashley narrowed her eyes at him.

"I need to see these babies for myself."

"Why?" Ashley frowned. "Does everyone in your family have a heart-shaped birthmark on their butt?"

"Ashley, he wants to see them once before he signs away all claim to them. That's just wrong." Mitch grabbed the bag and helped Laurel to her feet. "I'd advise you so, if I were your lawyer, Halford."

"Ha. But you're not my lawyer, Kincaid." Wyatt took a red baseball cap from a rack near the door and put it on Ashley's head.

"Is that true, Wyatt?" Ashley demanded, while Wyatt took another hat and put it on his own head.

"Can we debate this in the car?" Laurel waddled toward the door.

"Gabby, you and Grandma Gen are in charge." Mitch gently pushed Wyatt and Ashley out of the way. "And if that doesn't strike fear into someone's heart…"

"Dad. I can handle it." Gabby saluted and raised the mop in triumph.

"Of course she can," Mitch muttered. "She's twelve going on twenty-two. Let her run the credit card machine. Let her approve reservations online. No social media, Gabby. I mean it."

Wyatt chuckled as he followed them out the door.

Ashley hung back. "Grandma Gen is going to be hung over. She won't get out of bed until this afternoon. Don't wake her. Don't even wake her when we call to tell you the babies have been born."

"Really?"

"Ashley!" Wyatt called from outside.

"What am I worried about?" Ashley hugged Gabby. "You'll be fine. Just you and Devin and the rest of the Monroe clan." She hurried out the door.

"I hate you," Gabby called after her.

DESPITE THE FACT that both Wyatt and Ashley wore baseball hats, and that Wyatt had a black eye, they were still recognized at the hospital in Ketchum.

By staff. By family members waiting for babies to be born. By curious passersby in the hall when they went to check on Holden in the cardiac unit, who had a clear bill of health, other than a bout with anxiety.

Of all the days to be fawned over and handle photo requests. Ashley's patience dangled from a very thin thread. Wyatt kept his arm draped over Ashley's shoulders, and they leaned into each other, hat brims pulled low to avoid more attention.

She and Wyatt found an empty couch and slumped into it. "I guess our social-media campaign did its job," Ashley said. "Nobody has looked at us and questioned why we're together."

Down the hallway, Laurel labored. And she wasn't one of those women who labored in silence. Ashley gritted her teeth and forced herself to take shallow breaths, as if she were her sister's labor coach.

"Are you kidding me? We go together like peas and carrots." Wyatt patted her thigh.

"We could." Ashley was feeling emboldened by Laurel's change of heart last night and Wyatt's heroic charge to the rescue this morning. Mitch had been in no shape to drive. "You never answered my question about playing a secondary role as a father or in my film."

"Would you kiss me if I said I'd given both some serious thought?" He turned the bill of his hat around and nuzzled her ear. "I'm having an emotionally draining day and need some TLC."

She elbowed him back. "All you've done since you've come to Second Chance is mull things over. At some point, you have to make a decision."

"Like I said this morning…" Wyatt began. "I need to see—"

Laurel let out a primal scream.

"Oh, no. No, no, no. This is torture." Ashley

tried to hide her face in Wyatt's broad chest but only succeeded in knocking her hat off.

"I need to see the babies, okay?" Wyatt brought her face in front of his. "And then I'll tell you. I'll tell you anything and everything."

"I meant it's torture that I can hear Laurel down the hall." Ashley cringed at a particularly sharp scream. "But I'll hold you to that, too."

A nurse poked her head into the waiting room. "For Monroe?"

Wyatt and Ashley stood.

"Come with me." The nurse spun away, walking quickly.

Ashley clutched Wyatt's hand. "Laurel must have wanted you to witness the birth." She just hoped she could manage to stay in the room without falling to pieces.

A scream peaked, followed by a woman's shouts. "Get my husband in here. Right now! He did this to me."

They passed the room with the screaming, upset woman in labor.

"Where are we going?" Ashley glanced back. "I thought that was my sister."

The screamer's husband sprinted into the room, followed by what looked like two grandmas-to-be.

Wyatt wrapped an arm around her and smiled.

The nurse half turned. "We're headed to the NICU. Your nieces were born about twenty minutes ago."

"I am so relieved." Ashley settled into Wyatt's side as they moved along quickly.

They went through a series of doors until they came to a glass wall. Beyond the partition, several babies were in incubators. Laurel sat on a stool in between two. She gave Wyatt and Ashley a weary smile as Mitch took pictures with his cell phone. Their nurse escort went inside, scrubbed down and then wheeled the incubators close to the window.

The two little girls were wrapped up tight in blankets with pink beanies on their heads. Bright red hair fringed their caps.

Wyatt leaned closer to the glass, clearly eager.

The details of their features registered. The shape of their lips. The tilt to their tiny noses.

"Oh. My. Word." Ashley turned slowly to Wyatt. "They look just like you."

LAUREL WAS ASSIGNED a room in the hospital. Once the nurse had her settled in bed, she passed out from exhaustion.

Wyatt could relate. He was exhausted.

I'm a father. That part of the day hadn't really sunk in. Babies who looked like him. Babies who he'd helped create. Babies who needed him to keep their best interests in mind.

Mitch, Wyatt and Ashley joined a slumbering Laurel in her room as they waited for the twins to be brought in for a brief visit under a nurse's supervision. Dr. Carlisle said they were doing well and breathing on their own. If all went well in terms of weight gain and health, they could go home in a week.

"When you get back home, the signed paternity papers will be on your kitchen table," Wyatt said firmly. He didn't think he'd let go of Ashley since they'd entered the hospital. At his announcement, she yanked his hand like a bellpull.

"You couldn't find it in you?" Unlike Wyatt, Mitch spoke in a whisper. "Disappointing, man."

"We don't have to do anything today," Ashley said softly. "Except discuss. You promised me answers to questions once you saw the girls."

"Hazel and Eleanor." Mitch took Laurel's hand without waking her.

"No." Wyatt's grip tightened on Ashley's. He'd never asked what they were going to name the babies. Not once. "Not Eleanor."

"I hardly think you're in a position to argue about their names if you don't plan to sign on to being a part of their lives." Mitch gave him a dark look reminiscent of the day they'd met. "Do you know how many months Laurel and I have talked about names?"

"Hope," Wyatt said.

"Excuse me." Mitch looked to Ashley for a save, since Wyatt was clearly confusing him.

"One of the girls needs to be named after my mother. Hope."

"She died of lung cancer several years ago," Ashley explained to Mitch.

"Hazel and Hope." Mitch gave him a curt nod. "But don't be surprised if Laurel writes *Hope Eleanor* on the birth certificate."

"Birth certificate…" Wyatt looked to Ashley, clung to Ashley. He'd been able to joke in the waiting room. But not here. Not now. Now he could barely find his own voice. "Their father's name is…Mitch Kincaid." It was the hardest line of dialogue he'd ever delivered.

"No," Ashley said, tugging his hand again.

"We can wait," Mitch said. "Laurel doesn't

have to write the father's name on the paperwork right now. It can even be amended later."

"No," Ashley said again.

Wyatt took her face in his hands. "This is
what's best for Hazel and Hope. A chance
at a normal life outside of the circus that is
mine. I'll be their favorite uncle Wyatt, whose
title was earned because he was their father's
good friend."

"No," Ashley said a third time, gripping his
hands and pressing them against her cheeks.
"This isn't what you want."

"You know what I want," Wyatt said softly,
dying a little inside. "I want to be the highest-
paid actor on the planet, the actor every man
dreams of being and every woman dreams
of being with. I can go on being difficult and
charging an annoyance fee, breaking box-
office records and paydays." He drew a shallow breath, preparing to say the words that
threatened to break him inside "Hope…
and Hazel will be fond of their uncle Wyatt.
They'll be proud of me. And they'll love
Mitch, their daddy."

"Man, I really hate you right now," Mitch
choked out.

"You will regret this," Ashley told him,
tears dampening her cheeks and his palms.

He already was. "But I won't change my mind."

Because he'd finally realized what the right thing to do was.

CHAPTER SEVENTEEN

"THEY DIDN'T TAKE that well," Wyatt said to Ashley as she drove them back to Second Chance. Mitch and Laurel were going to spend the night in the hospital.

"I don't blame them," Ashley said. She was so disappointed in Wyatt. "I haven't taken it well, either."

Wyatt made an unintelligible sound. He was angled away from her, staring out the window. "It's for the best."

"They're going to look like you, Wyatt. And at some point, they're going to put two and two together and realize you aren't just their uncle Wyatt. And then what?"

"And then they'll have Mitch and Laurel to explain things to them."

"That is such a cop-out." She took her hat and swatted him with it. Not hard enough to hurt, but hard enough to make her feel better. "It's hard to believe you were encouraging me to get out of my shell and you won't get out of yours. No sidekick roles. No fatherhood. You can't make action movies when you're sixty."

"I know several sixty-something actors who'd argue that point." Wyatt sat up and turned his back to the door.

"I don't plan on being a has-been," Ashley said staunchly. "I plan to be an actress people still want to see when I've aged gracefully."

"Here we go," Wyatt said wearily.

"I plan on doing work that is well respected."

"Multi-award-winning," they both said at the same time.

Ashley took her hat off again and swatted at him, but he deflected her swing with ease this time. "Are you making fun of me?"

"No." He looked gaunt and sad, nothing like the vibrant Wyatt Halford who'd sauntered into Second Chance to squelch a rumor.

"We need comfort food." Ashley pulled into a burger joint, one of those local one-offs that were family owned. She ordered them burgers, fries and shakes, and then pulled forward to pay at the window.

"Hey, aren't you famous?" The young cashier who took Ashley's money couldn't place her. "Oh, but he's Ian Bradford!"

"Yes," Ashley said, turning to Wyatt to

raise her eyebrows. "She couldn't even remember my name."

"And she only knew me by my most famous role."

Ashley smiled, and it felt like her first real smile in days. "Better than your least famous role. Jeez, we're almost has-beens."

He gave her a half smile.

"Can you autograph this bag for me?" The cashier snapped their picture with her phone and handed her a bag and pen.

Fan satisfied, they were given their food and drove off.

"You should be happy," Wyatt said after he'd devoured his burger and before he swiped hers. "We've had our picture taken so many times today. Great PR for your festival and movie."

Ashley shrugged. "But the most important photo is the one you took of Hazel and Hope. Maybe when we come back tomorrow, you can hold them."

She drove up the mountain highway, and Wyatt fell silent, finishing her fries and her milkshake.

"I made a mess of things, didn't I?" Wyatt stared out the window. "That's what my father would say."

"I think you should focus on what your

mother would say." The woman he rarely talked about. The woman she felt was the key to understanding Wyatt.

"What my mother would say." Wyatt's voice sounded empty. "I… She… Seven years ago, the doctors gave her three weeks to live. I came home to see her, which shut down the movie I was starring in."

Ashley approached the last curve before the top of the pass, waiting to hear what else Wyatt would share with her.

"Mom was happy to see me. My sisters, too. Dad was… He sat in the corner of her room at the hospice and refused to talk to anyone."

Ashley could guess where this was going. "They wanted you back on set." Film productions were expensive and full of moving parts. There'd be little to do if the lead actor wasn't available.

He nodded. "Mom wanted me to go. And it was only supposed to be for a few days. Five at the most." Wyatt didn't sound like himself. Or maybe he did, because deep down, he was a man with a tremendous heart, one that could be hurt. And he was letting that pain spill into his words. "She died on day three. My father didn't speak to me at the funeral."

"He wasn't speaking before that," Ashley pointed out. "He was probably grieving."

"My sisters said they understood, but I could tell they didn't. I wasn't there for Mom at the end. And they were disappointed."

"You weren't there for them," Ashley gently chided. "When you lose someone, it's those who gather round that need love and support. When my grandfather died, he was ready. It was the family who wasn't prepared."

"Maybe." Wyatt rubbed his hands over his face. "Does it matter? Nothing I did healed that rift."

"Nothing as in whatever you bought them out of guilt. A house? A car? A…recliner?"

They reached the summit and started their way down the mountain into Second Chance. The roof of the Lodgepole Inn was visible above the treetops and the white church spire in the field where the wedding was to have taken place.

"Hey—" Wyatt sat up "—didn't anyone cancel the wedding?"

"WHAT THE HAY?" Ashley slowed the car as they approached the stop sign in Second Chance. "They may have canceled the wedding, but it looks like they didn't cancel the party."

Wyatt recognized some faces in the crowd, including the silver-haired director, Jess Watanabe. The Monroes who'd gone horse-back riding clustered around the church, away from the rest of the guests.

Genevieve met them when they parked at the inn. "Come on up. The party is in full swing."

It was the right thing to do for their careers. They were trending on social media, and several outlets had put in requests for interviews. And, of course, there was the Jess Watanabe fence to be mended.

"We're not dressed for a party, Mom." Ashley glanced down at her jeans and T-shirt.

"No one cares." Genevieve gestured toward the gathering. "You can tell us all about the babies."

Wyatt could see Ashley was torn. He was dead on his feet, drained emotionally, but he wasn't going to let her brave the waters alone. "Come on. Let's circulate and then make our excuses."

"Wonderful." Genevieve hooked her arms through each of theirs and marched up the slope.

"Sober today?" Wyatt asked.

"Delightfully so." Genevieve nodded. "Cam

mixed up a wonderful hangover cure. It's the clearest I've felt in days."

"Cured of your obsession with Dad's date?" Ashley asked.

"Delightfully so." Genevieve nodded again. "She caught sight of your cousin Bo and had a case of instalove. Best news I've had in years."

They reached the first cluster of guests.

"Here's Hollywood's latest power couple." Ashley's father drew them into his circle of friends, leaving Genevieve huffing as he showed them off to other studio heads. "Ashley's launching her own production company. She hopes to focus on women-driven stories. Her first project is a western set here in the Idaho mountains." He gave his daughter a one-armed, sideways hug. "And you all know Wyatt and his penchant for action movies. I hear good things about his latest summer film. I'm sure audiences will forget that turn as a villain rather quickly. Why don't you two tell everyone what you two are up to?"

"Because you told them for us, Dad." Ashley spoke with such grace that it smoothed the barb in her words. She greeted everyone in the circle.

Wyatt was mostly ignored, which he

chalked up to exhaustion and his inability to make small talk.

After a few minutes, Ashley took his arm. "If you'll excuse us, we've had a long day at the hospital and my mother says we need to circulate." She was amazing.

Before he could offer his thanks, she'd guided them over to a nearby circle of Hollywood executives. Ashley's brother, Jonah, stood among them, looking like the cat who ate the cream. He'd probably been pitching script ideas like lobbed water balloons.

"Welcome to the producers' circle." A skinny man with too much energy peppered Ashley with questions about the progress on her film. "If you need any advice, just call me."

Wyatt was admired but mostly ignored. This time, he thought it was rather odd.

An older woman leaned in to whisper, "We're mostly indie film producers. We know we can't afford you for our passion projects. Most actors who sign on for an indie do so for barely above scale."

Wyatt knew that was more like a wish than truth, but he gave them a bit more effort, asking about their projects and earning a smile from both Ashley and Genevieve.

What? They thought he didn't know how to do this?

They went toward a group of directors next. Wyatt held Ashley's arm and steered her toward Jess. The multitalented, silver-haired director welcomed them both warmly.

"Hey, Jess." Wyatt gave the man a firm handshake. "I'm sorry about the way things went down. But you know, it's never over..."

Jess clapped a hand on Wyatt's shoulder. "I backed out of the project. There are other films in the works that interest me." He nodded toward Ashley.

"The Ballad of Mike Moody?" Wyatt glanced from Ashley to Jess. "Really? Why?"

The old director's grip tightened on Wyatt. "I've always thought you had more depth to you. And now that you're with Ashley, I can see it more clearly than ever. It would be an honor to direct this film." His hand fell away.

"Great." Wyatt straightened, feeling not so great. In fact, he felt a bit like Ashley's accessory, especially when Jess cut between himself and Ashley.

Genevieve was there to hook her arm through Wyatt's, as if he was the most important person in the circle, not Ashley.

The group fragmented. Ashley and a half dozen directors looking for work, and Wyatt and a half dozen directors looking for actors. How did he know? The pitches started.

"We're looking for someone who can play a retired navy SEAL whose car breaks down in a remote mountain town."

"Second Chance?" Wyatt joked, although it wasn't funny.

"That's so predictable," said another director. "I'm working on a horror film."

"Does the hero have a brainy sidekick?" Wyatt kept that smile on his face.

"Have you ever considered cozy mysteries?" said another.

"Only as bedtime reading." Who did these people think he was?

Their pitches became muffled background noise because one thing was becoming clear—Wyatt was no longer a hot commodity. Ashley was. And just as annoyance should be bubbling past his smile, Wyatt realized that he wasn't really annoyed. He was happy for Ashley. Proud even that he'd been a part of her journey to this point. At this point.

Emotion gripped his throat as firmly as it had at the hospital when he'd told Mitch whose name to put on Hope's and Hazel's birth certificates. He didn't want to step away from Ashley, not for a moment. But he hadn't wanted to step aside for the girls either. But he'd done so because it was the right thing to do.

Music began playing through speakers that must have been hidden behind flowers. A slow love song. A few people moved into an open space to dance. Ashley was still deep in conversation. Gabby stood on the edge of the crowd, not really belonging anywhere.

Wyatt approached her, half expecting the preteen to dart away when his intent was clear. "May I have this dance?"

Gabby held her head high. "Only if you'll forgive me."

"For bringing me to Second Chance and letting me see the babies?" For giving him a chance to fall in love with Ashley and feel for at least a short while that he was part of a community and a family again? "Of course I forgive you, Gabby. I just needed time to cool down."

"You may have this dance." She extended her hand.

He took it and led her to the dance floor, drawing her carefully in his arms because he'd suddenly become aware of a need to treat little girls with kid gloves. "You are going to break a lot of hearts, young lady."

She drew back to look at him before casting a glance toward Holden's teenage son.

"Just not this week." He smiled.

"I can't wait to get older."

"And I…" He spun her around and back into his arms. "I can wait, because these are the days when the true character and heart of a young lady shine through."

"This is why you have so many fans like me." She grinned. "Because you're poetic and kind, and, oh, the babies are super lucky to have you."

He didn't correct her assumption. When the song was over, he twirled her over to Devin. "I think it's your turn."

Gabby blushed beet red.

"That was so sweet." Ashley appeared at his side. "Maybe next year I'll crown you America's Sweetheart. Ready to go?"

"Yes."

It took them another ten minutes to break free of the guests on the fringe.

"Wyatt." Ashley placed a hand over his when he would have opened the door to the inn for her. It was reminiscent of how things had played out only a few days ago. At any moment, she'd kiss him. At any moment, he'd sweep her into his arms.

She didn't. He didn't. They didn't move.

"I want to thank you for making this possible," she said in a small voice. "You goaded me out of my shell this past week, whether you want to admit it or not."

"Some might say *bully*," he murmured, trying not to stare at her lips. "And for the record, you were already operating without a shell when I got here." It was the truth, and he took some joy in pointing it out to her.

"I realize that meet and greet over there was painful for you. My mother greased the wheels for me, not you. I know you felt like a sidekick, but you hung in there and I love you for it." Before he could thank her, she rushed on. "And I love you. I've known it for some time, and this isn't romantic or the way anything is supposed to go, but before you disappear into actionlandia, I thought you should know that."

No one knocked Wyatt Halford off-kilter. No one but Ashley Monroe, who loved him.

But she wasn't done with her speech. "I'd like to officially offer you the role of Mike Moody. I'll have my people send the non-disclosure agreement to your people in the morning. And I can assure you that whatever you decide about the role, I will be a professional about my feelings." Except her eyes were misty and she swallowed thickly.

Now was the time to kiss her and tell her he felt the same, except, how could he tell her that? How could he accept her love when he hadn't been willing to step up and love Hope and Hazel?

"Oops." Gabby skipped up the porch steps, destroying the atmosphere. "I didn't mean to intrude."

Ashley opened the door. Wyatt and Gabby followed her in.

"You'll consider the role?" Ashley asked, frowning slightly. She'd just declared her love and offered him a job, after all, and he'd said nothing about either one.

"Yes." It was a win.

She'd be shooting in Second Chance. Laurel and the babies would be in Second Chance. His stint as Uncle Wyatt could begin.

Uncle Wyatt.

The title felt heavy on his shoulders, but he thanked Ashley for the part and then excused himself, heading straight for his room. Noting the time Ashley mentioned that he needed to be dressed for the Old West Festival in the morning.

Once in his room, Wyatt broke down the inversion table and put together the antique bed. He needed to leave tomorrow before he did something incredibly stupid, like tell Ashley he loved her, too. She'd never agree with his decision regarding the babies, and it would break her heart, if he hadn't done so already. There had been tears at the hospital.

Gabby knocked on his open door. "You need to read this." She handed him a thick script.

"Where did you get that?" he asked.

"Ashley left it downstairs." Gabby shrugged. "She offered you the role and she probably won't miss it until morning. It can be our secret."

Wyatt knew he should turn her down. He was going to perform in the Old West Festival tomorrow, but he wasn't going to take the role of Mike Moody in Ashley's film. Not because he couldn't be a supporting player but because he'd changed his mind. He couldn't stand to be near Ashley and not be allowed to openly love her.

He bade Gabby good-night and settled down to read.

On his second time through the script, he received a text from Mitch. Or rather a picture via text. Laurel had filled out the birth certificates and entered Wyatt's name on the line where Mitch's should have been.

And then an explanation rolled in.

COULDN'T STOP HER. DIDN'T WANT TO, PAPA WYATT. WELCOME TO THE FAMILY.

Mitch and Laurel wanted him to be part of their family. He wasn't a threat to them or a nuisance. He was Papa Wyatt.

He went to the window, not to stare out into the night, but to look at his own reflection.

He was many things. And today, he'd earned the title of Dad.

His heart felt full, but not quite full enough.

"THAT WAS WEIRD." Gabby entered the apartment, shutting the door behind her.

"What was?" Grandma Gen sat at the table sorting business cards as if she was playing solitaire.

"Pretending I was sharing a secret when you told me to do it." Gabby went to the counter and cut a piece of wedding cake. "Plus it was lying. Ashley picked up her laptop and her copy of the script right after Wyatt went up to his room."

"I shouldn't have let you talk me into this." Jonah stood near the refrigerator, arms crossed and brows knitted.

Grandma Gen tsked. "We needed a script. How else were we going to make Wyatt and Ashley see reason, dear Jonah? By morning, you'll be a hero."

Jonah made his escape out the side door, calling over his shoulder, "By morning, Ashley will fire me, dear mother."

CHAPTER EIGHTEEN

"WHAT ARE YOU DOING? I was looking for you everywhere at the smithy." Ashley burst into Wyatt's room in full Letty costume—that flouncy pink-and-black dress. The double layers of costume were too cumbersome to run around in. She was hot, sweaty and breathless. At the sight of Wyatt, her stomach dropped. "Why aren't you dressed?"

"I overslept." He wore blue jeans and a T-shirt. He hadn't even put his cowboy boots on yet. He handed her a script. "It's brilliant. Beautiful, gritty, powerful. The blacksmith tries to save Letty from joining the gang and accidentally shoots her during an attempted robbery. It's a tragedy, not a romance."

"Yes." Ashley stared at the script. "Where did you get a copy? You haven't signed anything." And wait until she told Jonah what Wyatt had said about his script. Not that she had time to think about that now. "This isn't the script for today's performance. Tell me you learned your lines."

"I learned my lines, Ashley." He closed the door behind her. His Mike Moody suit hung from a hanger in the open closet. "I learned all my lines."

"Wyatt—"

"You should sit down." He helped her to sit on the bed. "You look lovely today. Beautiful. You glow."

"If you're buttering me up because you can't perform in the festival, Wyatt, I need to go find Rich and Jonah."

"Ashley. Ash." Wyatt got down on one knee, pushing her skirts to the side and then taking her hand. "I know you offered me the role of Mike Moody, Ash, but I want to read for the role of Jeb Clark, the blacksmith."

"But he hardly has any stunts or fights or shoot-outs." Things Wyatt's fans would expect. Things he'd told her he wanted to focus on. But wait. "You want to read for the role?" He wasn't asking for it to be handed to him?

"Let me explain. It's important." Except he merely stared at her, grinning.

"Wyatt, I would love for you to explain, but we have a performance in thirty minutes. At least tell me you're going to play Mike Moody today."

"Yes. I can play Mike today. In fact, I could

play him in the film version, too. It's just that I don't want to."

"I'm confused." Ashley drew a slow, calming breath, reminding herself that Wyatt had been through a lot in the past week and she shouldn't judge him for not behaving rationally this morning.

"Listen, Ash. Yesterday, when those Hollywood people were happy to meet me, every one of them was clambering to work with you, and the thought crossed my mind that I was standing in your shadow."

"Okay." Ashley tapped her antique wristwatch. "At least put on your costume while we talk." And didn't she sound like a problem-solving director or producer?

Wyatt stood and stripped off his T-shirt, revealing muscles and muscles and muscles to spare. He began putting on Mike Moody's shirt, tie and jacket. "But here's the thing, Ash. While I was in your shadow, I didn't resent it. I was proud of you and genuinely wanted you to succeed."

"That's…great?" Where was he going with this?

"I know it's hard to believe, but it's true." He snagged his trousers off the hanger and disappeared into the bathroom. "I should have told you when we were walking back to the inn, but I was thinking that since I was leaving that I probably shouldn't try. And then when you told me you loved me, I should have told you that I felt the same way—blindsided by the one person in the world who seems to recognize who I am and what my fears are." He poked his head out of the bathroom. "What are my fears, Ash?"

"Besides not playing a role with the most lines of dialogue." She tapped her chin, although she didn't have to think long. "I'd say you fear confronting your family about your mother's death."

He closed the door again. "See? You know me so well."

Then why was it just now sinking in that he'd said he loved her? Ashley got to her feet. "Can we run back through some of those last lines?"

"The part where I admit that I love you madly?" The door flew open and he stood there in Mike Moody's cheap western suit. "Yeah, I thought you'd like that." He placed his hands on her waist and spun her around the room. "But maybe we should wait to talk about that until I confess that I'm going to be Papa Wyatt to Hope and Hazel."

Ashley had to sit back down on the bed. She was so dizzy. "I don't understand."

He began putting on the old-west boots Laurel had found, which had lots of laces. She'd never seen anyone tie those laces that fast. "Last night, Laurel filled out the birth certificates with my name on them. And as much as it makes sense to be Uncle Wyatt, I just knew. The time to fight for my right to continue down the same old path had passed. I need to blaze a new trail, try new things, love out loud." He brought her to her feet. "Because I love you, Ashley. And I'm going to love those girls and be their second dad, because that's okay, too."

"I love you," Ashley said simply, because she did, and he was so larger than life that the simplest of words seemed to do.

And then he was sweeping her into his arms and marching down the hallway. "She loves me!" He set her down at the top of the staircase. "Does that mean she'll marry me?"

"She will indeed, because she loves you." That earned her a quick kiss.

They raced down the stairs together.

Mom stood near the check-in desk, smiling, which was not like her.

Gabby threw open the front door. "They're calling for you guys!"

Ashley and Wyatt didn't waste a second and hurried to the smithy through a thick crowd of fans who waved and cheered when they saw them but got out of their way.

Before they began the performance, Wyatt gave her a kiss that promised to love, honor and cherish. And when he was finished, he touched his forehead to hers. "For Jeb and Letty."

"For Jeb and Letty. And Hope and Hazel. And for us."

What an ending. What a beginning.

Wyatt kissed her again.

Ashley couldn't think because of all the crowd noise, but she could feel. And what she felt was the confidence of the right man at her side, one who was strong enough to stand alone or be in her shadow. One who believed in her, believed in himself, and believed that together they—and theirs—could reach for the stars.

EPILOGUE

One week later...

IT WAS A SMALL ceremony on a gentle slope next to a freshly painted white church in Second Chance.

There were two brides, two grooms and two very fragile babies, who were extremely lucky to have two very special dads.

There were no tents for privacy. There were no black eyes or bridesmaids, other than one twelve-year-old junior bridesmaid whose job it was to hold the bridal bouquets during the ring portion of the ceremony.

Two honeymoon suites had been prepared. One in an A-frame in the woods. One at the Lodgepole Inn, where plans were being made to expand the manager's apartment up into the second floor, complete with soundproofing.

There were few Monroes in attendance. Most had left town to return to their lives. Attendees were local friends and relatives. They were celebrating many things, not just this double wedding. Progress had been made on declaring some old buildings historical landmarks. There'd been a boost to the economy from the Old West Festival, an increase in tourism that continued a week later.

And then the bear decided to make an appearance, giving them all something else to celebrate.

"There she goes!" Roy announced, pointing across the river to the meadow where mama bear and her cubs were heading south.

A cheer went up, followed by the sound of laughter.

And two twin babies, who were new to the world, wondered to each other if every day outside the hospital was going to be so full of joy and laughter.

News flash: It was.

* * * * *

SPECIAL EXCERPT FROM

H HARLEQUIN
WESTERN

*Can small-town veterinarian Emily Fielding forget
how Wes Marlow once broke her heart and take
another chance on love?*

Read on for a sneak preview of
SECOND CHANCE COWBOY,
*a new story in Claire McEwen's
Heroes of Shelter Creek series.*

Emily took one more look around downtown Shelter Creek,
so pretty in the clear morning light of early spring, and
froze.

A tall man in a black cowboy hat was walking across the
street. His face was angled away, but he looked familiar.
Something in his profile, the tilt of his jaw, reminded her of
Wes. But that was impossible. Wes had left Shelter Creek
when they were in high school. And he'd certainly never
worn a cowboy hat.

The man glanced toward her, and instinctively Emily
ducked down behind her truck. This was ridiculous. This
guy couldn't be Wes. And even if it was, what was she so
afraid of? She wasn't the starry-eyed kid she'd been back
then.

She crawled a few paces forward so she could peek
around the front of the truck. The man had moved on. Emily
stood slowly, afraid Might-Be-Wes would turn around and
see her.

She meant to get in her truck and drive to her clinic. But
instead Emily started walking, keeping pace with the man,

staying just behind him on the opposite side of the street. The next building was the vast Tack and Feed Barn, located, as its name implied, inside an old barn. The man went inside. Emily waited for a few cars to pass before she dashed across Main Street and followed him in.

The comforting scent of leather, grain and dust brought her to her senses. What was she *doing*?

Heat rose in her cheeks. Good thing there was no one in the store to see her making a fool of herself, chasing after a cowboy. But since she was here, she might as well visit the saddle she'd had her eye on forever. Emily walked deeper into the barn until she came to the tack section. She found her saddle and traced her fingertips over the floral design etched into the leather.

She'd forgotten for a moment about the man she'd been following. And then suddenly there he was, standing directly in front of her. A small squeak escaped from deep in Emily's throat because she could see that under the brim of that black cowboy hat it *was* him. Wes Marlow.

Wes looked up at the sound, and for a moment he didn't move a muscle. Then he took a step in her direction. "Emily?"

His eyes were still the green she remembered. He had a slight smile on his face, but he didn't look happy. Instead he looked wary.

Emily had followed him on instinct. She hadn't considered what she'd do if the mystery man really was Wes. "Why are you here?"

Don't miss
Second Chance Cowboy *by Claire McEwen,*
available April 2021.

Harlequin.com

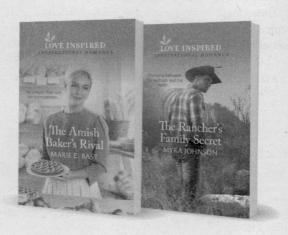

SPECIAL EXCERPT FROM

LOVE INSPIRED
INSPIRATIONAL ROMANCE

Rescuing a single mom and her triplets during a snowstorm lands rancher Finn Brightwood with temporary tenants in his vacation rental. But with his past experiences, Finn's reluctant to get too involved in Ivy Darling's chaotic life. So why does he find himself wishing this family would stick around for good?

Read on for a sneak preview of
Choosing His Family, *the final book in*
Jill Lynn's *Colorado Grooms miniseries.*

In high school, Finn had dated a girl for about six months. Once, when they'd been watching a movie, she'd fallen asleep tucked against his arm. His arm had also fallen asleep. It had been a painfully good place to be, and he hadn't moved even though he'd suffered through the end of that movie.

This time it was three little monkeys who'd taken over his personal space, and once again he was incredibly uncomfortable and strangely content at the same time.

Reese, the most cautious of the three, had snuggled against his side. She'd fallen asleep first, and her little features were so peaceful that his grinch's heart had grown three sizes.

Lola had been trying to make it to the end of the movie, fighting back heavy eyelids and extended yawns, but eventually she'd conked out.

Sage was the only one still standing, though her fidgeting from the back of the couch had lessened considerably.

Ivy returned from the bunkhouse. She'd taken a couple of trips over with laundry as the movie finished and now returned the basket to his laundry room. She walked into the living room as the movie credits rolled and turned off the TV.

LIEXP0121

"Guess I let them stay up too late." She moved to sit on the coffee table, facing him. "I'll carry Lola and Reese back. Sage, you can walk, can't you, love?"

Sage's weighted lids said the battle to stay awake had been hard fought. "I hold you, too, Mommy."

Cute. Finn wouldn't mind following that rabbit trail. Wouldn't mind making the same request of Ivy. Despite his determination not to let her burrow under his skin, tonight she'd done exactly that. He'd found himself attending the school of Ivy when she was otherwise distracted. Did she know that she made the tiniest sound popping her lips when she was lost in thought? Or that she tilted her head to the right and only the right when she was listening—and studied the speaker with so much interest that it made them feel like the most important human on the planet?

Stay on track, Brightwood. This isn't your circus. Finn had already bought a ticket to a circus back in North Dakota, and things hadn't ended well. No need to attend that show again. Especially when the price of admission had cost him so much.

"I'll help carry. I can take two if you take one."

"Thank you. That would be really great. I'd prefer to move them into their beds and keep them asleep if at all possible. If Reese gets woken up, she'll start crying, and I'm not sure I have the bandwidth for that tonight."

Ivy gathered the girls' movie and sweatshirts, then slipped Sage from the back of the couch.

Finn scooped up Reese and caught Lola with his other arm. He stood and held still, waiting for complaints. Lola fidgeted and then settled back to peaceful. Reese was so far gone that she didn't even flinch.

These girls. His dry, brittle heart cracked and healed all at the same time. They were good for the soul.

Don't miss
Choosing His Family *by Jill Lynn,*
available February 2021 wherever
Love Inspired books and ebooks are sold.

LoveInspired.com

LIEXP0121

Love Harlequin romance?

DISCOVER.

Be the first to find out about promotions,
news and exclusive content!

f Facebook.com/HarlequinBooks

y Twitter.com/HarlequinBooks

◎ Instagram.com/HarlequinBooks

℗ Pinterest.com/HarlequinBooks

You Tube YouTube.com/HarlequinBooks

ReaderService.com

EXPLORE.

Sign up for the Harlequin e-newsletter and
download a free book from any series at
TryHarlequin.com

CONNECT.

Join our Harlequin community to
share your thoughts and connect
with other romance readers!
Facebook.com/groups/HarlequinConnection

HARLEQUIN

Heartfelt or thrilling, passionate or uplifting—Harlequin is more than just happily-ever-after.

With twelve different series to choose from and new books available every month, you are sure to find stories that will move you, uplift you, inspire and delight you.

HNEWS2021